LATE NIGHT LOVE

CHAYLA WOLFBERG

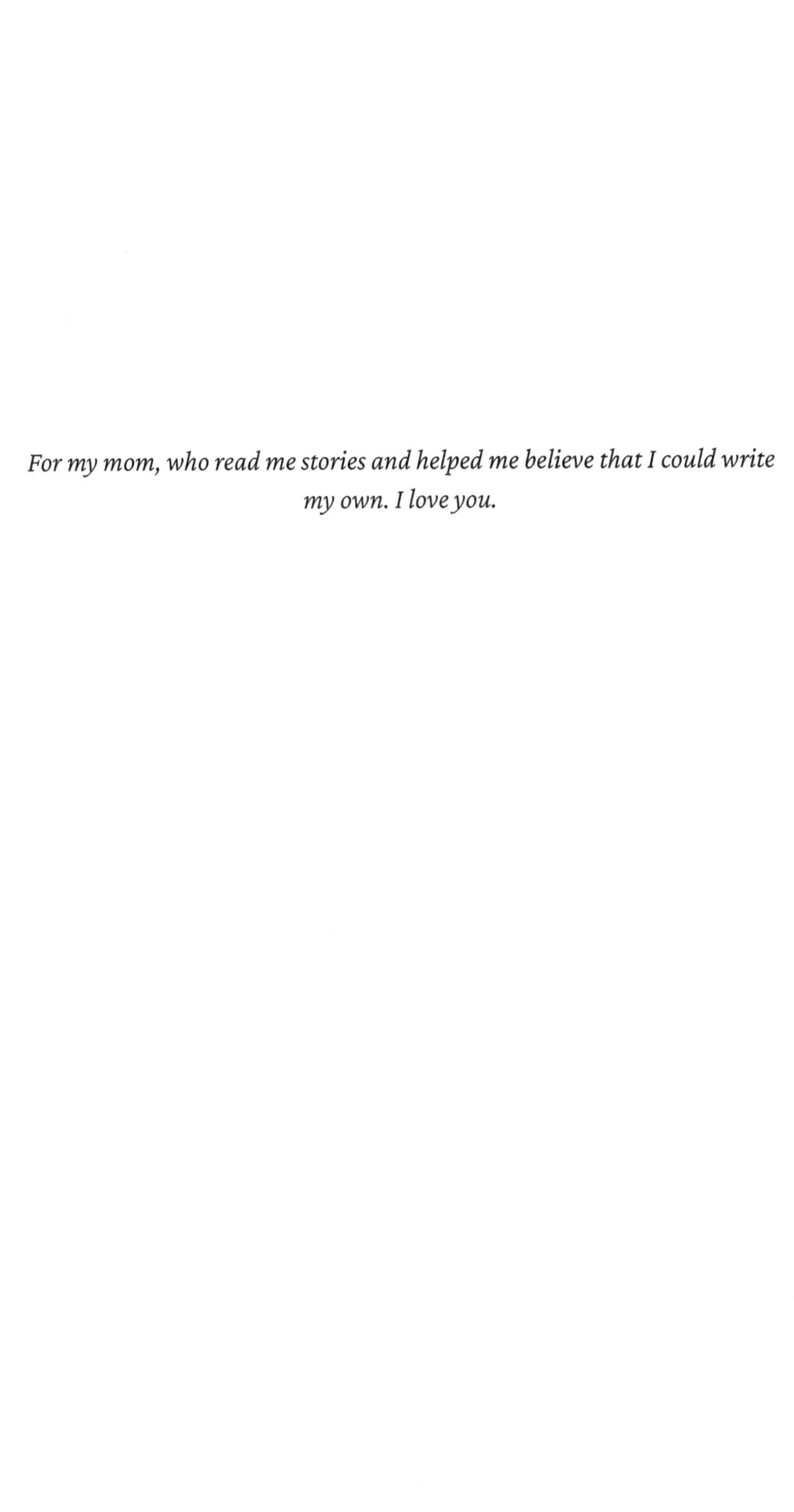

For my mom, who read me stories and helped me believe that I could write my own. I love you.

1

Even after six years as a writer for *Live From New York*, something about stepping across the threshold of the *Weekend Update* offices makes me feel like I don't belong.

No one is entirely sure why the writers of the *Weekend Update* segment have their own specific offices. They're not any different from those of the other *Live From New York* writers and cast members. It makes the *Update* feel exclusive. Which it is—in the sense that the current *Weekend Update* co-hosts love to exclude me.

I've barely spent any time here, since the men whose office it is have yet to give me the time of day. They've spent six years ignoring my jokes, ignoring *me*, and I'm here to find out why.

I've wanted to be a writer on this show since I fell in love with it as a miserable, friendless middle schooler. My parents let me stay up to watch the show every Saturday, and it was the highlight of my week. Slowly, the show became more than a source of joy and laughter. It was where I learned. I didn't care about politics until I laughed at the show's political sketches without even realizing it, I got an education in what was going on in my country. But it wasn't just the social commentary that I adored. It was the silliness and the way that famous hosts were suddenly humanized as they played along with audacious comedy bits. All of it served as a reminder that there were people out there who were just as weird as I was, who shared my sense of humor.

And at the center of all of that was my favorite segment. I loved the whole show, but I worshiped the *Weekend Update*: watching the hosts banter, seeing the recurring characters, and the ways different pairings played with the format, bringing their own personalities to it, building off each other.

As I got older, writing for *Live From New York* became less of a dream and more of a goal. I spent high school and college writing comedy, sending in submission packets every year when I graduated and praying for the day I was hired.

When that day came, I almost didn't believe it. It seemed impossible that after years of watching from afar, I had finally done it. I was in. It felt like the beginning of the rest of my life.

That was six years ago. Since then, I've made a name for myself as one of the best sketch writers on the show. I even won an Emmy last year.

"Oh, is that the coffee order? Thanks, Ellie," Chris Galloway calls from behind his desk, not even bothering to look up from his laptop when I enter the room.

A fucking Emmy, and this walking Ken doll can't be bothered to remember when I've set a meeting with him.

Chris, lovingly nicknamed the forgotten fifth Chris because he's hot enough to compete with the rest of them. He's even dated some of their co-stars, and yet he's still humble enough that every time someone uses that moniker, he playfully rolls his eyes and offers some variation of, "Come on, guys!"

My nicknames aren't polite enough to be said to my face. Must be nice.

My loathing for Chris has grown in me like a cancer. When I started, I was desperate for him to like me. Every time he'd give me so much as a brief nod or smile in the hallway, I wanted to jump for joy. He was everything I wanted to be: the host of the *Weekend Update*.

But that was six years ago. Six years of submitting jokes to the *Weekend Update*—every week—without a single one making it on the air.

That, and the realization that his *Update* co-host—and *Live From New York*'s head writer— Alex Nabakov was not the charming nice guy he so perfectly pretended to be on camera.

It took me only two minutes to learn that Alex was a disgusting human being. The first thing I heard him do was joke about hiding a video camera in the dressing room of that week's famous-actress host.

Even as my illusions about Alex were shattered, I held out hope for Chris. But with every year that passed of my success everywhere but the *Weekend Update*, that hope transformed into bitterness.

It was one thing to hate Alex. Everyone hated Alex. He flaunted his uncle's board membership on our network's parent company, couldn't write a joke to save his life, and treated anyone who wasn't a white man willing to laugh at his horrible comments like shit. As head writer, he set the tone for the rest of the show and made it a generally miserable place to work. At least for me.

But somehow, despite the fact that Alex had been his writing partner since college and his *Update* co-host for years, everyone loved Chris. They loved his grating aw-shucks everyman attitude. They loved his freckles, his height, and his self-deprecating charm, like Conan O'Brien if Conan was brunette instead of ginger and packed on what looked like a hundred pounds of muscle.

I knew this because I spent most of my time glaring at the back of his head, wondering how his pointed silence whenever Alex said something horrible made him a hero when he might be the only one who could call our head writer out without being fired for it.

Hating Alex came naturally to me. But hating Chris had become a fiery passion, a reminder that the toxicity of comedy wasn't just because of the toxic people but because of their enablers. Alex was trash, and everyone saw it, even if no one had the power to call him on it. But somehow Chris got a free pass, and no one seemed to have a problem with it but me.

Still, I'd asked Chris for this meeting instead of him because, as much as I personally dislike him, I can admit that he is at least funny. Not as funny as he could be if he removed the stick up his ass, but talented enough for two people. He had to be.

It was an open secret that Alex's nepo-baby status and partnership with Chris were the only reason he had found himself in the privileged position of head writer and co-host of the *Weekend Update.*

The silence has apparently stretched on long enough for Chris to look up, and I don't miss the annoyance that flashes across his face when he sees that it's me. He doesn't know that I hate him—that would require him actually having a conversation with me. But an intern with coffee is much easier to dismiss than a senior writer demanding answers about why he and his chauvinistic partner in crime have rejected every single one of her jokes for the past six years.

"Emily. Can I help you with something?"

"We have a meeting,"

"We do?" He glances down at his screen, double checking his calendar. "Oh, shit, we do. Sorry. You know how it goes."

"I don't think that I do, actually," I don't give him the satisfaction of agreement. "I don't know anything about what happens in this office. That's why I'm here."

"We mostly braid each others' hair and make friendship bracelets." A pithy dismissal, delivered with an infuriatingly charming grin. Damn him for being so handsome and charismatic. Life really isn't fair, and Chris Galloway is living proof.

"And reject my jokes."

"Ah." He swallows, his expression turning uncomfortable. Good. "Do you want to sit?" He gestures at the front of his desk before realizing that there is, in fact, no chair there. Chris stands, grabbing

Alex's chair and dragging it over. "You're welcome," he mutters after I sit down.

"I didn't ask you to fetch me a chair," I retort.

"Doesn't that make it even more chivalrous?" He smiles again, and I get the sense that that smile has gotten him out of countless situations. I can practically see Chris throughout his life, charming teachers and authority figures, skating by on good looks and boyish charm.

He's trying to do the same thing to me, and it only pisses me off more.

"What's wrong with my jokes?"

He sighs, running a hand through his honey-brown waves. They become even more perfectly tousled, which shouldn't be scientifically possible. "That's a complicated question," His tone is placating, condescending, and it makes me want to pull his stupid hair until he gives me a straight answer.

"That's why I asked you for a meeting."

"And here I was, thinking you just wanted to spend time with me." That grin again. Is he...no. He can't be.

He winks.

He's fucking *flirting* with me.

As if a few meager handfuls of attention from such a handsome man will make me forget all of my troubles.

I give him my sweetest smile. "You got me." He looks relieved, and I continue, "I just have, like, the biggest crush on you, and the only way I could think of to ask you out was to request a meeting." I lean forward as his expression grows more perplexed, his brows knitting together. "All I do is think about you, Chris. My office is covered in pictures of you, and sometimes, late at night, I—"

"I get it," he growls, his face an extremely satisfying shade of vermilion.

"No, you don't," I scoff. "You have no idea what it's like to have the thing you've wanted since you were a child kept from you by a pair of idiotic assholes."

"Well, you didn't have to be a bitch about it."

The word hangs between us, and I wait.

But he doesn't apologize. He doesn't even have the decency to look embarrassed. Why should he, for calling a bitch out? Because clearly any woman who dares challenge him must be one.

"Bitches get shit done, Galloway."

"I think you should leave."

"What, before my knight in shining armor apologizes?"

"I'm finding myself decidedly not sorry." He glowers at me. "You're wasting my time, Beckerman. Get out."

"Not until you tell me why."

"It's because you're a bitch." We both turn at the voice coming from the office door. Alex Nabakov saunters in, smug as ever, and I know it's over. Any chance I might have had at pleading the case for my *Update* pitches is gone now. Chris might be a dick benefitting from a supremely unfair system, but when it's just him, he's always been fair.

"Excuse me?" I hiss.

"Me-*ow*," Alex chuckles, making his way over to his desk. "Geez, calm down, Emily. You're never going to make it in this industry if you can't handle a little constructive criticism."

"And how, exactly, is calling me a bitch constructive?"

"Well, maybe you could try to be less of one?" Alex suggests.

I look at Chris, and he looks down. Of course he does. I wish there was someone else in here with me to bear witness. This is the real Chris Galloway. A goddamn coward.

"So, try to be less of a bitch, and then you might consider my material?"

"Exactly." He pauses, trying very hard to look thoughtful. "And maybe cut out the crazy feminist shit."

Last year, I scrapped a sketch idea about menstrual cups when Alex loudly announced at the table read that it was gross. Funnily enough, Alex and Chris wrote a sketch the week before about a fake product that could measure other men's penises while guys peed next to each other at a urinal.

The things I could have said. But I didn't, because I thought that I needed Alex to like me. Every week, I woke up thinking this would be the one where they would finally pick one of my jokes for the *Update*.

They were never going to like me, or respect me. And I'm done fucking trying.

I know I'm spiraling into something dangerous, but I've reached the end of my rope. All of my hard work, the blood, sweat, and tears that I've poured into *Live From New York* since I was first hired, and the two of them are standing in my way.

I'm done.

Well, I can't quit. I think leaving *Live From New York* would physically hurt me, not to mention the satisfaction it would give my mother, who has been convinced since I first started that the show was making me miserable.

It wasn't the show. That was all Chris and Alex.

There's also the mortgage on my condo, one I bought after my Emmy in a rush of idiotic joy. Rush being the key word, because I agreed to a very quick closing period that came back to bite me in the ass when an inspector declared it "unlivable" and requiring at least a month of renovation. That was three months ago.

I can't leave the show. But I also can't continue doing nothing. I'm mad. I'm fucking furious. I watered myself down in an attempt to be someone more palatable to men with control over my future, and it didn't matter.

"So, we're done here?" Alex asks. Well, it's phrased like a question, but he clearly doesn't expect a response. "Oh, and can you tell Faith we'll send her the final draft tonight for her to check?"

He *would* ask me to do something for him that he's perfectly capable of doing himself, like I'm his assistant.

"To check for what?" Faith Hernandez is another writer on the show, and a cast member. Why on earth would she be checking their work?

"Typos. Duh."

"You make Faith check for typos?" A fitting reminder that if it's bad for white women, it's worse for women of color.

"She offered," Alex replies.

My gaze swings to Chris, and once again, he says nothing. His face is so carefully blank that I find myself almost missing the shameless charmer of a few minutes ago. At least that would be *something*, compared to this utter lack of reaction to something objectively horrible.

"You know what?" I say, a plan beginning to form in my head. "Let me."

"Really?" Chris looks understandably skeptical.

"Yeah," I try to look demure. "You guys are right. I have been a bitch. But I want to change."

Chris doesn't look convinced, but he clearly doesn't argue with Alex.

"Dude, you're the best. And I love that attitude. Keep it up, and you'll go far." It takes every ounce of my self-control not to sarcastically thank Alex for that sage life advice.

I'm never going to change their minds. But I can do something undeniably bitchy. After all, I have a reputation to live up to.

It's almost too easy to replace one of the already written *Update* jokes with one of my own. Alex doesn't even bother having me send them back to him after I've proofread. I just pass the final jokes along to the teleprompter.

I didn't change much. And I put it at the very end, where it will hopefully go unnoticed until it's too late.

Now, I'm watching the final few minutes before the segment begins, hoping I don't look too excited. Chris and Alex go through the motions, finding their seats and getting mic'd up. Alex gets a final dusting of powder on his nose and forehead. He doesn't thank the makeup artist. Chris does.

But thanking someone is easy. Standing up to an asshole, one whose power helped your career just as much as it helped his? That's hard.

The show starts, and I watch them run through the lines preceding mine. Anticipation unfurls in my gut, my blood pounding in my ears as they get closer and closer to my line. When Chris delivers the joke directly before the one I snuck in, every part of my body goes taut. It's a different kind of nervous than how I've felt before my sketches were aired, and not just because no one else knows what's about to happen. It's different because this is the *Weekend Update*. All I've ever wanted since I started as a writer was to have one of my jokes make it on the *Update*.

I wish it was happening differently. But desperate times, and all that.

Alex pauses for laughter before he begins to read. "A new study has found that men with large penises are at a higher risk for several forms of cancer and long-term health issues," he pauses for a beat, and my breath hitches in my throat as I wonder whether he's going to finish the joke. "It was paid for and conducted by my new charity, Size Doesn't Matter."

How do you like me now, Nabakov?

2

There's a breath of silence before the laughter hits. It's the loudest and longest one of the night. They all assume Alex is in on the joke.

Except, he's not.

I wait for Alex's hurried "this has been the *Weekend Update*," his frantic push to get the cameras cut out so he can throw a temper tantrum. Or maybe Chris will be the one to pull the plug. He's used to cleaning up Alex's messes.

Except, neither of them does anything. They sit there, frozen. Chris with shock, and Alex with anger.

No, not anger. Rage. A vein throbs in his forehead, his face turns red, his chest heaves.

"Who did it?" Alex breathes, his voice scarily calm.

"I'm Chris Galloway, this has been the *Weekend Update*," Chris says hastily, trying to save face. But it's too late. Because Alex is standing, and the cameras are still rolling.

"Who the fuck did this?" Alex shouts, his vengeful gaze sweeping across the room. I don't know whether to be relieved or insulted that it doesn't even stop on me. He doesn't think I'm capable of doing something like this.

"It was a mistake." Chris places a hand on his friend's arm, but Alex shrugs it off.

Alex's lips curl into an ugly sneer. "No, it wasn't. *Someone,*" he spins slowly, his expression growing maniacal, "Thought they could embarrass me. By spreading *lies.*"

Of course he cares more that he was forced to make a joke about his penis being small on live television than the fact that someone managed to sneak a joke he and Chris didn't write onto the teleprompter.

"It doesn't matter." Chris looks frantically into the camera, but apparently Alex's abhorrent behavior has finally caught up with him, because no one has stopped recording. Our crew knows as well as I do that he deserves this.

Alex's nice-guy mask is coming off.

This, I didn't anticipate. I thought he was a better actor. I was content to have this be a little prank, something that no one but the *Live From New York* staff ever knew happened in a way it wasn't supposed to. Alex would be pissed and embarrassed, but he would hide it from the world the way he always did.

Instead, he's melting down in front of a live studio audience.

"It doesn't matter?" he screeches. "It's a fucking lie!"

I realize that I'm just on the edge of the *Update* stage now, out of the wings. I'm not the only one who has drifted forward. Other cast and crew members who were watching are gathered beside me, watching the show. Hopefully, enjoying it as much as I am.

And then Alex's hand reaches for his belt, and my jaw hits the floor.

He unbuckles it, reaching for the top button of his pants, and yanks them down his legs.

And suddenly Alex Nabakov is standing in his *red silk* boxers, on live television, and no one can do anything but stare at him in frozen shock.

"MY PENIS IS ENORMOUS!" He shouts, gesturing towards his groin for emphasis. "And I'll fucking prove it!"

He's reaching for the top of his boxers, when—

"Shut it down. *Now*," Jessica Braugher's arrival spurs everyone into action. She doesn't shout. She doesn't have to. When you're the most powerful person in comedy, everyone listens.

The blinking red light turns off, signaling the live feed is down, and still, no one speaks. Even Alex has gone silent, his hand still frozen on the hem of his boxers.

"You're fired."

"You can't do that," Alex protests. "My uncle—"

"Can't save you from this. You just screamed the f-bomb and took off your clothes on live television. You're done here. Put your pants on and get out, or I'm calling security." Jessica fixes him with a look of utter disgust. If I were on the receiving end of that from the woman who created *Live From New York*, I'd probably melt. But Alex only looks shocked. He was probably convinced that his privilege would protect him forever. It would have, if he didn't have a sore spot between his legs.

"And just so you know, it's always the ones with the smallest packages who feel the need to act like the biggest dicks," Jessica adds, a final nail in the coffin.

A few cheers rise up from the gathered crowd, but she shuts them down with a single look. "The rest of you, we have thirty minutes of show left. Get back to work." And then she stalks off.

Alex is gone. It seems too good to be true, but it is. He's done. We're free. And I was the one who brought him down. Not that I would ever claim credit—that would make me the next one to get the ax.

Suddenly, I feel the heat of someone's gaze on me. I turn, and Chris is staring with narrowed eyes. My stomach plummets.

He knows. And he looks even more angry than Jessica.

It only takes fifteen minutes for me to be summoned to my execution.

I drag my feet as I walk through the halls towards Jessica's office, savoring my last glimpses of the place I'd dreamed of working for so long.

Five seconds. That was how long my hope lasted, when I thought Alex was gone and I was staying. Five seconds of imagining what this show could be without his horrible influence. What *I* could achieve.

Actual jokes on the *Weekend Update* that were supposed to be there.

You will never learn your lesson. My eyes catch on framed photos of famous sketches. I had a good thing here. I had everything I could have wanted on this show, except for the *Update*, and I threw it all away for one laugh at Alex's expense. Was torpedoing his career worth it if mine is going down with it?

It's a familiar pattern of mine: act first, think later. Tell the joke, go too far, lose everything.

When I was six, I convinced my younger cousin to eat a hot pepper from our garden and had my Polly Pocket dolls taken away for a month. At ten, I called my fourth-grade teacher by her first name in front of the entire class and got sent to the principal's office, and at thirteen, I called child protective services when my parents wouldn't let me go to the midnight premiere of New Moon.

The first time I was ever fired was when I was twenty-two. I was a fresh, optimistic college graduate convinced that a few open mic nights would catapult me straight on to Live From New York. During the day, I worked at the Jewish Federation of New York City. As an assistant in their fundraising department, my main responsibility was calling people who had previously donated and trying to get them to do so again. It was a job that shouldn't have left much room for creativity. I was given a script that mentioned many of the wonderful things the Jewish Federation did. I embellished on it, to my own downfall.

"Please consider matching or increasing your donation to the

Jewish Federation of greater New York City. Our Jewish space laser is in desperate need of repairs," I tried on Karen Ettelson, who promptly hung up.

"We need your help to reach this year's financial goal, and we'd really prefer not to steal any more money from the National Mint than we have to," I pitched Earl Helfand, who actually spent a good ten minutes playing into the bit with me until I saw my supervisor coming and had to actually ask him if he was renewing his donation. Which he did, although probably not due to my efforts. Or rather, lack thereof.

"Inflation has caused the price of gentile infant blood to double, and with Passover around the corner, we need all of the financial assistance we can get. If you're unable to contribute money, perhaps you'd be interested in volunteering to help us bake matzah infused with the blood of Christian infants for families that may not be able to afford their own?" In hindsight, I should have known that I crossed a line with that one. But I couldn't help myself. I didn't just want to be funny. I wanted to be different, to challenge people and defy expectations.

Humor saved me and damned me. Growing up, I was the girl who made weird, borderline insulting jokes under her breath. Maybe if I'd been a boy, I would have been the class clown. If I were hot in the way that high schoolers valued, I might have even leveraged my jokes into some kind of popularity. But I was unfashionably curvy and had braces until I was seventeen. More importantly, I was deeply insecure in the way that most high schoolers are, and it undercut any inroads towards friendship that my sense of humor might have made.

Live From New York has been no different. I don't write well with others. My success on the show is mine and mine alone, for better or for worse. For the first two years, I tried. I tried to work with the other writers, but it became clear that my perfectionism and nitpicking made me an intolerable writing partner. Understandably and rightfully so.

I can hold a mirror to myself. I've never been blind to my faults. I've learned to accept them, to live with them, even if they isolate me.

Even if they've left me so alone that I don't have a single friend on this show to ask about my idea. Not a single person to tell me that it was stupid. I had to find that out for myself when it was already too late.

I pause in front of the door to Jessica's office.

"She's an idiot. What did she think would happen?" The outrage and frank assessment in Chris's voice makes me wince. "And Alex—"

I knock loudly before Chris has time to launch into an impassioned defense of his best friend. That's the last thing I want to hear right now.

"Come in," Jessica calls, and I push the door open. She gestures for me to have a seat in the empty chair next to Chris's. He turns around to look at me, and the poison in his expression nearly has me staggering back a step. Not just because it's so violent, but because it's so unexpected. Maybe it's just because the point of comparison was usually Alex, but Chris has a reputation around *Live From New York* for being even keeled. Easygoing. Likable. Basically, everything I'm not.

My hatred for him was always rooted in his lack of reaction, his unwillingness to stand up to Alex that no one but me seemed to give a damn about. And here he is, full of the righteous anger that part of me kept expecting him to focus on his co-host. Instead, it's turned on me.

My own fury rises to match it. I'm not delusional enough to think that anything I say or do in this room will convince Jessica not to fire me. But maybe I don't have to go down without a fight. Maybe something I say here will get through Chris's thick skull and help *LFNY*'s future.

At least as a work environment. Chris and I have never seen eye to eye comedically. I can count on one hand the times he's laughed at one of my sketches at a table read, and the same can be said of my reaction to his. His style of writing…it's safe. Boring. He writes sketches about dogs and the dads who didn't want them, crazy ex-girlfriends, and worst of all, *sports*. I rolled my eyes so hard they almost fell out of my head at this week's table read, when I had to suffer through one about airplane food.

He writes as if he's trying not to ruffle any feathers. I write with the express intent of not just ruffling those feathers, but blowing them straight off the bird.

I sit, lifting my chin and ignoring Chris's expression of disgust. Fuck him. I never cared what he thought of me before. No reason to start now.

"So," Jessica stretches that word out for longer than two letters should be capable of being stretched, tenting her fingers on her desk. "You fucked up, Emily."

Her words instantly fill me with shame. Chris's anger was one thing, but I actually respect Jessica. "I know that what I did was…unorthodox."

"It was morally repugnant," Chris snaps.

"So is 90 percent of what comes out of Alex's mouth, and you never gave a damn then," I retort.

"You should be ashamed of yourself."

"Really?" I wish I could raise a single eyebrow so much right now. "Me, and not the man who was about to take his pants off on live television?"

"You got Alex fired!"

"*Alex* got Alex fired," I hiss. "I'm not responsible for a grown man's mental breakdown over a joke hinting that he has a small penis."

"I'd say it was strongly implied." Jessica shakes her head. "But that's not what we're here to discuss,"

"What?" Chris demands.

"Good," I reply at the same time.

"But you're firing her, right?" he adds. "You have to,"

"Excuse me?" She pulls off the single eyebrow raise flawlessly.

"I'm sure I didn't just hear you tell me what to do on my own show, Christopher."

He blanches. "I'm sorry."

"I should fire you," Jessica says quietly, and my stomach lurches, until she continues. "But I'm not going to."

"What?" Chris and I exclaim at the same time, although he's outraged and I'm relieved.

"Thank you so much, Jessica," I beam, feeling the weight of anxiety lifted off my chest. "It won't happen again."

"It won't have to. Because I'm putting you on the *Weekend Update* desk."

For the second time tonight, my mouth falls open.

I may have dreamed about being a *Weekend Update* anchor when I was younger, but that dream was quickly crushed when I started on *Live From New York* and couldn't even manage to get a joke onto my beloved segment. And, at the risk of sounding self-pitying, the reality that my size sixteen body wasn't exactly the kind that usually made it from behind the camera to in front of it.

Chris makes a strangled noise. "No."

Of course, he would rob me of enjoying the moment my wildest dream comes true.

"That joke almost lost you your job. But it's also getting you a promotion, because it's the biggest laugh I've heard on the *Update* this entire season. The biggest laugh of this season, unfortunately."

Unease settles into me. *What does that mean?*

"Please, Jessica." Chris looks horrified. "You can't."

"Sorry, Galloway," I say. I can't help the triumphant smirk on my face. Well, maybe I could help it, but I don't want to. "You had your chance."

The corners of Jessica's mouth turn up ever so slightly. "You misunderstand me, Emily. Chris isn't leaving the *Update*. You're going to do it together."

"No," I breathe, my elation evaporating. I look at Chris, and our eyes meet. For once, we're in agreement. This is the worst possible scenario. "We...we can't."

"We have nothing in common."

"I'm not asking you to get married." Jessica says.

"I hate his jokes," I say emphatically.

"I hate hers more," he adds.

"He's an asshole."

"She's a disrespectful loose cannon."

"He's a pushover," I fire back.

"She's never even been on TV before!"

"He's an empty-headed flirt who spends more time trying to get into actresses' pants than he does writing."

"That is *not* true," Chris growls. "I don't spend any time trying to get into anyone's pants. I don't have to," he adds smugly.

"Oh, spare me," I spit. "Do you not remember when you insinuated that I only made a meeting with you to spend time in your oh-so-incredible presence?"

"I wasn't serious."

"Because you're never serious!"

"Excuse me," We stop arguing and turn to Jessica. I expect her to look horrified, quickly realizing that she's made a terrible mistake, but instead she looks...delighted. "Save that arguing for the cameras,"

"You...you want us to fight?"

"I want you to *spark*," she clarifies. "I want *Update* hosts who actually have chemistry,"

"Alex and I had chemistry," Chris protests.

"I bet you did," I mutter under my breath.

"You and Alex had nothing," Jessica sighs. "Chris, you're talented. But you've spent your entire career playing second fiddle to Alex. No one wants to watch Gaston and his little sidekick."

"Le Fou," Chris supplies. "What? It's a classic," he adds defensively at our looks of surprise, the tips of his ears turning slightly red with embarrassment.

"Right. My point is, I think you both have a lot to learn from each other," Our expressions must change, because she continues, "Don't look so surprised. Emily, you're a strong writer, but you don't know how to compromise. And Chris, all you've done is compromise yourself to placate Alex. You're not the only one. We didn't have a choice, because of his fucking uncle," Jessica sighs. "His display today gave me no choice but to fire him."

"But...that's a good thing, right?" I ask, because Jessica doesn't look pleased over losing his dead weight.

"It should be." She rubs her temple. "I don't know if either of you have noticed, but this show has been experiencing a ratings problem."

"Because Alex turned it into a self-flagellating garbage fire," I say. "But he's gone now, so it's fine, right?" *It has to be.*

"It's not. Things weren't great before Alex, but he made them worse. He was the only thing saving us from the chopping block. Alex wanted to work on this show, so his uncle kept us alive."

"What are you saying?" Chris asks.

"I'm saying if we can't turn things around next season, it's going to be our last," Jessica replies.

It can't be true. *Live From New York* is a television institution. The most successful comedians in the world got their start here. The most legendary entertainers and performers in the world clamor for a spot on this stage. How could that possibly go away?

"No," I choke. "That's not true."

"I wish it weren't." Somehow, seeing the pain and disappointment in Jessica's eyes is what makes it real for me. I clench the sides of the chair as my heart plummets into my stomach. *I cannot let this happen. I will not let this happen*, I promise myself.

"So, we 'spark'," I make sure to use air quotes. "On the *Update* and get people talking,"

"Not just on the *Update*. I never said anything, because I didn't exactly anticipate Alex's exit, but the two of you were my top choices to take over as head writer,"

I might swoon. *Weekend Update*, head writer, and no more Alex? This is the best day of my life.

Well, it would be if not for the guy sitting next to me, raining on my parade.

"Her?" He looks incredulous.

"Bold words from Alex's designated ass-licker."

"See!" Chris waves his hand at me. "It won't work. We'll kill each other."

"I hope you don't. A murder trial is the last thing this show needs." Her mouth quirks upwards in a sardonic half-smile.

"I can't do this. There's no good outcome. Either we fail and the show gets canceled, or we succeed and I'm stuck working with *her*," Chris cries.

My brain hadn't quite gotten that far yet, but he makes a compelling and horrifying point. "We can't do that forever." We probably can't even do it for a single season.

"Fine," she sighs. "Just for one season."

"And then what?" I ask.

"I suppose I'll choose one of you to stay on the *Update* and be head writer," And the other one gets a demotion. Chris and I exchange determined looks. Whether or not she knows it, Jessica has just thrown down the gauntlet. It's a competition.

"Stop it," she says. "I see that look on both of your faces. I want you to work together and become better writers for it, not compete against each other."

"Of course," I reply, unconvincingly.

"Definitely," Chris sounds even less believable than I do.

Jessica sighs again. "Try to remember that if you don't make this show popular again, there's not going to be anything left for you two to fight over." She stands. "I've got to get back for the end of the show. You can reach out to my assistant if you have any further questions."

Jessica leaves, shutting the door behind her.

Chris and I rise to our feet at the same time, turning to face each other. "I hope you didn't spend all the money in your trust fund, because when Jessica chooses me as head writer, I'm *so* firing you," I say.

"Not if I fire you first."

"Over my dead body."

"Don't threaten me with a good time," he spits.

"You know, it's not too late to quit," I taunt him. "Come on. You know you're not cut out for this without Alex using his family connections to get you ahead."

"Sounds like you're desperate to take me out of the running," he replies, his smile far too cocky for my liking.

"I'm not desperate for anything," I retort. "And if you want a fight, that's fine. I'm not afraid of losing this job to you."

"May the best man win."

"Oh, she will."

"It doesn't matter if I say man or person. Either way, it's not you,"

And then he walks out, slamming the door behind him.

3

T*hree Months Later*
"That's it, I'm cutting you off."

"You can't," I protest, hugging my juice box close to my chest.

"Those are for my children." My cousin Rachel wiggles her hand at me. I slump further down into her couch, but reluctantly hand over the apple juice. She's lucky that her four-year-old twins, Amy and Alex, are so cute. Otherwise, I would be much less willing to share juice boxes with them.

"I've always considered myself your surrogate child."

"I'm going to do you a favor and never tell your mother that you said that," Rachel sighs. "Aren't you supposed to be babysitting?"

"Isn't that what Josh is for?" Alex and Amy are currently at the park with Rachel's husband.

"It's not babysitting when they're his children," she scoffs. "You're the worst babysitter we've ever had, and one of them tried to hit on Josh in front of me."

"The patriarchy is so toxic for young women."

"He was a man," Rachel replies drily. "Remind me the latest on your condo situation?"

"It remains the worst financial decision of my life," I reply grimly. "And I was convinced to do a full remodel."

"Oh, honey." She squeezes my shoulder. "I don't want to say I told you so, but..."

She told me so. Everyone in my family told me so, which only made it more thrilling. I wanted to prove that I was a real adult. I'd lived well below my means since starting at *Live From New York*, thanks to the financial advice of two Holocaust survivor grandparents and two who'd survived the Great Depression. So the condo purchase and subsequent renovations weren't bankrupting me, but if not for the generous raise my dual promotion to head writer and the *Weekend Update* desk had earned me, they might have come close.

A promotion that should be the highlight of my career, and yet I can't even enjoy it, because it means working with Chris fucking Galloway.

The doorbell rings, and Rachel and I exchange glances.

"Tracey?" she asks.

"Tracey," I sigh again.

"Hi, Aunt Tracey," Rachel says, opening the door to reveal my mother. "What are you doing here?"

"I was in the neighborhood."

"You live on Long Island." I give her a suspicious look.

"Well, maybe if you answered my calls, I wouldn't have to surprise you like this," she says, and I wince. She's not wrong. My mother and I usually talk at least three times a week, but I've been avoiding her all summer. If we did, she would ask me about the promotion, and I'm incapable of lying to her. I've tried, but she sees right through it. And discussing my anxiety over working with Chris would only lead to her favorite topic of conversation: not-so-subtle hints that maybe working on *Live From New York* isn't the best thing for my well-being.

I don't know how to tell her that this has become bigger than my happiness, that the very future of the show is at stake. If she knew how much pressure I was under, she'd do everything in her power to get me to leave.

My mom has helped me through the darkest times in my life. But sometimes I worry that my past struggles with anxiety have left her unable to see me for who I am now. In her mind, I'm still the girl who called her crying every day of my first three months of college and panicked if I went a single calorie over the limit on my tracking app. But I'm not. I've healed and grown stronger, and yet I still don't know how to tell her that without sounding ungrateful or making her think that I don't need her.

"I'm sorry. I've just been…busy," I say evasively.

"Really? Because Rachel seems to think all you've done this summer is wear a hole in her couch cushions."

"Et tu, Brute?"

"I need to…answer an email." She avoids my gaze, practically sprinting down the hallway towards her bedroom. Clearly, Rachel is as bad at lying to Tracey Beckerman as I am.

"Sit." My mother pats the aforementioned couch, and I do as she says. Her hand comes to squeeze my shoulder. "I've missed you. Usually, summers are the only time your father and I get to see you."

"Don't worry. The guilt trip is working."

"You're avoiding me." Her brown eyes soften. "Tell me what's going on."

"It's the promotion,"

"Is it too stressful for you?" she interrupts.

"No. I mean, not in and of itself. It's just my new coworker. We… we don't exactly see eye to eye,"

"Oh, the handsome one who was on the *Weekend Update* before? The one who dated that actress?"

"You'll have to be more specific. He's dated *many* actresses. The man is incapable of keeping it in his pants," I reply snarkily.

"Don't insult your new partner."

"What? It's true."

"Well, there's nothing wrong with dating." *That* she says pointedly, and I roll my eyes.

"If you bring up grandchildren, this conversation is over."

"Fine, fine." She puts her hands up in a placating gesture. "I just worry about you. You're my only child. I feel a certain responsibility for your happiness. And I don't know if this career is bringing you that."

"I can't just quit, Mom," I remind her. "I've been working towards this for years. Even if it kills me, I have to try."

She frowns at me. "If it kills you? Really? I know how important this show is to you, Emily, but is it worth the cost of your happiness? You give so much of yourself, and what have you received in return? Do they value you for all that you do?"

"I got a promotion," I reply defensively. "And I get to be a *Weekend Update* anchor," In a very underhanded and unorthodox way, but still. She doesn't have to know that.

Her face softens. "I know, honey. And I know how much you used to want that."

"I always wanted it," I admit. "I just pretended not to because I never thought it was going to happen."

"But is it going to make you happy?"

"One single thing isn't going to make me happy. That's not how life works,"

"I'm aware. I'm thirty-five years older than you, Emily. I know how life works. What I want to know is if things are going to be different. I've spent the last six years listening to you complain about this dream job of yours. And I can't just let you choose suffering because you think writing on this show is what you've always wanted."

"It *is* what I've always wanted," I reply defensively.

"No, Emily," she pauses, placing her hand on my arm. "You wanted to be happy. You wanted to be at peace. And you wanted to find love, and a family."

"I have those things." I try not to let her words sting, those reminders of all the other milestones in life that I thought would simply appear as I got older.

"Oh, is there a boyfriend hiding in here that you haven't introduced me to yet?"

"You're turning into a cliche."

"So are you. And I would say this if you were a man, too. I don't want you to work your life away and realize in five years that you don't have an identity outside of it."

"I don't want that either. But I barely have time to date, Mom. Maybe...maybe I'm not meant to be loved that way."

She swats my arm. *Hard*.

"Ow!"

"Don't you dare speak about yourself like that." she gives me a threatening look. "You deserve everything that you want in life."

"Right now, I want to focus on *Live From New York*," As in, trying to save one of the only things I've ever loved from cancellation.

"Maybe that's for the best. Sometimes it's when you're not looking at all that your person comes to you. You know, before my grandmother passed, she told me that she was going to send my husband to me. And three weeks later, I saw your father at Zabar's, and I just knew." Her eyes grow misty.

My mother and I share several things: a stubborn streak, mouths like sailor's, an inability to put up with bullshit, and our love for love. She was the one who handed me my first romance novel when I turned thirteen. I'd been in our library and reached for the second book in the Bridgerton series, *The Viscount Who Loved Me*. Being a sex-positive queen, my mom didn't stop me from reading it and instead told me to ask her if I had questions.

As a graduate of the American public school system, I can attest to the fact that romance novels taught me more about sex, consent, and pleasure—specifically, female pleasure—than sex ed ever did. And they taught me about love. Maybe for some people, it would be weird to swap smutty book recommendations with the woman who gave birth to you. But for us, romance has always been about joy. Romance novels promise a happy ending, the knowledge that by the time you finish reading, everything will work itself out. When I didn't know how to feel that way about my own life, those books were what I turned to.

"So, just send me my husband," I tease her.

"I've been trying." She sniffs. "For the past six years, ever since you turned twenty-four and your biological clock started ticking—"

"*Mom!*"

"I know, I know, you froze your eggs. That's not the point. I've been trying. I don't think it's my fault anymore."

"Oh, so it's somehow mine? Don't you think if I met the man of my dreams, I'd know? Like with you and Dad?"

"It doesn't always happen that way. There are a dozen paths a love story can take, Emily."

"Well. When mine starts, I'll keep you updated," I promise, humoring her. Maybe there is some truth to the right person finding you when you aren't even looking, but right now, I hope that he doesn't find me. I need to get my shit together before I'm ready to fall in love.

Just before midnight, Rachel knocks softly on the door to my room. I'm half asleep, my e-reader propped up on my chest, wearing my favorite oversized Brandeis sweatshirt.

"How're you feeling?" she asks, closing the door behind her with practiced carefulness. Once Amy and Alex are down for the night, no one wants to risk waking them up. She climbs into the bed and wraps an arm around me. I let my head rest against her chest and breathe shakily, setting my e-reader aside.

"Anxious," I admit, the words muffled slightly as I speak them against her shoulder.

"Did you take your meds?"

"Yup." I first started suffering from anxiety and panic attacks in college. Rachel was the one who suggested to my parents that I would benefit from something more than continued therapy, that maybe medication could help me deal with the waves of despair that I couldn't control.

In her usual fashion, my mother immediately commandeered the process. She called me every day to see how I was feeling, making sure that the medication was helping. She even booked a surprise trip to visit me, driving from Long Island to Waltham. And when my body changed, she listened to me cry for hours on the phone about how my worst fears had come true. Listened, and then reminded me in her usual no-bullshit way that gaining weight was a natural part of life and, if it came about because my anxiety has lessened, something to celebrate.

"You're going to be fine," she says, sounding so sure of herself that I almost believe it.

"I can't be fine." I shoot up, nudging her with my foot. "I have to be perfect."

Rachel yawns. "Yes, that's a very reasonable requirement to have for yourself on your first day in a new role."

"It doesn't matter if it's reasonable. Either I'm perfect, or *Live From New York* is over." She reaches over to squeeze my hand as the uneasiness inside me leaks into my voice. "What if I'm not good enough?"

"You are," she reassures me, stroking my hair with one hand. "And it sounds like things on the show have been going in the wrong direction for a long time. If you can't turn things around in one season, that's not your fault."

"You're right. It's Chris's."

"That is not what I meant."

"But it's true! He's basically Alex 2.0. They've been running this show into the ground since I started. Chris wouldn't know a good joke if it bit him in the ass."

"I thought you said he was talented."

I roll my eyes. "Compared to Alex. That's like saying he's young compared to Joe Biden."

"I don't know. Maybe he'll surprise you," Rachel suggests.

I snort. "The only thing that would surprise me about him is if he's even dumber than he looks." If there's any justice in the world, that would be very. For someone to be as objectively handsome as Chris Galloway and also smart…well, to quote my *bubbe*, God doesn't give with both hands.

"Can I give you some older-cousin wisdom?" she asks.

"Does it matter if I say no?"

Rachel laughs, kissing me on the cheek before stretching theatrically and standing up. "Not really."

"Fine," I say, snuggling into the covers. "But you have to tuck me in."

"Deal." She does, making sure to check for monsters under my bed. "I know how much this show matters to you. I know how much you want to save it, and I also know that when you care about something, you put a lot of pressure on yourself. I'm not telling you not to do that. I just want you to remember that you can't control everything."

"I can try."

She gives me an unimpressed look. "Sure, if you want to make yourself miserable. Chris isn't a good partner. The network wants to cancel the show. Those things might never change."

"Now you're just scaring me."

"That's life," she pauses. "We've had it easier than most. There's a lot of things to be grateful for. I know you've had your struggles, too, but I really want you to try to enjoy this. As the person you forced to be your only audience member when you pretended to be on the *Weekend Update* through all of middle school, I know how big of a deal this is to you. And head writer? Emily, you've worked your entire career for this. It would be really sad if you were too focused on the things that are out of your control to enjoy it."

"I'll try," I promise as she blows me a kiss, closing the door behind her.

Before I go to bed, I let my eyes rove around the room I've made my own. Pictures of me and Rachel, my college improv group, and all of my favorite *Live From New York* sketches. The same flimsy pieces of paper I printed out in high school so that I could look at them when I didn't want to get out of bed in the morning, when the fear of what others thought of me and questions of whether I'd ever truly be happy swirled across my brain and made it impossible to think straight.

The show helped me laugh at my problems. It taught me that the funniest things were those that we all share, the anxieties and inse-curities that make us human. I sometimes worry that I have too many of both.

Being on the *Weekend Update* is beyond my wildest dreams, and it's also extremely terrifying. Even though I'll technically have a part-ner, he wants nothing to do with me. I'm essentially alone.

And if we fail, it won't just be the knowledge that I couldn't save this show that means so much to me that haunts me. Existing in a world without *Live From New York*…the very thought of it fills me with dread. I love our show. I love the creative freedom, the adren-aline, making giant celebrities play along in jokes. I love the energy backstage as everyone prepares to go live, knowing that I get to be part of that.

Try to have fun, I say to myself after I shut off the lights. And I want to. But it's going to be hard to enjoy myself while carrying the knowledge that if Chris and I can't pull this off, *Live From New York* and all of the magic it's created will cease to exist.

4

The next morning, my anxiety wakes me up four hours before I actually have to be in the office. I pull out every trick in my arsenal to try to fight the looming panic: I meditate, I go to the gym, and I listen to my pump-up Taylor Swift playlist as I get ready. But it doesn't help, not really. Nothing can erase the knowledge that I'm about to walk into one of the most stressful situations of my entire life. And I'm doing it alone.

By the time I'm back from the gym, Rachel and Josh have already left to go to work and drop the twins off at kindergarten, respectively. Rachel did slide an encouraging note under my door, which was incredibly sweet. I tape it to my mirror as I get ready, looking at her reminder for constant reassurance as I apply my makeup.

"You are Emily fucking Beckerman. You've got this," I read aloud. And although I am in no way certain that I do got this, saying it aloud does help.

Or, at least it did, until I was on the subway careening towards the office. I tap my foot against the disgusting train floor, full of nervous energy. At least I look good in my favorite pair of raw-hem jeans, platform Converse high tops, and a black T-shirt. I briefly considered other shirts, but then I checked the weather and remembered that New York at the end of August and high nerves are a pit stain-inducing combination that even the strongest antiperspirant can't fully combat.

The subway screeches to a halt at my stop, and for a moment, I wonder what would happen if I just…didn't get off. If I kept going, and ran away and joined the circus. Or started working at a law firm, somewhere I'd meet a nice Jewish boy who my parents would adore. I could have a different life. An easier life.

The hesitation lasts only a moment. That's not me. I'm not the person who runs away when things get hard. I've worked my entire life to get to where I am today. I won't give this up without a fight. Not when the entire future of *Live From New York* is at stake.

Live From New York has never felt like *my* show, even though I've been writing for it for six seasons. With Alex in charge, it always felt like it belonged to him. Seeing my sketches on the air never changed that. He went out of his way to make sure everyone knew that he was in charge. But no longer.

Whatever happens this season, I'll still be able to say that I had one season as head writer. One season behind the *Weekend Update* desk.

It's more than I ever thought I'd get.

And that reminder helps ease some of my nervousness, replacing it with fizzing anticipation.

I exit the subway, pushing my way through the crowds as I make my way towards the building. The place where all the magic happens. Growing up on Long Island, I forced my parents to take me here every time we were in the city. It was a holy pilgrimage. I would just stand and stare at the building that housed all of my loftiest dreams, imagining that one day I might have a place there.

Now, I do. I'm here. I have the career I dreamed of. What would little Emily think, seeing me here now?

She would wonder why it took me this long to get behind the *Update* desk.

I sidle through the lobby, smiling at the security guard as I swipe my ID badge. I force myself to walk with purpose as I step onto the elevator. Although I've worked here for six years, today, everything feels different. Alien. Brand new. And not in an entirely bad way. With that newness comes promise. Things do not have to stay like they were. They can be better. *I* can be better.

Better than Chris Galloway, at least.

When the doors sweep open, I take a deep breath, letting the familiar scene of the offices wash over me. It's not a particularly sexy space. The furniture is outdated, the desks are messy, and you're more likely to see someone in sweatpants than a suit. But if you look closely, you'll notice the Emmys stacked on the shelves, framed posters of iconic sketches, and the pictures of celebrity hosts and musical guests. Our show is the kind of place where Harry Styles sits on a comedy writer's busted yet comfortable couch and gets pitched jokes. I don't know how much I believe in a higher power, but the energy here...every time I step off the elevator, I feel it. A little crackle in the air reminding me of the genius that has happened in these halls.

The *Weekend Update* office is at the end of a long hall, lined with pictures of *Update* hosts past. I don't know if it's just my anxiety, but it feels like they're all looking down on me, wondering what made me think I deserve to follow in their footsteps. Taking bets on whether I'll crash and burn, on if I'm going to be the reason that their portraits are all taken down.

"I've got this, you guys," I whisper. They still look like they don't believe me. I don't blame them. I don't really believe me, either.

It seems as if the hall goes on forever. I finally reach the door to the *Update* office. Pushing it open without knocking fills me with dread. It doesn't feel like my space. It feels like the place I could never get into, that last barrier between me and my goals. And I don't even know if I want to make myself at home the way I probably should.

Yes, I'm going to be spending a lot of time here. I should nest. But it all feels so temporary. And it kind of is. Even if Chris and I somehow manage to save the show from being canceled, only one of us is staying at the end of this season.

I step inside, feeling as if I've crossed some invisible barrier. My things from my other desk have been dumped on top. I run a finger across the wooden surface, thinking of all the people who have sat here and written jokes before me. If I sit here long enough, can I absorb their skill and wisdom through comedy osmosis? I place my cheek against the desk, willing some of that energy to infiltrate its way into my body.

"What are you doing?" Chris asks from the doorway.

"Nothing!" I jump up, smoothing my hands along the front of my clothes. "Just, uh, unpacking."

"Right." He makes his way over to his desk in a few short strides. Has the office always been this small? When it wasn't mine, it somehow felt bigger, but now it's practically claustrophobic. Our desks are barely three feet apart. Chris's hip barely brushes mine when he makes his way past me to sit down, and I nearly jump out of my skin.

"These don't have to be this close together," he mumbles to himself, dropping his navy backpack to the floor and surveying our desks with his hands on his hips. Chris goes to push his forward, but then the chair in front of it bumps up against the beat-up navy couch. He tries to tug it back, but then he can't even manage to pull in his chair to sit down. The desk is against the wall on the other side, and then there's me. "Can you move yours?"

"That desperate to get away from me?" I joke.

"Yes," he responds without hesitation, surveying the furniture as if he's playing a game of Tetris. There's our desks, with a chair in front of each, two couches, and a small coffee table. "What if we moved that chair to my side?" We do, but then the edge of my desk bumps up against the enormous wooden bookshelves lining the walls on my side of the room, the ones without the couches. They're full of binders, presumably scripts from shows past, with one empty row left.

I try not to take that last, singular row as some kind of cosmic sign.

There's nowhere to go. Nowhere to hide. Just us, together.

Maybe I should say something. Extend the proverbial olive branch. We might not like each other personally, but hopefully we can at least agree that the future of the show is more important than all of that.

"Chris, I—" Before I can finish my sentence, he walks out.

This is ridiculous. Gone is the easygoing, seemingly empty-headed charmer who attempted to flirt me into submission in this very office. But maybe that was never real. It strikes me, suddenly, how little I know about this person that I'm about to be spending all of my time with.

Who is Chris Galloway? More importantly, who is he outside of Alex Nabakov? Maybe he was just as downtrodden and suppressed as the rest of us. Maybe once he gets over the way I one-upped him by sneaking a joke into the *Update* that performed better than anything they'd ever written, he'll be grateful that I got rid of Alex.

Or maybe he was content to ride Alex's nepo-baby coattails for the rest of his career and will hate me forever now that he actually has to work instead of just batting his eyelashes at whichever beautiful, famous women his choice of career put him in a room with this week.

I steal a glance at his desk, and then one at the door. If I want answers about who Chris is, there's one place in this building they might be. If I'm lucky, maybe even a secret diary full of his most private and deeply embarrassing thoughts that I can use to blackmail him into going along with my ideas.

He's still not back. Fuck it.

I walk the few steps over to his desk, my footsteps light even though I'm completely alone. It's unsurprisingly sparse. No pictures of friends or family or a significant other, no knick knacks or tchotchkes, not even so much as a pack of gum or box of tissues. Does the man not have seasonal allergies or occasional bouts of stress-related crying? Ugh, of course he doesn't. That would require having feelings that don't originate from his dick. Well, not the seasonal allergies part. Still, the only thing even hinting at a personality is a Red Sox bobblehead. I glance around, confirming I'm alone even though I already know that I am, and then I pick it up.

Suddenly, I hear the soft echo of footsteps and practically jump back into my chair.

He stands in the doorway, pauses, and then asks, "Why are you holding my bobblehead?"

"What?"

"You're holding my bobblehead."

I look down and my hands and realize that I am, in fact, holding it "Whoops," I reply breezily. "Let me just put it back,"

"Why were you touching my stuff?"

"Um. It was an accident?" I hold it out to him, and he snatches it back.

"You accidentally picked something up from my desk?" Chris narrows his green eyes at me. He has even more freckles now, and his hair is slightly more golden, probably from spending time outside over hiatus.

"I needed something to do, since you disappeared on me," I pause. "Or maybe that was how it worked with you and Alex. He left the room and you did all the writing, and then let him take the credit?"

"I'm flattered you think I'm capable of doing all that."

"Don't be. I didn't say it was good writing."

He scowls. "I think that's for the best. If you think something is good, it's probably an offensive mess."

"Better an offensive mess than a bland disaster."

The scowl deepens. "Just because something isn't risky doesn't make it bland."

"I'd rather take a risk and miss than write boring jokes because I'm afraid of failing."

Some emotion that I can't place flashes behind his green eyes. "Failure isn't an option."

"Finally," I lean back in my chair, "Something we can agree on. And on that note, we should probably discuss strategy for this season. I know we're not each other's first choice when it comes to writing partners—"

"You'd probably rank somewhere after Doris." Doris is one of the janitors.

"Right. But I'd rather suffer through working with you for a year than be responsible for *Live From New York*'s cancellation, so here we are. How should we get started?"

"Don't worry about it."

"What does that mean?" I ask warily.

"It means," He doesn't even look at me as he speaks. Instead, he pulls his laptop out, setting it on his desk. He takes his time signing in and opening his email. "Don't worry about it. I have things handled."

"That's not how this is supposed to work," I fume. First, Alex iced me out of the *Update*, and now Chris is doing the same. I can't let that happen. No matter how overwhelmed I feel or how many times I doubt that I can do this, I know the only way to truly get past those feelings is by starting. Once I start, it won't feel so impossible.

"Oh," Chris pretends to consider my point. "I don't care."

But I can't do that if Chris keeps doing...this.

He sighs, as if I've been bothering him for years and not just a few seconds. It's not even bothering. I'm just trying to do my job —*our* job—and he acts as if that's some kind of annoyance. And that sigh. I don't know if it sounds loud because it is or because of this small space we're in, but either way, it makes my skin crawl. "Look, Emily, maybe if this whole cancellation threat wasn't happening, I'd have time to mentor you. But right now, you're only in a position of power because Jessica is desperate to save this show. So what I need from you is to stay out of my way."

"*Mentor* me? We're at the same level!"

"We're not, though. You've never been on camera before. I might not have had the title, but I was basically head writer alongside Alex." He says smugly.

"If I were you, I wouldn't be bragging about the way your best friend let you do his job for him, but you do you." I may be out of my depth when it comes to the *Update* and being in charge of all the other writers, but I've had plenty of successful sketches on the air. I won an Emmy. I won't let him mansplain this job to me.

"He's not my—you know what, never mind. I won't let you get under my skin. Just stay out of my way and let the only one of us who actually knows what they're doing get this done."

"I know what I'm doing."

"Sure you do."

Somehow, I miss the flirty Chris. At least he was nice. "Jessica put us here to work together, not so that I could watch you type,"

"Then don't watch me."

"Well, I have nothing else to do." I turn my chair fully towards him, propping my chin on my hand and giving him my full attention. Every second of staring has him turning more and more tense, but he refuses to budge. Instead, he does something equally irritating. He turns the volume of his laptop up to full blast, so that I can hear the aggravating ping every time he gets a new email.

But it's not just the sound that's irritating me. Why is Chris's inbox blowing up if mine is a ghost town, when we essentially have the same job?

I could ask Chris, but I have the niggling suspicion that's exactly what he wants me to do. So I call IT instead.

"Oh, I see what's going on here." The IT tech pauses after I explain the situation. "We had to freeze your inbox for the day to deal with a phishing situation."

"A phishing situation?" I'm no tech whiz, but even I know better than to click on those emails.

"Yes, it looked like you clicked an email link for…," she trails off.

"Um. It looks like the link in question was titled, 'Chris Galloway sex tape?'"

"Was it?" I grit my teeth, turning my attention back to my smirking coworker.

"It wasn't anything serious. We should have you back online in a few hours."

"Thank you." I hang up, wondering if there's smoke coming out of my ears. "How, exactly, did you get into my email?"

"I have a friend in IT," Chris shrugs.

"That's a severe violation of company ethics," I protest, hating how much I sound like an employee handbook. "And a dick move in general. And poorly planned, because I would never be interested in watching your sex tape." Wait. Does that mean he has one? Or did he just make it up? And how willing am I to sacrifice my dignity right now and Google it?

"Yeah. You sound *very* uninterested."

"Who was it with?" Hopefully someone much less famous, otherwise the tape would come up under her name. Then again, it wouldn't be the first time an important woman is reduced to her sexual partner.

"It doesn't exist." Chris looks horrified.

"I guess if it had, I would have heard about it before now," I say, more to myself than to him.

"Do you really think I'm the kind of person who would have a sex tape?"

I look him up and down. "Kind of, yeah."

His face turns slightly red. "You're slut-shaming me."

"I'm not the one who called you a slut. And I'm pretty sure that's just for women. Men who have a lot of sex don't get shamed for it."

"Except you're doing it, right now."

"So, you admit that you have a lot of sex," I crow, pointing a finger at him.

"I...I don't want to talk about this with you now. Or ever." The tips of his ears have turned bright red. "I have a lot of emails to answer," he adds nastily, reminding me how we arrived on this conversation topic in the first place.

"I can't believe you did something so underhanded. I should report you."

"I should report *you* for being a hypocrite," he retorts, and I flush with shame. Of course. If we're talking about doing shady things to get ahead, I don't have a leg to stand on. "In case you forgot, this is a competition."

"I didn't forget." How could I? And now, he gets to be the one to control the narrative. Literally. Every introductory email and day-one issue that he handles, by himself, will make me look like I don't know what I'm doing. Or worse, as if I've *let* him speak for me.

"Good. Because I'm pretty sure I just took the lead."

If looks could kill, we'd both be dead right now.

5

"I need to talk to you." I can't tell if Faith Hernandez is surprised, confused, or a bit of both when I knock on the door to her office.

"What's up?" I don't think I'm imagining the irritation on her face. Faith and I both have strong personalities, and we've butted heads on more than one occasion. But I'm determined to turn over a new leaf.

Also, Chris has declared war, and I need allies. It's Wednesday now, and those two days have made it clear that the rest of the cast and writers consider Chris the rightful heir and me the usurper. And unfortunately, I can't blame his little email scheme, although it certainly didn't help.

People like Chris, and they don't like me. If I'm going to be taken seriously as head writer, I need to win them over. Or at the very least, earn their respect.

"I'd like to write together."

"Aren't you supposed to be working with Chris?" She looks at me suspiciously.

"That is...not going well."

"Color me surprised," she snorts. "Collaboration isn't really your strong suit."

I resist the urge to wince. I'd come up with this plan hoping my promotion would give the other writers some faith—pun not intended—in me. But clearly, that's not enough for a second chance. Not when I've made it clear in the past that I was much happier working on my own.

If I want a chance, I'll have to earn it. "It hasn't been. But things will be different now."

"Why?" She raises an eyebrow at me. "Because you say so?" Faith sighs, looking over my shoulder as if to make sure we're the only ones around. We are. "The other writers and cast members don't trust you. Not just because of what you did to Chris—someone we consider our friend—but because you're impossible to write with."

She's right. My anxiety and perfectionist tendencies have always made collaboration difficult for me. I was the kid who did all the work on group projects because I didn't trust anyone else to get it exactly right. And I did the same thing when I started on *Live From New York*. I was a new writer, and yet I tried to commandeer the process whenever I wrote with others. The idea of relying on others for my success terrified me.

It still does. But writing sketches on my own isn't going to cut it anymore. Being head writer means that I don't get to just take credit for the things I submit and pat myself on the back if they're good. It means that the welfare of the entire show is my business. I have to help everyone else and make the show as a whole stronger, not just my own pieces of it.

And no one trusts me to be able to do that. Why would they? Look what I did to Chris. Look what I did to them. When I slipped that joke onto the teleprompter, some small part of me thought it would make me a hero. I'd be the brave vigilante who got back at someone we all hated. But I forgot that the ends don't always justify the means.

Alex was just as awful to everyone else on this show, and no one else stooped to what I did. I'm not heroic, I'm selfish and self-destructive. And everyone around me is just waiting for me to implode, because it's what I do.

"I know you don't have any reason to trust me. Especially considering how I got this promotion. But I want to be good at this job, and you're a great writer, Faith. I want to work with you. I think together we could do really great things."

"That's a nice speech, Emily. I might even believe it if Chris hadn't already told me this would happen,"

"What do you mean?"

"He told me that Jessica's pitting you against each other. And as fucked-up as that is, it's no better that the only reason you suddenly want to write with me again is to save your own ass."

"That's not true," I protest. "I don't care about the competition. That's all Chris. He cares more about getting rid of me than he does about the future of this show."

Faith rolls her eyes at me. "The future of this show? Really? This is *Live From New York*, not some last-minute pilot pickup. I think we'll be fine."

She doesn't know. When Jessica told Chris and me to keep the news about the potential cancellation to ourselves, I thought she meant for the summer. I thought she was just waiting to tell the rest of the cast and writers on her own terms. But apparently, she's not going to.

"Don't you want things to be different? Chris wants to keep playing it safe. He wants to do everything just like Alex did."

"Chris isn't Alex," Faith says defensively.

"No." Whatever Chris is, he's not quite that. But there's a lot of space between 'not as bad as Alex Nabakov' and 'doing what's right for *Live For New York*'. "But they were writing partners for a long time. I think he might be afraid to take risks." Especially with the future of the show on the line.

What he doesn't understand is that those risks are exactly what we need to save *LFNY*. Maybe he won't believe it coming from me, but if someone like Faith said so? He trusts her. It could make a difference. It could be *something*, at least.

Faith only shrugs in response, looking infuriatingly unconcerned. "He's new. Change happens slowly around here, and if Chris thinks it's best to keep things going in the same direction for now, I trust him. It takes time to adjust to being head writer. Give him a few seasons, and he'll be more comfortable stepping outside of his comfort zone."

The problem is that we don't have time. But I can't tell her that.

What follows is more of the same. I stick to the senior level writers. Maybe our newer staff members would feel compelled to write with me just because I'm head writer and I asked them to, but I don't want to put them in that position. And I need to focus on winning over the power players to my side before I target everyone else.

By Thursday night, I've asked everyone, and been rejected by them all. I'm out of options. Our first show is in just over a week, and it's going to go exactly the way Chris wants it to.

I see it all play out in my head and I'm powerless to stop it. The other writers will cut him slack because they like him and he's new to being head writer. They'll go along with his plans, without realizing that the time they're so convinced will iron things out is a luxury that the show no longer has.

I'm screwed. Because if I can't win over the other writers, that means...

That means I have to win over Chris.

"I hear you've been trying to convince my friends to betray me." Speak of the devil. I look up from my computer as he strides into the office, practically with a skip in his step. Unbelievable. I hate how comfortable he is. I want to be getting under his skin as much as he's getting under mine.

He's wearing his usual work uniform of faded jeans, sneakers, a tee, and an unbuttoned flannel long-sleeved shirt. On anyone else, I'd think it was cute, but Chris could be standing in front of me naked and I'd only be able to think about how deeply I hate him.

"They're very loyal. You're lucky."

He smiles at me. The sight of it makes my skin crawl. Everything about me drives him insane. The way he falls into his chair, his loud typing, his weird little snort-giggle that he does when he's reading something that he finds funny. And yet, my future depends on him. I'm going to have to throw away my pride and beg Chris to let me write jokes for the *Weekend Update*. Between that and my sketches, I'll be able to inject at least a little bit of fresh energy into our show. Hopefully it'll be enough.

The *Update* will be the tricky part. Chris can't stop my sketches from making it into the show, as much as he must want to. Jessica would smell a rat if one of the head writers suddenly found herself unable to get anything on air. But I was getting sketches on the air when Alex was in charge, and it still wasn't enough. One or two good moments don't make a difference if the rest of the show is boring.

We have a golden opportunity to set a new tone not just for the *Update*, but for the whole show, and Chris is wasting it. The press release went out at the beginning of this week announcing my promotion to head writer alongside him, and that I'd be joining Chris on the *Update* desk. We're only on air for a short segment, but what we do with that time is going to get attention. If we stick with the same old same old, that attention will go away, and it will be ten times harder to get people watching the show.

"Why did you even bother?" he asks as he grabs his laptop from his backpack. "You had to know people wouldn't choose you over me."

"It's not about choosing a person. It's choosing the direction we want the show to go in."

"Well, everyone chose me," he gloats.

"I'm aware," I reply, my jaw tightening. I can feel his smugness radiating across the room, invading the space, practically suffocating me. I wish I could escape this stupid office. Go anywhere else, write, get out of my head. But I can't, not without looking like I'm running away.

"Don't take it personally." He leans back in his chair, stretching his long legs in front of him. "I just have more friends than you. Probably because I'm actually a nice person."

"At least I'm honest," I snap.

He sits up straight. "What the hell are you talking about?"

"You're lying to everyone!"

A muscle feathers in his jaw. "About what, exactly?"

"Just that small matter of our potential impending cancellation."

"Oh," he exhales. "They don't need to know. I'm handling things."

"Yeah. You keep saying that. But what if you're wrong? What makes you think that you know better than everyone else here?"

"They trust me. You should, too."

"Do you know what everyone I asked to write with told me?"

"That they'd rather stab themself in the eye with a succulent? Or dive into a swimming pool filled with piranhas? Or make out with a spider?"

"Do spiders even have lips?" I pull out my phone to google it before realizing what a bad idea that is, considering how bad my arachnophobia is. The less I know about spiders, the better. "Never mind. No, they did not hurl childish insults at me."

"My insults are not childish."

"They're incredibly childish, but don't try to change the subject. Everyone told me to give you time," I pause, letting my words sink in. His jaw tightens and he runs a hand absentmindedly through his hair, blowing out a frustrated breath. "A few seasons, to chart your course and figure out how to separate yourself from Alex and what kind of head writer you want to be."

"I am separate from Alex."

"He was your partner, Chris. Somehow, your reputation hasn't suffered for it, through some sorcery on your part."

"Not being a dick to people isn't sorcery. And I can't help it that I'm well-liked." Unbelievable. He *still* doesn't understand what I'm saying.

"You're going to be the most hated person in this building when the other writers and cast members find out that you knew we might get canceled and didn't tell them."

"Jessica told us not to tell."

"She did," I give him a knowing glance.

"If you think everyone else needs to know, then go ahead."

"And that would work out perfectly for you, wouldn't it?" I snap. "We both know I'd be fired for that. I'm here by the grace of Jessica. If I fuck that up, I'm gone. But you? She can't get rid of you. You're the only one of us who knows what they're doing."

Chris's eyes widen at the compliment, but his expression hardens once more once he understands my meaning. "You want me to tell everyone."

"If they knew how much was at stake, maybe they'd feel differently."

"You mean, they'd listen to you," he scowls. "Because that's exactly what *you* want, for me to break my word to Jessica and make the rest of the staff think we have to take unnecessary risks. You don't think it's the right thing to do. You're just trying to trick me again and make me look bad in front of everyone."

"This isn't about you!" I cry. "I don't want to make you look bad. You're not important. What's important is keeping this show from being canceled, and I'm the only one who seems to care."

"If I didn't care, I would have thrown you a bone and let you get a few jokes in, if only so you'd leave me alone."

"Wow, *thanks*," I seethe.

"But I can't do that, because you'll ruin everything that I've built," he continues.

"And you don't think a little bit of ruination is a good idea?" I protest. "Things aren't going well, and yet for some reason you're convinced that doing exactly what Alex was doing before is going to keep *Live From New York* alive. It's not. We have to change. We have to evolve and be different. That's the beauty of a show like this. And you're just wasting that, all because you're afraid of taking a risk that doesn't go well. Guess what? We're at rock bottom and have nowhere to go but up. Maybe not everything we try will work, but at least it won't bore people to death."

His handsome face twists into a scowl, even as he pales slightly. If I wanted to, I could probably count every freckle visible on his skin. "I don't want to be the guy that got *Live From New York* canceled," Of course. He's scared. He wouldn't be clinging to Alex's way of doing things if he wasn't. And I get it. But I need him to see beyond his own personal hatred of me, to actually hear what I'm saying and acknowledge that I'm right.

"I don't want that for either of us," I say quietly. I shift my chair towards his side of the room, ever so slightly, shrinking the distance between us. Trying to reach out a hand to him, pleading with him to take it. "Can't you see that we're fighting for the same thing?"

"The difference is that you're wrong and I'm right," he replies defensively.

"Why can't you at least give me a chance? We can see what works. We can fix this together. It doesn't have to be Chris's way or Emily's way. Jessica promoted me so that we could combine our strengths. The best of you and the best of me is what this show needs."

He pauses, and I wait with bated breath, hoping he'll give me an opening. For a second, I think I see him considering my words. But then he closes himself off again, and I feel that little flicker of hope inside me die once more.

"I can't, Emily."

"You won't," I reply hotly.

"Why do you have to be like this? Why are you so stubborn?" Chris shouts. "You have the better deal here! You get to sit next to me and do the *Weekend Update*. You get all of the credit without having to do any of the work."

"Maybe, if my greatest aspiration was to tell *your* jokes on the *Weekend Update*."

"Too bad this is bigger than you." He knows just where to hit me.

Those words sound just like the ones already living in my own head, telling me that I don't deserve this. That I'm choosing my own glory over the good of the show. That I should let Chris have control because he said so, and he's more experienced.

But Chris is a jerk, and so the voice in my head must be, too.

"Look, I'll make sure you stay on when I'm head writer next season." Unbelievable. The condescension dripping from his every word, the way he phrases it as if he's doing me some enormous favor. Does he know that he's only making things worse? Or is Chris Galloway truly ignorant enough to believe that he's being helpful? "You'll have your chance, once you earn it like everyone else."

"Like *you* earned it?" I sneer. "Everyone likes you, but they also know that the only reason you're here is because Alex had a well-connected uncle, and you were Alex's lackey."

His face contorts with fury. "You have no idea what I've given up to be here."

I roll my eyes. "I'm playing a tiny violin for all of your white male Ivy League sacrifices,"

"You're impossible to have a conversation with. This is why no one likes you."

His words don't hurt me. I refuse to let them. At least not when he can see. I'll fall apart later, when I get home and have to face the truth.

He's right.

I'll just have to do what I always do when my personality gets in the way of my success. Work twice as hard, and be twice as good.

It's not the easy way, or the enjoyable one. But clearly it's the only option for someone like me.

"I'm sorry," Chris's apology drags me out of my downward spiral. He rubs the furrow between his brows, sighing deeply. "I shouldn't have said that."

"I've said worse," I shrug.

"We both have," he sighs. "It's just a lot. I thought I was ready for all of this, but I'm a little overwhelmed."

"Let me help you."

Chris's green eyes narrow. "The last time you helped me, it didn't go so well."

"I don't know," I smile. "Wasn't there some small part of you that kind of enjoyed it?" Wasn't there a version of Chris, however many years ago, who didn't like being under Alex's thumb? Who saw him for the terrible person that he was?

He bites back a grin. "Maybe it was...entertaining." The expression softens his face, and for a moment, I see a different Chris come through. Someone I might actually want to be friends with.

Then his phone buzzes, and that tiny bit of vulnerability is gone. "I have to take this."

"I should get started on that whole helping-you thing," I pack my bag up quickly. "See you tomorrow!"

"Wait—Emily! I didn't say what I needed help with," he calls after me, but I'm already gone.

I know exactly what I need to do to help us both.

6

I get in early the next day, giving me a good two hours before Chris usually arrives to conduct my deep dive. I watch the sketches he's written, his and Alex's past *Update* segments, and even manage to stumble upon some of Chris's earlier articles for the Harvard Lampoon. It's sad, seeing just how much of Chris's voice was lost when he partnered up with Alex. But it does give me hope. If Chris was a different writer before Alex—one who I actually find marginally funny— maybe he can be one after Alex, too.

"Between this and going through my desk, I'm beginning to grow concerned."

I nearly jump out of my chair when I hear Chris's voice behind me. *Fuck.* I'm watching one of his and Alex's earliest *Update* segments, because of course that's what he would catch me doing.

"It's not what it looks like." I turn slowly to face him. He's leaning over my chair, just slightly, and yet that small invasion of space has goosebumps rising across my skin.

"I don't know." The corners of his mouth drag upwards. "It seems like we might need to get human resources involved."

"This is strictly professional curiosity," I say defensively. "I wanted to see how much of your past writing work was you and how much was Alex."

He leans slightly closer, his face drawing closer to mine. "You could have just asked."

"Yes, because you were so forthcoming and cooperative."

"And you were?"

I scowl. "You started it."

"To answer your question, most of it was me." Chris leans forward more, until his head is hovering directly next to mine in front of my laptop. "And this tab?"

I blanch as he points to an article about his most recent ex-girlfriend. "I didn't mean to click on that." And I barely even read all of the details of their breakup, which apparently left her devastated. Why any woman would date Chris, much less miss him, is beyond me, but clearly several have—and they all seem wildly out of his league.

"Really, Beckerman?" He shakes his head at me. "You must have been at least a little bit curious about my past as an empty-headed charmer."

"I'm not. I'm curious about who you were before Alex got you under his thumb."

"And what did you find?" he asks, his voice dangerously even.

"You were talented."

"I'm a pretty successful guy. Don't sound so surprised."

"I'm not surprised. I'm sad."

His expression tightens. "I don't need your pity."

I snort. "I don't pity you. Clearly, you chose riding Alex's coattails over cultivating your own skill as a writer. That tells me all I need to know about what kind of person you are."

Chris clenches his jaw. "Well, if you've already made up your mind, I guess I don't need to waste my breath trying to change it." He steps back, putting distance between us. "So, was that the whole purpose of your deep dive? To remind yourself how much you hate me?"

"I don't need a reminder about that. I was trying to find... common ground. Comedically." And I failed. Sure, his old material was kind of funny, but it was still completely different from my style. Our senses of humor will never mesh. But maybe when he sees how much better my jokes do, he'll realize that his way is wrong. "Don't worry. My efforts were unsuccessful."

"That's a relief. If I had anything in common with you, I'd be concerned for my future," Chris replies. "When you offered to help me yesterday, was this what you had in mind?"

I swallow. "No. I actually...I wrote some *Update* pitches that I'd like to share with you."

"*Update* pitches," he repeats.

"They are part of my job."

"And you already wrote them?"

"Last night." I was up way too late working on them. I don't know why I bothered, when it seems clear enough that he'll never take me or my writing seriously. But I can't shake that burning desire to prove him wrong.

For the future of the show, of course. Not because I need any sort of personal validation from him.

"So, you spent this entire morning researching my writing to see if we had anything in common even though you'd already written all of your pitches?" Well, when he puts it that way, it sounds bad. I had told myself I would try to win over Chris, but I found myself physically incapable of writing anything that aligns with his definition of comedy.

"I wasn't trying to cater to your sense of humor. I was trying to write good material. Jessica didn't promote me to write the way you write. She promoted me to write the way *I* write." Technically, she promoted both of us so that we could compromise. But that's clearly not happening, so my only option is showing Chris why my way is better.

"Jesus, Emily. You might just be the most arrogant person I've ever met."

I have to hold in a laugh, and not just because calling me arrogant when he used to be writing partners with Alex is hilarious. Anyone who spent five minutes inside my head, surrounded by swirling insecurities and paranoid thoughts, would know that I'm the furthest thing from arrogant. I'm terrified. But I would rather Chris think that I'm the most confident person in the world than admit any of that to him.

I'm not stupid enough to flaunt my biggest weakness in front of my greatest enemy.

"Look, can I just give you these pitches?" I ask.

"Fine." He sighs, sitting down at his own desk, which is still disconcertingly close to mine. I wonder if the office felt this small when he was sharing it with Alex.

"Okay. I read this article about the orgasm gap, so maybe we do an *Update* bit with this bro type who's giving sex tips but clearly doesn't know what he's doing, and then he can't even find the clitoris."

Chris turns bright red. "We— we can't say that," he splutters.

I frown. Is he...surely not. A man over thirty who's had as much sex as he has isn't *embarrassed* by that word? "What? We can't say clitoris?" He flinches. "Oh, my god. You are such a child!"

"What, just because I don't want to talk about the..."

"Because you can't even say it," I interrupt.

"Of course I can," he mumbles something inaudibly under his breath.

"I didn't catch that. Can you say it a bit louder?" I cup my hand over my ear.

"Clitoris!" Chris shouts.

I smirk. "I hope for the sake of the women you've slept with that even if you can't say it, you at least know where it is. And what it looks like."

Chris's expression shifts in a flash, his eyes turning smoldering. And even though I don't like the man, the intensity behind his green eyes has my stomach doing funny things. "Trust me, Beckerman. If this conversation were happening in the bedroom, you wouldn't be asking that question."

I suddenly find myself incapable of drawing breath. It's been too long since anyone but me and my vibrators have touched my own clit. Chris is an experienced seducer. He's tried to flirt me into submission once before. But it won't work. And as soon as I can form sentences again, I'll tell him exactly that.

"Cat got your tongue?" Chris asks, eyes glinting with devilish amusement.

"Hardly," I clear my throat. "Now that you've managed to say the word aloud, what are your thoughts on the pitch?"

"It's inappropriate."

"Why, because it's on a woman's body and not a man's?" I demand.

"Do you even want to tell a joke, or did you just want to get in a fight with me and the network about sexist double standards?" Chris asks.

"So you agree it's sexist!"

"Of course it is," he replies, his voice full of exasperation. "But do you really think it's a good idea to die on that hill when the entire future of *Live From New York* is in jeopardy?"

Damn it. He's right. "Fine. What about a character who's a snake expert and he comes on to talk about why snakes make great pets, but he's fully covered in snake bites, and as the bit goes on we realize that he's actually super afraid of the snake?"

"So, your brilliant ideas involve either doing battle with Standards and Practices or live animals," Chris sighs. "This is late night television, not a circus."

"Fine," I grit, refusing to let him get under my skin. That's exactly what he wants, to make me feel stupid. I won't let him. We're equals here, even if he refuses to admit it. "I also think it would be fun to find some ways to deliver jokes that shake up the traditional *Update* hosting setup. We could do a segment where we read jokes that the other person has written for us that we haven't seen before."

"That's not a bad idea," Chris says.

"I'm sorry, I think I just hallucinated," I pause. "Did you...did you like something I pitched?"

"It was better than the snake."

I ignore that. "Okay, great. Maybe next week, when it's closer to, we can sit down and come up with some ways to put this into practice? Maybe we introduce the segment and each do one joke, and then if it goes well we can build it up into something bigger. I—"

"I didn't say we were going to do it."

"What? But you said it was a good idea!"

"Okay, don't put words in my mouth. I said it wasn't bad. And maybe once we've solved our ratings problem, we can do one of your little experiments." His voice drips with condescension.

"My ideas," I correct him. "And you have no right to act like they're any less valid than yours. Jessica promoted me for my voice, not to be a little drone writing jokes in your style." *Like you did for Alex*, I don't have to add. From the thunderous expression on his face, he knows exactly what I mean.

"Jessica isn't thinking clearly. Her show is under threat of cancellation, and she's throwing shit at the wall to see what sticks to save it."

I suck in a breath, hoping the physical ache of hurt I feel from his words doesn't show on my face. "I am many things, but I'm not shit. I'm a fucking talented writer, and we both know that Jessica has never panicked a day in her life. She made this show. Things have faltered, but she knows what works. I wouldn't be here if she didn't think I could make *LFNY* better." And she's pretty much the only person not related to me who actually believes I can do this.

"You're only going to make things worse."

"So you're telling me not one of these pitches is any good?"

"It's not a question of good. None of these ideas are right for the *Weekend Update*. The *Update* has a rhythm to it that works for a reason. We can't just blow that all up, not when there's so much at stake."

"I'm starting to think this rhythm is just jokes that aren't written by me," I mutter darkly.

"Look, I've told you what I want from you."

"You haven't told me anything!"

"Exactly," he smirks. "That's what I want from you. Nothing. Show up next Saturday, say the jokes on the teleprompter, and let me handle things."

"That is *not* what I was promoted for."

"I don't care." Chris looks me up and down, dismissing me altogether. I hate how angry he makes me feel. "*Live From New York* matters to me, and I am going to do everything in my power to keep it from being canceled,"

"I feel the same way." If he weren't so stubborn, he could see that my comedy is the future and his is the past. He's so afraid of doing anything that Alex wouldn't approve of that he's going to run the whole show into the ground.

"Great. Then you keep writing whatever you want to write, I'll approve one of your sketches a week—whichever is least offensive— and then all you have to do is sit next to me during the *Update* and read lines off of a teleprompter." His unfairly attractive mouth curls up into a smirk. "Do you think you can handle that?"

"No! I mean, yes, but that's not going to help the ratings. Sticking to the same things that this show has been doing for years is the reason why we're in this position in the first place. People are bored!"

"Because of the quality of the writing, not the style," he repeats. "Change isn't always a good thing."

"You're scared," I breathe, understanding dawning on me. "You haven't written without Alex since you were a freshman in college, and you're afraid that you can't do this without him."

"I'm not scared," Chris exclaims. "You have no idea what you're talking about. I'm in charge now. I'm the boss, and I'm telling you to stay out of my way so I can handle this."

"You're not my boss," I hiss, leaning forward. The wheels on my desk chair follow me, causing me to drift over the invisible median between us and into his space. Only slightly, but by the look of disgust on Chris's face, you'd think I just climbed into his lap.

"Next year, I will be. If I even let you come back." He takes his foot and physically pushes my chair back over. "And I'd prefer you stay on that side of the room."

"You can't do this. You can't shut me out." I sound desperate, and I hate that, but I'm desperate. Nothing is getting through to him.

"And how do you think you're going to stop me?" He smirks. "Tattle to Jessica? Do you really think that's going to make her want to choose you over me for head writer next year?"

Fuck. He's right. Running to our boss at the first sign of trouble will only make me look like I'm weak and incapable of handling things myself.

He's trapped me perfectly. I have everything I ever dreamed of on this show, and yet it's more like something out of my nightmares. The thought of sitting behind the legendary *Update* desk and being forced to read jokes that I had no part in writing fills me with dread.

"And don't even think about trying to fuck with the teleprompter again," he adds. "I've given the whole crew strict instructions not to accept anything from you."

"I wasn't going to do that." I was definitely going to do that. It was my first thought after he revealed his evil little plan to isolate me from both of my new jobs. I hate that he's two steps ahead of me. I hate that we're one day in and he's already beaten me. Or at least, it feels like he has. "I guess it's not personal, right?"

"Oh, it's definitely personal." He fixes his gaze on me, his eyes vibrating with intensity. "You fucked me over. And even if you hadn't, even if I actually liked you as a person, why would I want to help you? The worse you look, the better chance I have of keeping this promotion."

"You're right." I shake my head. "But I thought you might actually care about the future of *Live From New York* more than you cared about yourself. I guess I was wrong."

He stiffens. "I care about the show too much to let someone like you ruin it."

"You're doing that well enough on your own," I laugh bitterly. "When's the last time you've overheard people talking about *Live From New York* in a bar, or a coffee shop, or at a restaurant?"

"I don't eavesdrop on people."

I roll my eyes. His loss—there's nothing more fun than overhearing an interesting conversation. "That's not the point. Do your friends who don't work here talk about the show, if you even have any? Your parents? Your siblings?"

"My family has nothing to do with this." His entire body vibrates with tension.

"Chris, I care about this show. You care about this show. But I'm starting to feel like the people who work here are the only ones left who do. When I was growing up, I didn't tell people that I wanted to be on TV, or that I wanted to be a comedy writer. I told them that I wanted to write for *Live From New York*. Saving this show means everything to me. And your plan isn't going to work. I would have preferred to work with you instead of against you, but since that's not an option, we can go head-to-head."

"And how do you propose we do that?" he asks.

"You write your *Update* jokes, I write mine. And may the best *person* win," I add, echoing his words at the end of last season. "We hate each other too much to be objective. We'll let the people decide."

"Nice try, but no. I'm not letting you ruin even half of the *Update*."

Shit.

7

That night, I find myself walking through the halls without even realizing where my feet are taking me. Now that I share a space with Chris, I don't have anywhere in this building that I can be truly alone. A place that's just *mine*. The *Update* office is the furthest thing from that right now.

Every time I think I might be getting through to Chris, he lets me down again. He's so hard-headed, so convinced that he's right and I'm wrong, and nothing I say or do will change his mind. He wants me to compromise with *him*, when he should be compromising with me.

I know how to save this show. But if I can't get him to listen, will it even matter?

I'm so distracted by my thoughts that I bump into someone without realizing it. "Oh my god, I'm so sorry! Are you okay?"

"Totally fine." I don't recognize the girl standing in front of me. She looks familiar in a way I can't place, although she can't be older than twenty-one. "I'm Zoe. I'm one of the interns. Emily, right? It's nice to meet you."

"I wish it were under better circumstances," I joke. She's tall, with freckles and long blonde hair. "Sorry, I've been a bit distracted."

"Are you busy right now?"

I almost laugh. It seems like a ridiculous question for an intern to ask the head writer of *Live From New York*. I should tell her that I am, in fact, busy. I should pretend to have my shit together in front of her so she can see me as a strong, capable woman in a position of power. But I don't want to be alone with my thoughts right now.

"I'm not," I admit.

"Great!" Zoe grins at me. "Then you can help me fix the printer."

"I should be upfront and let you know that I have never touched the printer before." Our printer is state of the art—it has to be, considering how many trees we cull through sketch printouts—but I have yet to meet a single non-intern who knows how to work it.

"Oh, that's fine." We reach the printer room, which also houses a much smaller and easier to use color printer and enough boxes of paper to last through a zombie apocalypse. "Actually, I just have to press a button and let it update for a few minutes, but I thought you might want a little privacy. No one ever comes in here."

"Thank you," I sigh. "I share an office now, so it's nice to have a little bit of breathing room."

"I have something that might cheer you up." She grins at me before stepping to the side of the printer. "It's technically an intern secret, but I think I can make an exception for you." I follow her, and notice a small mini-fridge.

"A secret fridge? Did you come up with this?"

"I was told it's been here as long as anyone can remember," Zoe leans down, rummaging through its contents. "What are you feeling? Diet Coke? La Croix? CBD-infused adaptogen seltzer?"

"La Croix is perfect. Do you have tangerine?"

She stands, passing me a cold can before cracking her own open. "That's my favorite, too,"

"Right? But I'll drink anything except for cran-raspberry."

"The worst," she shudders. Zoe finds a seat, leaning up against the wall and stretching her long legs out.

"So, are you in college?" I ask, joining her.

"Yup. I'm a sophomore at NYU."

"A sophomore? Wow, it's impressive that you got an internship here that early on," I wince, realizing how condescending I must sound. "Not that you don't deserve it or anything."

"Does anyone?" She cocks an eyebrow at me. "My intern responsibilities are mainly fixing the printer, going on coffee runs, and making sure we have enough Diet Coke for Jessica. I'm pretty sure a robot could do it."

"Well, I wouldn't want to hang out with a robot."

"Really? I kind of would." She sighs wistfully. "But yes, to answer the question that you were too polite to ask, I got my foot in the door a bit prematurely thanks to connections. I can't tell you who, though, or I'd have to kill you."

"Fair enough."

"Plus, it's just not classy. Half the other interns run around blabbing about how the CEO of the network is their step-uncle or Jessica's cousin's sister used to babysit for them. *I* prefer to cultivate an air of mystery."

"I can respect that. It's hard to get a spot here without connections. Probably because of our glamorous work environment," I add as the printer begins to shake slightly with the effort of whatever it's doing.

"Don't worry, that's normal," Zoe says confidently. "Can I ask you a question?" She doesn't wait for my response before she continues. "Why are you *really* hiding in here with me?"

"Because I hate my new writing partner," I pause, shocked at my own honesty. "Did you sneak a truth potion into this sparkling water somehow?"

She shrugs. "I just have that effect on people. You're talking about Chris, right?"

"Yeah. Do you know him?"

"Okay, I may not have gotten this internship entirely on my own merit, but I do know who Chris is."

"How do the interns feel about him?" I ask, trying not to sound like I'm fishing for gossip.

"He's nice," she says casually. "Polite, always says thank you. Makes a point to learn everyone's name."

"You can tell a lot about people by how they treat the people working under them."

"That's true. But you can also tell a lot about someone by how they treat the people working with them,"

"Yeah," I sigh, taking a long sip of my drink. "We've gotten off to a rocky start."

"Because of the teleprompter thing?"

"How do you know about that?" I ask suspiciously. No one knows —Jessica made sure everyone who did know kept it under wraps. She didn't want it getting out and putting a dent in the show's image.

"I was friends with one of the interns from last season."

"Well, it wasn't just about the teleprompter. I think he blames me for Alex getting fired."

"Why? It was the best thing that ever happened to him. Comedically, at least," she adds, running her hand along the lip of her La Croix can, looking as if she's deep in thought.

"You think so?"

"I know so. Alex is poison. He was dragging Chris down," Zoe says with surprising ferocity.

"I wish someone would tell him that."

She cracks a smile. "Have you tried?"

"Yes," I wince. "It did not go over well. He thinks I don't know what I'm doing, just because I haven't gotten anything on the *Update* before."

"You haven't? And you got the hosting gig?" Her eyebrows shoot up. "Sorry. Not implying that you don't deserve it, just...wow."

"I submitted something every week," I admit. "I used to pretend to be a *Weekend Update* host when I was a little kid. I was obsessed with *Live From New York*, but with the *Update* especially. I didn't think I'd ever be an anchor, but I wanted to write for it so badly."

"And you never got the chance?"

"Nope. That's actually the reason I switched the joke out. I had set this meeting with Chris to talk about why I couldn't get anything on air. Alex crashed it and told me it was because no one liked me."

"God, he's the worst. What did Chris do?"

"Nothing," I laugh bitterly. "He never stood up to Alex."

"Not everyone finds it so easy to confront people who are so close to them when they're so manipulative."

"Maybe. But he's free now. I don't know why he's so desperate to carry on Alex's legacy. I wish I could get through to him."

"Hmmm." A small, devious smile creeps across Zoe's features. "I have an idea. But it's a little...unorthodox."

"Please. You're talking to the girl who got Alex Nabakov to say he has a small penis on live television. I'm open to anything."

"That was so good! The look on his face was priceless," Zoe sighs happily. "I wish the show was like that every week."

"See! See!" I gesture to the empty room around us. "That's exactly what I've been trying to say. People don't just want to watch the same shit over and over again," I sigh, slumping back against the wall. "Any chance you'd feel comfortable telling Chris that?"

"Definitely not. But I think I know how to get him to listen to you." Her green eyes twinkle with mischief. Oh, I *really* like her. "You need to annoy the shit out of him."

"I think I already do just by existing."

"That's a great first step, but you need to take it further. Chris shouldn't even be able to concentrate. Make him so pissed that he can't work, and then tell him that you'll stop if he gives you what you want."

"Really?" I ask skeptically. "You think that'll work?"

"As a younger sister, I'd say it's a tried-and-true method."

"Ah. I'm an only child, so I haven't been exposed to this particular technique before. But it sounds promising."

"It'll work," Zoe insists. "Trust me."

"I do,"

The printer makes a noise, and she sighs. "That means it's done updating. You can hang out here as long as you need to, but I unfortunately have to get back to work."

"Thank you."

"It's not a problem. I'm glad to help."

"No, seriously. I've been feeling pretty alone here since I got promoted, and it's nice to know that I have someone in my corner."

"I'm rooting for you, Emily." She smiles. "I think you've got this."

And I don't know if it's Zoe's special brand of confidence or if I just needed to hear someone who wasn't a blood relative say those words, but I'm starting to believe that I just might.

The key to annoying Chris will be to create a work environment that is deeply uncomfortable without being overtly hostile.

Step one: candles.

I arrive fifteen minutes early the next morning to set up and light the seven scented candles I brought with me. I place them on nearly every surface of our shared office, except for Chris's desk. So, technically he has no reason to complain.

When he gets in, I don't take my eyes off of my computer screen, but I can feel the mood in the room shift. It smells weird. The candles are overpowering, and they're all different scents: vanilla sugar, tobacco and vetiver, lavender honey, lemon verbena...smells that would be pleasant enough separately, but together are cloying, overpowering, and more importantly, utterly distracting.

He sniffs. Once, and then twice. But he doesn't say anything when he sits down.

Fifteen minutes in, he coughs loudly. Five minutes later, he sneezes. Or at least, he pretends to. It sounds slightly fake.

I track every second of his discomfort, soaking it in, absorbing its power. Letting it make me stronger.

After an hour, he attempts to open the window behind us. Chris reaches for the latch. It doesn't move, and when he leverages his body to try and get it to budge, his hips bump the back of my chair. He lets out a growl of irritation, but he doesn't stop. He continues pushing and pulling. Chris yanks on the latch and then falls backward with a particularly aggravated grunt. He falls directly into my chair, causing me to bump against the desk.

"Oof!"

"Sorry," he breathes. "I just want to get some fresh air in here," he says pointedly, staring at the candles.

"Didn't work?" I swivel around. My body, not the chair, since there's not even enough room to turn the wheels with how close he's standing to me. My question is answered when I see the aforementioned latch in his hand, completely broken off from the windowsill.

"I'll ask an intern to make a maintenance request."

"What about Zoe?" I ask innocently, knowing she'll do everything in her power to delay said request. At least I have one ally.

"What about Zoe?" Chris asks, some emotion I can't identify flitting across his face.

"Uh, she could be the intern? Do you have a problem with that?"

"Of course not," he replies. "I don't care who we ask. It just needs to get done."

"I'll handle it," I offer. "What, no thank you?"

"I'm not going to thank you for solving a problem that you created," Chris replies.

"I wasn't the one who broke the window."

"I wouldn't have *needed* to break the window if you hadn't polluted our office with these candles."

"You don't like them?" I ask innocently.

"I would like one candle. But seven? It's an assault on my senses."
His eyes practically spark with irritation.

"Unfortunately, I don't think an 'assault on your senses' is an actual assault," I make sure to use air quotes, relishing the way his face grows even redder.

"Maybe not. But *this* has to end one way or another."

It turns out, one way or another involves Chris blowing out each candle every time I leave the room, and me lighting them again. The thought of him blowing out each candle one by one gives me so much satisfaction.

That lasts all of Tuesday and Wednesday. Thursday, he comes up with a different solution.

"You have to put those out," Chris returns triumphantly from lunch with Lauren, our human resources representative, in tow. "It's in the bylaws!" He lifts up a very thick employee manual. "Page ninety-seven, subsection three."

"Why not just ask me to put them out?"

"You never asked?" Lauren gives him a pained look. "Emily, can you please put those candles out?"

"*He* has to ask me."

Chris sighs dramatically. "Emily. Can you please put the candles out?"

"No. I don't want to," I smile.

"Tell her why she has to!" he says to Lauren. "Please."

"It does violate building policy. No open flames. Apparently there was an incident with Willie Nelson and a joint that almost burned down the whole building in the late seventies."

"Thank you, Lauren." Chris smiles smugly at me. "Are you going to extinguish those monstrosities, or shall I?"

"I'm going back to my office," she mutters, slamming the door shut with much more force than necessary as she leaves.

"That must have been a gripping read," I nod at the employee manual still in his hand. "You really made it through ninety pages of that just to find something to use against me?"

"I had to protect my peace somehow." He extinguishes the candles one by one, making his way around the room, until he reaches my desk. He leans over it, blowing out the final candle, and I feel the slight gust of his breath against my shirt. "Next time you want to make a change to our shared workspace, ask."

"Oh, I will," I smile up at him, resting my chin in his hand.

"This wasn't what I meant and you know it," Chris storms into our office earlier than usual.

"What are you referring to?"

"This!" He shows me his phone's home screen, currently cluttered with multiple texts, all from me, each one making a different request.

> EMILY
>
> Can we organize the old scripts by host sex appeal instead of year?
>
> Can we move all of the artwork on the left wall three-quarters of an inch to the left, and all of the artwork on the right wall two inches right?
>
> Can we get some throw pillows for the couches?"

"They could use a little sprucing up."

"Emily, I don't have time for this." Chris exclaims, rubbing his temple. "Do whatever you want,"

So, I do. I spend all of lunch on Friday moving every piece of furniture in the office slightly off center.

"This is ridiculous," Chris hisses Friday evening, after losing an entire afternoon of work. He stood up every five minutes, trying to figure out what was off and why he couldn't seem to focus. And then when he finally figured out that it was the furniture, he spent the better part of an hour dragging everything back into its correct place.

"It's not my fault your buttons are so easy to push," I return.

"They are *not*," he protests, his chest still heaving slightly from his unplanned manual labor.

"Are you sure? Because you look a little...flustered." I wave a hand over my face, and he puts a hand to his. There's a thin sheen of sweat across it. It actually makes him look sort of ruggedly handsome, but I'd never tell him that. "Hot *and* bothered. Have you had a productive week, Chris?"

"You know the answer to that," he growls. "I've spent all week dealing with you. *You* made it impossible to do my job. Is this another one of your revenge schemes? Since I'm not giving you enough control, you're going to sabotage me and let the whole show fail out of spite?"

"You're not giving me *any* control."

"You didn't answer my question."

"No. I don't want revenge. It's not all about you."

"Are you driving someone else to near insanity, then? Because it feels pretty damned focused on me." He runs a hand through his hair in frustration. "What will it take to get you to just leave me alone?"

"Well," I fold my hands on my desk, trying not to let him see how easily he's played into my plans. "Since you asked, I want half of the *Weekend Update* jokes."

His jaw twitches. "I told you before. No."

"Then tomorrow, I'm bringing my three essential oil diffusers. And if you thought those candles had strong fragrance patterns, you ain't seen nothing yet."

"I'll give you one joke."

"Half."

"Twenty-five percent."

"Half," I pause, checking my phone. "Wow. Already seven on a Friday night. Did you have weekend plans? Maybe a hot date with a woman willing to overlook your personality?"

"I don't have a date," he glares at me. "I can stay here all night."

"But do you really want to?" I ask, attempting to bat my eyelashes at him. "All night, alone with me," The bane of his existence. His left eye twitches.

I don't know whether to be flattered or insulted that spending that much time with me is such a strong threat.

"Fine! Fine. You win, you insufferable creature." He glares at me. "Half of the *Update* jokes. But just for this week."

"After this week, my jokes are going to be all anyone wants to hear." I hope he can't sense how false my confidence is.

"But no clitoris," he warns me. "I can't get into it with Standards and Practices. They're a headache."

"Deal," I smile widely. "And, because you teed it up for me so nicely, I believe 'no clitoris' is what all of your sexual partners tell their friends after they're finished hooking up with you?"

"Yeah," he rolls his eyes. "I walked right into your trap."

"Yeah, you did," I smirk. "Twice now, actually."

"What do you..." His mouth falls open. "You weren't just annoying me because you enjoy it, were you?"

"Well, I did enjoy it." I lean back in my chair, crossing one leg over the other, an exact imitation of his favorite pose. "But no. I had a goal. As you love to remind me, we're in competition. And if I have to play dirty to win, then I will."

"So, the gloves are off." Chris narrows his eyes at me. "Good to know." He sits down, opening his laptop. He raises his hands to type but then pauses, swiveling to face me. "You might have won this round, Beckerman. But I wouldn't count on it happening again."

"I don't know. I think it's a win all by itself that I get to go enjoy my weekend because *I* actually got my work done." And if my plans consist of ordering sushi, drinking cheap red wine, and reading the latest Sarah MacLean novel, well, he doesn't need to know that. "Bye, Chris," I wave sarcastically.

"I'll see you on Monday." It's more a threat than a promise, but I still feel his eyes on me for all of my short walk to the door.

He knows what I'm capable of now. Good. I was growing bored of being underestimated.

8

When I get to the office on Monday morning, Chris is already there, typing away. He doesn't even bother to say hello. Without the distraction of finding ways to frustrate him, I'm left to focus on my sketches. Well, sketch. I haven't even started to think of my *Update* jokes. Those tend to get written last-minute because they revolve around current news events, and I'm fine with sticking to that pattern, because now that I have permission to write, I suddenly find myself unable to come up with any.

My jokes are going to be on the *Weekend Update*. And I'll be the one telling them. If they're bad, I can't blame Alex, or Chris, or anyone else. The fault will be entirely mine. I spent all weekend consumed by nightmare scenarios of what my first appearance on the *Update* might be like: complete silence, booing, even a version where an angry mob of *Live From New York* fans chase me out of the building.

"What's the plan for Wednesday?" I ask Chris.

"What do you mean?"

"For the table read."

"Oh. I'll handle it."

"What a shocking twist of events," I say sarcastically.

"Look, Beckerman." He turns slightly, giving me an unobstructed view of his green eyes and the iciness behind them. "I gave you half the *Update* jokes. That's all you're getting from me. Everyone knows you're head writer in name only, so just try and learn something. Maybe it'll come in handy at your next job."

"Fine," I seethe. "I *will* learn. But not because you told me to. Because I need to know for when I'm the only head writer next year."

He grins.

"Stop smiling like that," I snap.

"Sorry. I'm just picturing what my life will look like when you're not in it. Gives me goosebumps."

I respond by lobbing a crumpled-up piece of paper at his head. Unfortunately, it misses, landing on the side of his desk.

I spend the rest of the day and all of Tuesday stewing in my own anxiety. Chris spends both days mostly out of our office. Probably off writing with everyone else who hates me. I sigh, leaning back in my chair, stretching out my legs. "This is pointless," I mutter to myself.

I'm not getting anywhere. I have my *Update* joke pitches that Chris barely looked at and one sketch. That'll have to be enough. I'm not even particularly worried about my submissions. It used to be that I couldn't even fall asleep when I got back from the office the night before a table read. Now, I'm not even thinking about that. I have bigger worries. Like the fact that I'm going to be on live television in a matter of days.

I need to distract myself.

~

Twenty minutes later, it's clear that my initial strategy of pacing back and forth down the hallway isn't going to do anything aside from wear a hole in the carpet.

It's a special kind of torture, wandering through the halls, listening to snippets of laughter and shouts of excitement from behind other people's closed doors. They're sharing sketch ideas, sharing laughter, sharing friendship, and I'm alone.

I have no one to blame for that but myself. I chose this. I couldn't find the words or the courage to explain that my difficulties communicating were actually acute anxiety. By the time I'd had enough therapy to work through those issues and find a better, less sensitive version of myself, I was too afraid to reach back out. I told myself I didn't need to. But I wanted to.

I still do. But I tried, and it didn't work.

I can't control what the other writers do. But maybe I can do *something* to make myself feel better before I finally force myself to leave.

My feet carry me down worn carpet, past tiny offices and the empty kitchen area, all the way to the door that separates our office space from the stage. Technically, we aren't supposed to be back here. But I'm head writer now, even if it's in name only, so I might as well get some use out of that title. Especially since it looks more likely by the day that it will only be mine for the year.

The first thing that strikes me is the quiet. I breathe in that scent of sawdust, savoring the soft tip-tap of my shoes against the wooden floors. I've never been back here when it wasn't total mayhem, full of people running around doing all of the work it requires to prepare a show. The emptiness feels almost eerie, and yet I'm glad for it. I don't want anyone witnessing what I'm about to do.

I make my way over to the main stage, stopping myself before I enter through the wings. I've never really fantasized about hosting *Live From New York*—my ambition was always to be a permanent part of the show—but it's too tempting to resist. I reroute myself, climbing up the small set of stairs at the back of the wings that takes me to the host door. I pause in front of it, gathering my courage.

"Ladies and gentleman, please welcome your host, Emily Beckerman." I cry in my best announcer voice.

I pretend to hear clapping and hollering as I push open the door, waving to invisible band members as I descend the small staircase and then make my way to the top of the stage.

"Wow, what an honor to be here." I begin, but it doesn't quite feel right.

If I did host *Live From New York*, it would be a triumphant return.

"What an honor to be back!" That's better.

"What are you doing?"

"Ah!" I jump a foot to the left, nearly falling off the stage. Faith is staring at me from the wings, arms crossed over her chest and a bemused expression on her face.

"What are you doing?" she repeats.

"Uh...practicing?"

"Last I checked, your name wasn't Sarah Michelle Gellar." She raises an eyebrow at me.

"Well, I'm not hosting *this* week. She is. Obviously," I laugh nervously. "I was just...going slightly stir crazy alone in my office. And then I got back here and I couldn't resist."

"Do you want to host one day?" Faith walks over to me, joining me as we sit down on the lip of the stage, our legs swinging over the edge.

"I don't know."

"It's just that you never expressed any interest in doing anything but writing."

"I wanted to be on the *Weekend Update*," I admit. "That was my first dream. But I..." I pause. "I didn't really think that was possible for someone who was my size,"

"I didn't think it would be possible for me, either," Faith says. "A fat, gay Mexican woman."

"It was even harder for you, and you didn't give up. I did."

Faith shrugs. "I wanted to, sometimes. I started as a stand-up. It was so toxic towards women and people of color, to anyone who didn't fit in a certain mold. I had a lot of people telling me I'd never succeed."

"You proved them wrong."

"I proved myself right." She stands, dusting her hands off on her pants. "Come on. This isn't helping."

"I must have looked ridiculous."

"Nah, we've all done it. Trust me. But you're not going to be here on Saturday." She heads for the wings, in the opposite direction that we came from. I follow her until we reach the *Weekend Update* desk.

Faith flicks on a light, and my stomach bottoms out. Here, empty, under the fluorescent glow, they look almost holy. I step forward, hesitantly running my finger over the top of it.

"Sit down," Faith urges. I do, and then she nods at me, crossing her arms over her chest. "Okay. Now tell me a joke."

"You don't have to do this, you know."

"What, you're too good for my help?" She frowns.

"No! No," I shake my head. "That's not what I meant at all. I just...I don't want you to think you have to help me."

"Why, because you're head writer?" Faith smirks. "I know I don't have to help you. I want to."

"Why?" I ask, tracing a pattern on the top of the desk. I slide my chair forward. My chest is nearly level with the top of the desk. The chair is clearly still set for Chris or Alex, someone much taller than me. Another little reminder that I don't belong here. "You're team Chris."

She snorts. "What is this, a Twilight fan club? I'm not team anyone."

"You didn't want to write with me."

"Because I didn't want you to boss me around. This is me bossing *you* around. That, I'm okay with. Now, tell me a joke."

"An *Update* joke?"

"Any joke."

I pause, thinking of one of my pitches. "A diabetes medication called Ozempic has gone viral for its popularity among celebrities when used for weight loss. Side effects include extreme bloating, diarrhea, nausea, and realizing that being thin won't make all of your other problems go away."

Faith chucked. "Not bad. But you rushed through it. You have to talk more slowly, and make sure to pause for laughter."

"If there is any," I mutter.

"Go again," she instructs. We run through that line several more times as Faith gives me instructions.

"Slower!"

"Look at the camera."

"Don't smile like that, you look constipated."

"I think that's just how I smile," I frown at her.

"Okay. Pretend that you're sharing a little inside joke with someone. They're sitting across from you in a crowded room, so you can't be obvious, but just a tiny smile so they know you're in on it."

I try a few different options until she finally approves one. "That's it!"

"Yes!" I leap up, reaching across the desk to high-five her. "Wow. I think I might actually be able to do this."

"At the very least, it won't look like it's your first time on television," she grins. "That's not nothing."

"Seriously, thank you. I don't know what I would have done without you. This just made me feel so much better,"

"Good." Her expression softens. "I'm glad I could help," she yawns. "I'll see you tomorrow, okay?"

"See you tomorrow," I echo, sitting back down. I spend at least another hour practicing, getting used to the *Update* desk. It's not the same as how it will feel in front of a live audience, with Chris at my side rooting against me, but, as Faith said, it's not nothing.

And maybe the more time I spend behind this desk, the more I'll start to believe that I really belong here. That this isn't all some crazy dream that will slip through my fingers. It can't be. I won't let it.

It's nearly midnight by the time I get back to my office. It only takes a few minutes for me to grab my things. Chris's stuff is all still here, but it's not like he wants me to hang around and say goodbye.

I'm walking down the hallway when I hear voices coming from ahead.

"You've been avoiding me." It's Chris. He doesn't sound angry, just slightly irritated.

"I'm busy."

I pause, trying to place the second voice. It's a young woman, but it doesn't sound like any of the writers or cast members.

"And you told me not to act like I knew you," she continues.

"Yeah, while we're in the office. Not outside of it. I've barely seen you."

"Well, I'm here now."

"Do you want to get a late dinner?" There's such hope in his voice as he asks, it takes me aback. The voices go closer, and I stop, looking frantically around for a place to hide so that I can continue eaves-dropping. Luckily, there's a broom closet behind me. I duck inside, careful not to knock over any of the cleaning supplies.

"I already ate."

"Zoe..." My stomach drops. Zoe. Are they...together? Why else would Chris be getting dinner with an intern? Is this new, or did he get her hired on the show because they're together?

Zoe's a sophomore in college. Twenty-two at the oldest, poten-tially even twenty. Not even legally able to drink. We celebrated Chris's thirty-third birthday last year. I wonder how they met, what she saw in him.

Well...as much as it pains me to admit it, I can see what Zoe might have been attracted to. Chris is good-looking. It's not my opinion or anything—*I'm* certainly not attracted to him—but his handsomeness is just an objective fact, like how his eyes are green and his hair is golden brown and his jaw is strong in a way that sharpens his features even as his freckles soften them.

"Chris, by your own rules, you shouldn't even be talking to me." He must be the secret important connection that helped her get hired. I can't believe she lied to my face when she said that she didn't know Chris. Was helping me antagonize him just a joke to her?

"You haven't called me back."

"I'm *busy*," she snaps. "It's not easy, having an internship and taking classes. Not everyone can be their own boss."

"Technically, Jessica is my boss."

"Whatever," she replies.

"Don't *whatever* me."

"Don't tell me how to act!"

"I can't keep having this conversation with you," he says.

I know I shouldn't be listening in on this, but I can't help myself. Besides, they're basically right in front of the closet door now. If I revealed myself, that would only make things so much worse. Better to stay hidden so they'll never know I heard this.

"You don't listen to me." she cries. "Or other women, clearly,"

"What's *that* supposed to mean?"

"Why are you ignoring Emily's ideas?" she counters.

"You talked to Emily?" His voice goes cold. "Don't do that."

"God." Although I can't see through the door, I have a strong hunch from her tone of voice that she's currently rolling her eyes at him. "You're such a child."

"She's the child! She basically annoyed me into giving her half the *Weekend Update* jokes..." he trails off, putting two and two together. "Was that you? Did you tell her to do that?"

"I merely suggested that making you unable to concentrate in your workplace would earn her a faster concession. Basic torture and interrogation principles, really."

"What kind of classes do they teach at NYU?"

"I like Emily, okay? She's nice. She actually kinda reminds me of you."

He makes a noise of disgust that I really don't like. "I'm nothing like her. She suddenly thinks she knows best. She doesn't."

"Why, because you do?"

"Yes. At least about this."

"Well, all the other interns think she's a total badass," Zoe says defensively, and warmth fills my chest. She might be dating Chris, but she's not afraid to stand up to him. And who knows, maybe hearing this from someone he actually likes—maybe even loves—will be the thing to get him to listen. "We've watched Alex's meltdown so many times. It was epic."

"That's only because you didn't have to deal with the aftermath."

"You shouldn't have had to, either," she pauses. "Have you talked to him?"

Chris pauses. "No. He asked me to quit the show, too, and when I refused...he made it clear that our friendship was over."

Seriously? I knew Alex was a jerk, but I thought he at least looked out for Chris. Instead, he hung the one person who liked him out to dry. And Chris stood up to him. I know the little bubble of hope rising in my chest at that knowledge is dangerous, but I can't help it.

"I'm sorry," Zoe says quietly. "You didn't deserve that."

"Why do you think Emily and I are alike?" Chris asks, quickly changing the subject. I don't know when I became less agonizing to talk about than Alex, but it feels like a small victory.

"You're both crazy stubborn. And you're obsessed with this show, especially the *Update*. Why else would she keep submitting jokes to you and Alex, every single week, even though you never used any of them?"

"How do you know all this? Did you guys do a joint therapy session or something?"

Zoe does something that makes him yelp. "No. We sort of just bumped into each other, and she confided in me. She's been having a tough time."

"She *is* a tough time." That one hits me in the gut. I wish I could shake that label of being difficult. But I don't know how.

In some ways, it is true. I *am* difficult. I work hard, and have high standards. At least, that's how I would be described if I were a man.

But I also let those high standards fuel my anxiety. I let myself take out that stress on other people and treat them like they aren't good enough. Maybe there's a way to change that part of myself, that part that I don't like, without losing the part that I do.

"Stop avoiding the question. Did you really reject her jokes?"

"We did."

"Were they bad?"

"I...I never read them," he admits. Zoe makes a noise of disgust. "I know, I know. And I fucking stood there while Alex told her the reason we rejected them was because no one liked her, like a goddamn coward. As I'm sure she told you."

"Well, not the coward part." She frowns up at him. "But it sounds like you at least already know you did something wrong. So can't you try to work with her now?"

"Fine. But only so she stops annoying me."

"I'm the only one who gets to do that," Zoe says happily, and something twists inside my gut at their casual intimacy. Probably just jealousy that I don't have anyone in my life like that.

"Let's go get dinner." They walk away, and I slump forehead-first against the door to the closet.

This is a good thing. Zoe fought for me. They'll go off to dinner, and he'll come in tomorrow in a great mood, ready to try with me to make his girlfriend happy.

That sinking sensation inside me is only from wishing Chris had agreed to stop icing me out because he wanted to, not because Zoe asked him.

That's what this nagging unease inside me is about. It has to be.

My first table read as head writer feels no different from all the ones that came before it. I sit next to Chris, but he doesn't even bother to introduce me as the other head writer before things kick off. Sure, I've been working with most of the people at this table for the past six years, but they know me as another writer, not as the leader.

Still, I don't make a scene. Jessica is watching, and I know better than to throw a tantrum about being sidelined in front of her. Chris and I need to at least seem like we're getting along. And we do. At least, at the table read.

What comes after is an absolute disaster.

When Chris, Jessica, and I adjourn to her office with that week's host, things go immediately downhill. The purpose of this meeting is to decide which of the sketches submitted at the table read will make it into Saturday's show.

"I think we should use Faith's first sketch as the cold open," I suggest.

"Absolutely not," Chris interjects. "We can't have that back-to-back with yours. We can't do two political sketches in a row." My sketch was about a clothing company designing bulletproof children's apparel to prevent school shootings, and Faith's involved George Santos doing messages on Cameo.

"Why not?"

"Because we just don't do that," he replies, clenching his jaw. "It's too much politics."

"Fine. What if we use the one about soft launching your new job as the cold open instead?"

"We should cut that one. It's too niche. Not enough people know what a soft launch is."

This is ridiculous. "Well, even if they don't, the sketch was well-written enough for them to understand the concept from context clues. So I don't think that's a problem."

"It's too weird. It's not big funny. We need a big funny sketch for the cold open."

"It got big laughs at the table."

"What works for a group of comedians doesn't always indicate what's going to work for the rest of the world." Chris's tone makes it sound like he's explaining gravity to a toddler.

"Then what's the point of even having a writing staff? Why don't we just outsource our sketch writing to the people of America if you think we're so out of touch?" I snap.

Jessica clears her throat. Chris and I pause our arguing, remembering that we have an audience. Sarah Michelle Gellar, this week's host, looks wildly uncomfortable as she excuses herself to use the bathroom.

Jessica is pissed. "We'll start with Faith's political sketch in the cold open, then follow with the one about gourmet dog food. Emily, yours can go after the second musical performance."

I try not to cringe. The sketches put after the musical guest's second song are second tier. My sketch is definitely too good to go there, but I can't exactly contradict Jessica. Especially not when it's clear that this is a punishment.

"Chris, which one at the table was yours?" Jessica.

"I didn't submit one."

"Not even one you wrote with Emily?" We exchange guilty glances, and Jessica sighs. "Right. Here's what's going to happen. I'm going to take Sarah Michelle Gellar out for a very expensive lunch, during which you will put together a preliminary order of sketches for this week's show. When we get back, we're going to start this meeting over, and you're going to pretend that you like and respect each other. Do you understand?"

We nod, and she strides out of the room. Chris immediately slumps down in his chair. "Fuck," he mutters.

"Fuck," I agree. "You really didn't write anything?"

"I didn't have time."

It's Chris's own fault that he didn't have time to write a sketch, since he was too stubborn to work with me and insisted on doing everything himself. Still, that wouldn't have stopped Alex. Our old head writer would never have allowed a show to happen without any of his writing in it.

Chris put the show before himself. I still hate him, but I can respect that.

What I can't respect is his insistence on choosing the worst sketches from the table read for the show. We spend the next three hours fighting, and we make absolutely no progress. Finally, Jessica texts us that she can't delay her return any longer, and we're forced to pick the remaining sketches at random.

I can tell Jessica isn't happy when we make our suggestions, and rightfully so. She switches things around to her liking. So long as the host is in the room, she doesn't betray a hint of her anger, but Chris and I have worked with her long enough to know when Jessica is displeased. Today, she's furious.

And she has every right to be. We're supposed to be compromising. Instead, we picked the sketches for *Live From New York*'s first show of the season at random and forced our boss to clean up our mess. This show means everything to both of us, but our mutual hatred has left us so unable to compromise that we can't get anything done.

It's a horrible day, and it only gets worse when Jessica tells us that we have to stay late to shoot our credits sequences. Traditionally, *Live From New York* cast members have a few photos taken for their appearance in the show's credits, but Jessica decided to have Chris and I do ours together behind the *Weekend Update* desk.

Maybe she thinks forcing us to pose as a united front will make it so, but all it does is have us looking pissed-off and grumpy when we sit down behind the *Weekend Update* desk after hair and makeup.

"Come on, Emily. Just like you practiced," I whisper to myself as I wiggle my butt back and forth in the chair, adjusting.

"What did you just say?" Chris whips his head around.

"Nothing."

"Not nothing." his eyes widen. "How, exactly, did you practice?"

"I may or may not have pretended to tell jokes to an empty audience,"

"Well. I'm sorry that I missed it."

"Just ask Faith for a recap. She caught me."

"I hope she gave you an appropriate amount of shit."

"She did," I admit. "But she also helped me."

"She helped *you*?"

"I know, it's shocking that anyone would want to do anything nice for someone as unliked as I am."

"That's not what I meant," Chris pauses, something unreadable flashing across his expression. "I'm more shocked that you took someone's advice."

"I'm perfectly capable of accepting help from someone who's not actively trying to get rid of me." I inform him.

"Well, not *actively*. I'm stuck with you through the year." His words are serious, but there's a playfulness to his expression. It's the first time either of us have spoken about our forced proximity with any sort of levity.

"And I can tell how much you enjoy it," I roll my eyes.

"I don't know." Chris's lips quirk up in a small smile. "You have a way of keeping me on my toes."

There's begrudging respect in his eyes, and I find myself suddenly desperate to hold onto it. I open my mouth, wanting to say something but not sure what, terrified to break this fragile truce we've found ourselves in. But then the photographer arrives, and our temporary camaraderie ends as quickly as it began.

I smile for so long that my cheeks start to hurt, adjusting the angle of my head and tilt of my chin what feels like ten million times. I feel ridiculous. Suddenly, I picture myself on a subway ad, with poorly drawn devil horns above my head and an anatomically incorrect dick across my chest. I used to laugh at the graffitied ads in the subway—I never thought I could be one of them.

"Okay, now talk to each other," the photographer barks. "Laugh, tell jokes. I don't care, just make it look funny."

"Funny-looking is your specialty," I mutter under my breath.

"I've never had any complaints."

"Not to your face, at least."

"When I'm alone with a woman, she's not doing much talking."

I shudder at the thought. "Ew!"

"Hmmm." Without realizing it, I've shifted closer to him as we've talked. We're leaning in, heads together, as if we're friends having a conspiratorial conversation. He leans in, close enough that I can smell the slightly plastic aroma of stage makeup on his skin. He can't be wearing much of it, though, because I can still see his freckles.

"What does *that* mean?"

"Well..." He shifts slightly, angling his head to face me. I can almost taste the coffee on his breath as he exhales. "You did spend all that time watching my old videos. I'm just saying, your disgust seems...forced."

"Trust me, it's all natural." I force a laugh. Chris's eyes follow the motion, sliding up from my chest to my neck and then my lips as if tracking the specific movement of my breath in my throat.

"Keep telling yourself that," he smirks. My eyes catch the slight uptick of his full lips, the way that one motion makes him so handsome that my heart starts pounding.

"Your little fake flirting act didn't work on me the last time you tried it. It doesn't now." Who am I trying to convince, him or me? This close, I can almost feel the heat of his skin. I wonder what it would be like underneath my hands. It's as if I'm in a trance, unable to think of anything but him. Every detail of his face, the bobbing of his throat as he breathes...

"Okay, great," the photographer shouts. We jolt apart. I turn my body away, placing a hand on my heart as if that could quiet its pounding. What just happened?

I steal a glance over my shoulder at Chris, who looks just as shocked. It was probably nothing. It's been a while since I've been with anyone. This is just my body's natural reaction to closeness. Closeness to a very good-looking person, a person who I can't seem to remember why I'm supposed to hate.

"Great," I say quickly.

"Yup, great, glad we're good," Chris replies, sounding just as uncomfortable. "Are we done here?"

"Actually, I'm supposed to get a few of you in your office, too."

Chris practically sprints up from behind the *Update* desk, hurrying through the halls until we reach our office.

"It's not a race," I huff when he pushes open the door.

"The sooner we start, the sooner we can get this over with," he replies tightly, and I clench my fist at my side. Clearly, he hated our moment of closeness. Which is good, because so did I. In fact, I hated it even more than he did.

"Let's have you next to each other on the couch," the photographer instructs when she arrives. I sit down robotically, placing as much distance as possible between myself and Chris. "Maybe...get a little bit closer?"

"If that's okay with Emily." Chris directs the inquiry to the photographer, refusing to look at me.

"It's fine. Let's just get this over with." I say, echoing his words as we scoot into the middle of the couch.

"Okay," The photographer looks between us, clearly still unhappy. "Chris, maybe you can put an arm behind Emily? Emily, lean in a little bit closer to him? Make it look natural."

I feel like I've suddenly forgotten how to move my limbs. Chris is no better. Every moment of accidental contact makes him jump. His hand brushes my shoulder as his arm drapes over the couch. He's no closer than he was before, but the openness of that gesture makes something inside me turn heated.

My stomach dips as I look up at him. His freckles are a constellation, splattered across his nose and cheekbones. I look down at the hand on his knee and notice that his forearm is freckled, too, dotted with them beneath his body hair. They're even on his neck. My gaze dips lower, towards the top of his chest, and I wonder where else those little dots might appear on his body.

"A bit closer, Emily," the photographer instructs, interrupting my ogling. My cheeks heat as I drag my gaze away from Chris, wondering if anyone noticed. I do as she says, drifting closer. When the side of my body touches his, Chris stiffens.

"Stop being weird," I hiss through my staged smile.

"I'm not being weird," he grits his teeth.

"You look like you're in physical pain. If you pretend that you don't find sitting next to me on a couch to be about as enjoyable as being waterboarded, this will be over faster."

"Maybe if you weren't so fidgety, this wouldn't be an issue."

"I'm not fidgety." I am. Every time either one of us moves, I jump, shocked by the electricity of it.

"Can you look like you're actually comfortable sitting together?" the photographer suggests. "Aren't you two partners?"

We are partners. In name only, since we have yet to work together, but the rest of the world can't know that. Even if we have different ideas of what direction this show needs to take, we both know that much. The success of the *Weekend Update* hinges on the chemistry of its hosts.

"Fine," I huff, attempting to bat my eyelashes at him and almost dislodge one of my contact lenses. Our eyes meet, and every nerve in my body perks up, as if telling me to pay attention. I feel gooseflesh erupt across my skin, shivering slightly under the heat of his stare. There's something like shock in his green eyes. Surprise, as if this electricity between us caught him just as off guard.

"Now you look happy," the photographer crows. "Cross one leg over the other and angle your body towards her. And *smile*, both of you." The way she says 'smile' has an impressive "or-else" under-tone, reminiscent of when my mother told me to behave as a child. And, in all honesty, as an adult.

We do as she says. I try very hard to ignore the sweatiness of my palms and the skin behind my knees, and the way I can see Chris's chest rise and fall with every inhale and exhale. I try, and I fail.

Out of the corner of my eye, I see Zoe slip in the door and position herself behind the photographer. She gives us both an encouraging thumbs up, but it feels like an empty gesture now that I know she lied to me about her relationship with Chris.

"Okay, we're all set. Great work, you two," the photographer crows. Chris leaps up from the couch, and I try not to take it personally. Even though it's definitely personal. His gaze lands on Zoe, and then he looks away guiltily. This is ridiculous.

"Are we done here?" Chris asks.

"Yeah, you two do whatever. We'll clean up."

He heads for the door, and I follow him.

"You told me you didn't know her," I say once we're alone in the hallway.

"Who?" Chris continues walking.

"Zoe. The intern."

"I don't."

"That's weird, because I saw you two talking the other night."

"Did you?"

"Yes." I clench my teeth. "Why would I lie about that?"

"Why would I lie about knowing her?"

"Maybe because you're engaged in a secret and incredibly inappropriate workplace relationship with an intern?"

"What?" Chris stops in his tracks. When he turns to face me, he looks simultaneously horrified and repulsed.

"You heard me." I fold my arms over my chest. "Do you have any idea how bad it would look for *Live For New York* if something like that got out?"

"Don't worry about it."

I wish it were that simple. He's such a hypocrite, icing me out over my own moral failing and acting like he's some sort of perfect person. That's what's bothering me so much about this.

I shake my head at him disgustedly. "I can't believe you. I thought you were different. Did you get her the job on the show because you're dating? Or did you see her and decide you just *had* to have her?"

"First of all, the interns started a week ago, which is hardly enough time to start a clandestine relationship."

"It is if one of those people is the other person's boss and she feels like she can't say no," I counter.

"Does that sound like something I would do?"

"I don't know. Why else would you lie to me? I heard you talking, Chris. You know each other."

"It's none of your business." His jaw tightens.

"If it could impact the show, it's my business."

"It won't."

"I don't see how it wouldn't, if it gets out."

"Trust me," he says.

"You keep saying that, but I'm finding that you haven't given me any reason to."

"I don't need to give you a reason because I'm in charge here."

"What are you doing with her, Chris?"

"Just fucking leave it alone," he snaps. I step back, shocked by the vitriol in his words. "You don't know when to quit. You don't know when you've crossed a line. Or maybe you do, and you just don't care. Hell, maybe you enjoy it, because it's all you seem to do."

"That wasn't a denial."

"I don't owe you anything." He turns on his heel, striding away, and I can only watch him.

Every time I think we've made some progress and begun to trust each other, it blows up in our faces.

I can only hope that we're good enough at faking it to pull off our first show on Saturday.

10

When you're afraid of getting into cold water, people say the solution is just to jump in. If you go too slowly, it'll be too hard, and you'll chicken out. You have to take the plunge without thinking about it. Once your body gets over the shock and discomfort, you'll be fine.

That's what I keep telling myself as I sit in a makeup chair getting ready for my first show as a *Weekend Update* anchor.

Chris is in the chair on my right, ignoring me. We've barely spoken since our fight on Wednesday after the credits shoot.

"You need to stop moving," the makeup artist tells me. "Or I won't be able to finish your eyes."

"I'm trying." I try to sit still, but my leg is jiggling uncontrollably. I'm full of nervous energy, and it's going to manifest how it will.

"I can't do this right now." she sighs. "Come back and get me when you calm down, okay?"

"I'm sorry," I call after her as she leaves. I haven't even gone on television yet and I'm already disappointing people. This is not a good start.

"The polite thing to say would probably be that you don't need makeup, but you kind of look like shit," Chris says. He's not wrong. I've barely slept all week. Every time I close my eyes, all I can think about are the ways that my first television appearance could go wrong and end my *Update* career before it's even truly started.

"So do you." The bags under his eyes are as bad as mine, but he doesn't seem outwardly anxious.

He only shrugs in response, still infuriatingly calm. "That's what the makeup is for."

"Were you nervous before your first show?" I ask, the words falling out of my mouth before I realize how foolish I'm being. I've just revealed a weakness to Chris, one that he'll easily be able to exploit. But something about my potential impending humiliation has me confiding in the absolute worst person.

It's not that I'm worried about my *Update* jokes. I know I'm a good writer. But I've never been the person delivering the jokes before. I used to be hidden, and now I'm completely exposed.

Bone-deep terror sinks in, stopping my fidgeting but making me feel glued to the makeup chair instead. If I don't get up, I won't have to go on television and potentially humiliate myself.

"I wasn't wearing pants."

"What?" I gape at him.

"It's true. No one could tell because I was wearing dark socks and I don't stand up at all, but if you look really closely, you can see my bare legs under the desk."

"Is this a weird performance trick thing? Like, a reverse picturing the audience naked?"

"No, no. Keep your pants on. Please," he says, so quickly that I'm slightly offended. "I wasn't wearing pants because I peed myself. I told everyone it was because I drank too much coffee. Which I did, but the real reason was that I was fucking terrified. I had no idea what I was doing, and Alex kept making all these snide little comments, getting in my head, until I was so afraid that I lost control of my body."

"And you still stuck by him, even after he did that to you?"

"It wasn't his fault. And that's not why I'm telling you. I just...my first time on the show, I felt alone. And I don't want you to feel that way."

"Thank you."

Chris could have easily done to me what Alex did to him. He could have passed on the cycle of abuse and toxicity by making me feel more nervous than I already am. But he chose kindness. He chose vulnerability, and honesty. We've both fucked up, but when it counted, he chose to be different.

And that's a problem, because if I stop hating Chris, I might start liking him. We might start to work together and build something here.

Which will only make it worse when whichever one of us is chosen to stay on inevitably fucks the other over at the end of the season.

"I should go grab the makeup artist again," I say, breaking the silence between us.

Chris pauses, his eyes roving over my face in an almost clinical manner. "Let me try something." He walks over, not stopping until he's standing directly in front of my makeup chair. His legs brush mine, and a little zing shoots up my spine at the contact.

"I told you to stop flirting with me," I protest, but it comes out breathy and entirely lacking conviction.

"I'm not flirting with you." He leans forward, closer and closer to me, and I'm holding my breath, unable to think about anything but the space between us. Well, the lack of it. "Close your eyes."

"What are you doing?" I ask as he picks up an eyeliner pen. He removes the top.

"Do you ever listen?" His tone is playfully exasperated, like we're old friends acting out a familiar bit.

"Not if I can help it," I croak.

"Close them," he says again, more firmly this time.

My mind does not appreciate being ordered around.

My body maybe appreciates it too much.

"Hold still," Chris instructs, gently grasping my chin with his other hand. I'm too surprised to move as he begins to apply my eyeliner.

"What is happening right now?" I say, more to myself than to him. He finishes one eye and moves on to the other.

"Trust me. I know what I'm doing."

"Famous last words," I mutter.

Chris laughs softly, his face so close to mine that I feel the air against my skin as he exhales. He takes a step back, and my eyes fly open in time to watch him put the eyeliner down and reach for a tube of mascara. "Look up," he instructs.

His palm comes to grip my jaw, and I draw in a sharp breath. It takes everything in me to keep my eyes trained on the ceiling as he applies the mascara.

This can't be good for my pre-show jitters. My heart is beating faster than ever, my pulse fluttering in my throat, and I can't even think about how bad it is that my body is reacting this way to Chris of all people.

I'm too busy wondering how it would feel if I looked down. How it would feel to have his eyes staring into mine with that focus and intensity that he's using to apply my eye makeup.

Chris steps back again, picking up an eyeshadow palette.

"Where did you learn to do all this?" I ask when he leans in again, desperate to distract myself.

"My sister," he says as he begins applying the eyeshadow. "She was obsessed with makeup YouTube, and she made me watch it with her."

"I didn't know you had a sister."

"I do." Although it goes against all of my natural instincts, I stay silent, waiting for Chris to continue. He applies a different shade to the brush and spreads it onto the crease of my eyelid, before moving on to my other eye. "We weren't close until she was a teenager, and at that point, I would have done any girly thing that she wanted if it meant being a part of her life and having a better relationship with her."

I melt a little bit. I can't help it.

Chris takes a step back to compare my eyes. "I even let her practice on me. And no, I didn't take any pictures, sorry."

"That's unfortunate," I rasp, and it's an effort of will not to reach for him as he dumps the used brushes in the sink. "It looks amazing," I add when I catch a glimpse of myself in the mirror. It does, but I barely even look at myself before my eyes are dragged back to his face. "Are you two still close?"

"We are." His expression shutters, and I feel desperation sweep over me. I can't help it. At this moment, I'd do anything to make him smile again. Anything to wipe that blank, closed-off expression from his face.

"Is our five minutes of vulnerability and open communication wrapping up?"

Chris smiles then, although it doesn't reach his eyes. "I told you a story about my incontinence, with full knowledge that you could choose to use it against me."

"Unfortunately, you're so charming that I'm sure any attempt on my part to besmirch your good name would only backfire. You'd be celebrated for your vulnerability and rejection of toxic masculinity." When I look back up at him, he's smiling for real, and it induces a strange swooping sensation in my stomach. "What?"

"So you do think I'm charming."

I flush. "I can acknowledge that other people might think that. But I don't," I quickly add. "I see right through you."

His grin doesn't falter. "Or maybe I see right through *you.*"

"Whatever," I'm sure the dismissal in my tone is made less convincing because I can't hide my smile.

"Well, now that you look presentable, I guess I'll see you out there."

"Yeah," I wave him away. "Stop teasing me and let me get myself together before I have to go be on television."

Chris shoots me a look of surprise. "What, no biting retort? Beckerman, you've lost your edge. Don't go all soft on me now."

"I'm sure going soft is your area of expertise," I reply sweetly. At that well-timed limp dick joke, he retreats, leaving me with my thoughts. And there are many of them fighting for space in my brain right now.

I lean back in the chair, trying to calm my racing heart. I'm about as successful at that as I am at convincing myself that it's only due to pre-show jitters, and not at all from Chris's lips being so close to mine.

In what seems like no time at all, we're sitting behind the iconic *Weekend Update* desk, getting last minute adjustments to our hair and makeup.

"Can I have more of that deodorant, please?" I ask. The bright lights of the set and my nerves are not a good combination.

"Two minutes," A camera operator yells.

"Good luck," I tell him.

"We don't need it."

"One minute!"

"Stop jiggling your foot." one of our producers shouts at me.

"Shit, Sorry." I take a few deep breaths, trying and failing to center myself. Despite what Chris said before, part of me feels suddenly, startlingly alone. I shift in my seat, feeling suddenly uncomfortable. I move my hand to smooth down my blazer and realize that it's shaking.

Every insecurity I've ever had seems to be rising to the surface. My body, my face, my voice...all of it is about to be picked apart by people who don't even know me. Will anyone even care if I'm funny? Does that matter, if I don't have the right body or the right look? Was I kidding myself, thinking that a woman who looks like me could ever do this and be taken seriously?

Chris bumps my knee under the table. "Get out of your own head. It can't be worse than the last *Update*, right?"

I laugh shakily. "Don't you worry. I'm keeping my pants on."

"We're live in three, two, one," someone—I can't tell who—calls.

"Hi, I'm Chris Galloway, and let me introduce you to my new *Weekend Update* co-host, Emily Beckerman!"

"I'm excited to be here." I smile, hoping it makes me look charming and not constipated.

"The rise of artificial intelligence has many academic institutions concerned over how it might be used to write papers for students," Chris pauses. "Call me crazy, but I think papers should be written the old-fashioned way. By bullying a nerd into doing it for you." We agreed we'd each read our own jokes, so that one was his.

I start with one of my softer jokes. "A Colorado woman has filed a lawsuit against the TSA for confiscating her vibrator while she was going through security. She also complained that she didn't finish during her pat down."

Chris tries to start his next joke, but his timing is all wrong. The audience is still laughing. I steal a glance at him, noticing the irritation, but I can't tell if it's at the success of my joke or his own mistake. When it finally does quiet down, it takes him a few moments to notice. Then, he finally clears his throat and begins. "The White House released a statement this week confirming that President Biden failed his most recent driving test," Chris pauses. "But, hey, can being president really be that much harder than driving?" That joke gets a titter. I try not to look too boastful, but my first joke got a much better reaction than both of his.

I feel his foot tap mine under the desk and realize that I've been waiting too long to tell my next joke. "Recent extreme weather in South America has led to a predicted cocaine shortage throughout the United States. In completely unrelated news, this will tragically be our last season of *Live From New York*." That one doesn't get as big of a laugh, but I knew it wouldn't. It was a bit inside baseball for most people.

We volley jokes back and forth, each of us telling the ones that we wrote, but it still doesn't feel right. I can tell that, even with the adrenaline rush from being on television. We don't banter. It's obvious that we're on different pages.

"McDonald's and Wendy's are fighting on Twitter about whose burger is more popular. Burger King and Taco Bell are also fighting, over whose food gives you worse diarrhea," Chris says.

"Pharmaceutical companies have capped the price of insulin at $35 per month, earning the controversial industry some praise. I guess when you're responsible for the opioid epidemic, it's easy to look good by doing the bare minimum."

"Former President Donald Trump visited the site of a natural disaster in Missouri last week. He brought along his own natural disaster with him: his hairdo," Chris says.

I flick my eyes to the teleprompter and feel a mixture of dread and anticipation as I see my last bit of material appear on it. My most aggressive joke of the night. "As we approach elections in November, the issue of abortion rights is at the forefront of many voters' minds," I pause. Chris doesn't look at me, but I can sense his unease. Even though I was given free rein to write my half of the jokes, I know he hates that he doesn't get to control this. "There are many men out there writing laws about what women can do with their bodies. But in their defense, I'm sure it's hard to understand that many women enjoy having sex for pleasure and not just conception when you've never given a woman an orgasm."

Laughter erupts around us. I hear it as if I'm underwater. My ears are ringing. I feel like I have tunnel vision, and I can only see the teleprompter in front of me. And the laughter keeps going. It keeps going, building, and I am not alone. Not because of Chris, but because of *them*. The audience. The people here, laughing at something that I've written, enjoying it.

"Well, that's been the *Weekend Update*. I'm Chris Galloway." Obviously, Chris.

"And I'm Emily Beckerman. Thank you, and goodnight!" Obviously, me.

It felt like two different shows. We were on parallel train tracks, doing the same thing next to each other and not *together*. My jokes were great, and I'm proud of them, but it wasn't enough. We're going to have to figure that out eventually. But right now, all I can do is grin.

I did it. I take a moment, just one moment, to savor, to remember, as we wave to the audience before the cameras cut out.

Every other thought fades away as I commit it to memory: the heat of the lights on my face, the scratchiness of my suit, the cold wood of the *Weekend Update* desk under my sweaty hands. The thundering of my chest. The knowledge that, wherever else life takes me, I'll be able to say that I did *this*.

11

Despite having written on the show for two years, tonight marks my first time attending an afterparty. I never had many friends—any, really—among the cast and writers, and the thought of walking in and seeing a sea of people with no interest in talking to me, and being by myself...it brought up high-school levels of social anxiety that made me want to run in the opposite direction.

So, I did. I isolated myself further, and it got me nowhere. It felt like just another example of how much I'd failed, how little I'd been able to live the reality of my so-called dream job. Now, it's different, and not just because I took two shots of tequila in my office before leaving.

I changed out of my *Update* uniform into a one shoulder silver bodysuit, tight high-waisted black jeans and my favorite black ankle boots. I feel confident, powerful, and only slightly terrified. I don't know why the thought of walking into this party scares me more than going on live television did. I don't have an explanation for why my brain works the way it does, but I do know that separating myself isn't going to earn me any more writing partners. If I want to be a part of this show, I have to be *here*.

I push open the double doors of the trendy Italian restaurant we rented out. It's sumptuous and swanky in an old Hollywood way, with lush leather booths, enormous crystal chandeliers, and shiny parquet flooring clicking loudly under the weight of hundreds of stilettos.

Like a wave, the assembled crowd parts for me. I realize why: Jessica, from a corner booth off to the far right of the dance floor and in front of the stage, has risen. She's essentially a combination of Jesus and Moses. Jessica need only tilt her head in my direction and I know that I have been summoned. Chris is standing next to her, looking more nervous than I've ever seen him.

"That was some show." She takes a sip of her Diet Coke, and my stomach dips as Chris and I exchange uneasy looks. She definitely doesn't mean that as a compliment.

"It was our first show. It takes time to find the rhythm," Chris says defensively.

"Considering I *created* this show, I'm well aware of that fact," she snaps. "What I want to know is why your jokes sounded like they were written in separate rooms. On separate continents! What the hell was that? I hired you two to write *together*. I don't want Chris jokes. I don't want Emily jokes. I want Chris and Emily jokes."

"But—" Chris starts, but Jessica holds up a hand, silencing him. "You both know what you need to do. This is not a superficial partnership. I want your writing styles, working together. And if you two can't give me what I want, I'll find someone who will."

"It won't happen again." Jessica Braugher doesn't traffic in apologies, so I don't bother making one.

"No, it won't," Chris agrees.

"Great. Well, go enjoy yourselves." She dismisses us with a wave of her hand. I turn to Chris, but he's already walking away. We need to have a conversation, but if he doesn't want to do it now, I'm not going to chase after him.

"Emily!" Faith waves me over from a booth where she's sitting with two other cast members—Riley Greene and Mandy Nevis.

"Hi," I say awkwardly as Faith waves for me to sit down. "It's good to see you all."

"You were great tonight." Riley has always been the friendliest of the three. He has the kind of boundless energy that has never ceased to amaze me. He's equally cheerful first thing in the morning and at 3 a.m. the night before a show, always ready with a kind word or jokey greeting.

Mandy is a former college point guard with a legendary poker face, second only to Jessica's. She's the kind of person where you never know if a rumor about her is too crazy to be true. I heard that Adam Sandler once offered her a six-figure salary to be his full-time basketball coach, that she once shot down a joke idea from Benedict Cumberbatch when he was hosting and made him cry, and that she regularly parties with professional athletes. She certainly looks the part tonight, wearing a blue sheath dress with Air Force 1s. Her dark skin is glowing, and she's somehow managed to pull off a glossy nude lip and neon blue eyeliner.

"You look nervous," Mandy says, tossing her long, waist-length braids over her shoulder as she takes a sip of her champagne.

"*Mandy*," Faith whispers through her teeth.

"What? She does,"

"Oh, I am," I admit. "This may or may not be my first afterparty."

"That's so sad."

"*Mandy*," Riley elbows her.

"No. It's true," I say as Faith passes me a glass of champagne. "But I don't want to isolate myself anymore. And I promise not to be a dick if any of you want to write with me in the future."

"Turning over a new leaf?" Riley asks.

"I have a lot to learn," I take a sip of my drink. "But I'm trying. I don't expect any of you to pick me over Chris—"

"Oh, my god!" The three of them look at me with horrified expressions.

"Are you two still fighting?" Faith demands. "This is insane."

"You two just need to talk," Riley suggests. "Get to know each other. Become friends."

"It will be a cold day in hell before—"

"There he is!" Mandy raises her voice. "Chris! Come sit with us."

"What are you doing?" I hiss, sliding down the leather of the booth. But Faith gently drags me back up. I should have known better than to believe escape was possible.

"How's it going?" Chris asks awkwardly, sliding into the seat across from me.

"How do you think it's going?" Faith asks him.

"I think I need a drink," he says.

Faith passes him the bottle of champagne, and he takes a long sip directly from it. I stick my hand out. Chris raises an eyebrow at me, but hands it over all the same. I take an even longer sip.

"That was bad, right?" He drags a hand down his face.

"It was terrible." Mandy doesn't bother sugarcoating it. "What's going on?"

"You're being weird. You've been avoiding us," Riley adds.

"It's...complicated." Chris looks down. Who has he been spending all his time outside the office with, if not his friends?

Probably Zoe. My stomach clenches just thinking about it.

"How? This is what you always wanted, right? To be in charge instead of Alex," Mandy says.

"You wanted to get rid of Alex?" I blurt. "But I thought you guys were friends,"

Riley snorts. "I mean, so did Alex."

"I'm confused." I look between them.

"Well?" Faith asks. "Can we tell her?"

"Fine," Chris exhales.

"Chris hates Alex as much as the rest of us. But he couldn't do anything without putting his job on the line. So he mostly just talked shit about Alex to us,"

"Really?" my mouth twists. This is an interesting development.

"I thought I could fix things from the inside." Chris looks as if he's in physical pain, admitting this to me.

"And now you can. Now that Alex is gone, you have time to get this show back on track," Faith says. Chris's expression turns guilty, and it all clicks. He's been avoiding his friends because he can't tell them the truth.

"*Live From New York* might get canceled," Chris says. I nearly spit out my champagne. Riley, Mandy and Faith almost do their own spit-takes, as we all stare at Chris with shock. He's looking at me as he says it. I swallow, hoping the sudden fizziness in my veins is just from the champagne.

"So, what do we do?" Mandy asks.

"I don't know," Chris looks exhausted. "I'll try and be better, I guess."

"You can't do this on your own," Riley interjects. "You need us. You need Emily."

"Alex did it on his own."

"Aww. Do you miss me already?" As if Chris summoned him from the bowels of hell by simply speaking his name, Alex Nabakov—the perfect picture of sliminess—strolls over.

"Couldn't stay away, Alex?" Faith asks, her voice biting.

"I had to make sure this one didn't fuck everything up," Alex elbows Chris in the ribs. Chris winces, and I wonder how many times Alex has hurt him—emotionally and physically—under the guise of male friendship, of boys just being boys.

Anger bubbles under my skin, rising to the surface. But this time, I refuse to let it just simmer. I spent years under Alex's thumb. So did the rest of the people at this table. But he doesn't control us anymore.

I think of Chris telling me about his humiliating public urination as a way of calming me down before the *Update*. He made sure I felt comfortable. He did my makeup. Even with the competition between us, knowing that we were both walking out there trying to one-up each other.

I tap my knee against his, mimicking what he did to me before the *Update* started. *You're not alone.* It goes both ways. It has to. If I want Chris to trust me, I need to show him that I'm on his side. And now that I know his true feelings about Alex...that doesn't actually seem like a bad place to be.

"I can't believe they even let you back in here," I snap.

"Friends in high places." Alex smiles smugly, as if he knows how close I am to boiling over, and he loves it. He loves that he can poke me and provoke me until I explode, until I look like a crazy bitch and he looks like the victim. "I bet you miss them now. Maybe when *Live From New York* dies, I'll pitch my own show for the time slot. Finally get to run things without anyone telling me what to do."

So he knows that we might be canceled. Of course he does. "Well, *if* anything ever happens to *LFNY*, I look forward to tuning into the Alex Nabakov small penis hour."

Alex's face contorts into an ugly expression. Before he can open his mouth, Chris speaks. "Alex, you should leave," he says thickly.

"What? Don't you miss me?" He looks around the table, a lazy grin on his face, but no one returns his smile. Faith, Mandy, and Riley only look back at him with stony faces—a reminder that everyone sitting here sees right through him, down to his ugly, toxic core. "Fine. I have better people to talk to, anyway. Some of us have moved on to *real television*," he sneers, stalking off towards the bar.

"What exactly does he mean by real television? Because last I heard, no one wanted to hire him," Faith breaks the heavy silence.

"I heard he got an interview for a Law and Order spinoff, but the showrunners found him 'obnoxious and arrogant'," Riley shrugs. "Our agents are friends. I may or may not have begged for gossip."

"That's beautiful," Mandy smiles.

"I'm gonna grab another drink," Chris announces. He doesn't offer to get one for anyone else, or mention when he'll be back. He just stands and quickly walks away, bypassing the bar entirely for the hallway by the bathrooms.

"Emily?" someone says. I turn my gaze back to our table, belatedly realizing that I was staring after him. I shouldn't. I really shouldn't. But then I see Alex follow Chris down the hall.

"I have to go to the bathroom," I excuse myself. When I get to the hallway, I don't see them, but I hear voices down the bend in the corner. I follow the sound, stopping short before the hallway turns when I realize that from my current position, I can hear everything they're saying, but they can't see me.

"Why haven't you answered any of my texts? Why are you avoiding me?" Alex demands, his tone still skating that knife's edge between anger and something more terrifying. I take a half step closer, ready to launch myself around the corner as a barrier between them if it comes to that.

"I've been busy."

"Too busy for your best friend?"

"You were never my friend. All you did was push me down to make yourself feel better," Chris says hoarsely. My body acts of its own accord at his words, taking the final few steps around the corner to face them. Something like pride bubbles in my chest, hearing Chris stand up for himself. Not that I have any right to that feeling, but... I misjudged him. I thought he worshiped Alex. And he let me think the worst of him. He didn't trust me enough to tell me the truth.

Until tonight.

"You're going to mess this all up. You know that, right?" Alex sneers. "You only got onto this show because of me. Without me, you're nothing."

"Maybe. But I'm still here, and you're not."

Alex surges forward, as if he's about to tackle Chris, and I surge forward, putting myself between them. I refuse to let Chris stand alone against this prick for another moment.

"You stupid bitch," Alex spits.

I lean forward, staring him down. Refusing to let him intimidate either of us. "Alex, your grasp of the English language is horrifyingly lacking for someone still attempting a career as a writer. Find something more creative to say if you're going to insult me."

"Fuck you both, then," Alex staggers off.

"Are you okay?" I whirl on Chris, placing my hands on his arms without thinking.

"I—I'm fine." He doesn't look fine. He looks shaken. "Are you? He shouldn't have called you...that."

"You've called me a bitch," I can't resist reminding him.

"When you were acting like one," he says. I roll my eyes, but then he adds, "Not when you were defending me."

"I've never done it before." Our eyes meet. "I didn't hate it."

"I didn't hate it, either." An awkward silence settles between us, one that we break at the same time.

"I'm sorry."

"Chris—" My mouth falls open, the apology stunning me into silence.

"I'm sorry," he repeats, his voice soft but sincere. "I don't want to be like him."

"You're not," I bite my lip. "And I'm sorry too, Chis. We've both said shitty things to each other. But...maybe we could try not to? Maybe we could try to move on. And actually work together. At least, for the year."

"Right," he says quietly. "For the sake of the show."

"Exactly," I nod. We're nearly chest to chest now. Well, my chest is closer to the middle of his torso, considering how tall he is, even in my heels. I have to lean my head back to look at him. "But don't think this means you won me over," I add.

"You jumped in front of Alex to defend someone you don't even like?" The corner of his mouth curls up in a teasing smile.

"You looked like you needed some help," I scoff. "I was being chivalrous."

"What does that make you?" He leans forward slightly. "My knight in shining armor? My hero? My savior?"

"Did I save you?" I ask, my voice shaking slightly. My legs are threatening to do the same. Chris is so close to me. Too close, but I don't want him to back away. I don't want space.

I want him to call me his savior again.

"Emily," he whispers. Not Beckerman. Emily.

I don't know if I've ever liked anything more than I like the sound of my name on his lips.

"Chris?" We jerk apart at the sound of Zoe's voice. She's standing at the end of the hall. Shame rushes through me all at once. *He has a girlfriend, you idiot.* I can't believe I flirted with him like that. "Sorry. I saw you and Alex…"

"Meet me outside," Chris says tersely. She nods, walking away, leaving us alone again.

I wait for an explanation that doesn't come. And why should it? I'm only his coworker. He doesn't owe me anything. Any flirting that I thought was happening was only on my side—in my own head, influenced by my own delusions and too many romance novels, making me think that a few minutes of banter in a dark hallway actually meant something.

12

"I don't understand what you have against emotional support animals."

"I don't have anything against the animals! It's just an overdone joke," I retort.

"Says the woman who just pitched me three about global warming."

"I pitched you three jokes about *climate change*, and there's much more to say about that than people bringing snakes onto planes."

"Exactly! Snakes on a plane—the joke writes itself," he exclaims.

"That's because it's lazy."

"Just because something isn't weird and controversial doesn't mean it's lazy."

I groan, letting my head fall onto the cool wooden surface of my desk. It feels like we've been fighting for years, even though it's only Tuesday morning.

I thought that working with Chris would be as easy as simply deciding that we were going to work together. Instead, it's like pulling teeth, except the teeth are every single word in every one of the jokes that we write and I'm debating asking to be put under. A weak analogy, but my brain is tired.

We're incapable of agreeing on anything: the funniest synonym for technocrat, whether jokes about Elon Musk or Jeff Bezos are better, even the temperature of our office.

I got in first on Monday and changed the temperature to 72 °F. When Chris got in, he switched it to 70 °F. Totally fine. Barely an adjustment. But then after lunch, it had been lowered to 68°F.

"68°F is ridiculous," I protest.

"It's a perfectly normal temperature," he says.

"Well, it's my office too, and I run cold," I reply stubbornly. "Too warm is better than too cold."

"No one has ever said that! If you're cold, you put on a sweater. If you're too warm, there's nothing to do!"

"Take off a layer," I suggest flippantly.

"Are you telling me to take my shirt off?"

"I'm telling you to dress for the temperature I want this office to be," I retort.

The next day, I wear my coziest sweater, and when Chris steps out to use the bathroom, I crank the temperature from 65°F to 73°F. The heat flickers on and I sigh with pleasure, shedding my sweater. It takes him a few minutes to notice the shift in temperature when he returns.

When he does, he rushes for the thermostat, poking the down key repeatedly until he flounces back to his desk. I only stand up and stride back over, bumping the temperature from 62°F to 71°F.

For a few minutes, Chris types away at his laptop, pretending to ignore it. But he's annoyed. Oh, he's very annoyed. His foot is jiggling, faster and faster until he finally rises, so quickly that one of his knees knocks against the bottom of his desk.

"Ow. Damnit," he curses, shooting me an accusatory glance.

"It's not my fault that you're so tall," I don't bother looking up from my computer. Chris stomps back to the thermostat, jabbing the key so aggressively that I'm surprised it doesn't fall off. When the temperature reaches his satisfaction, he shoots me a smug look and returns to his desk.

I stand, and his shoulders tense.

"Don't play this game with me," he warns.

"What game?" I sidle a few steps closer to the thermostat, trying to keep an innocent expression on my face. But I can't help it—my triumphant grin breaks through.

"That's it!" Chris stands as well, making a break for the thermostat. With his stupid long legs, he reaches it an instant before me, and physically covers the panel with his body.

"I thought we were working on compromise."

"*You* were working on compromise. I'm already great at it," he insists, despite the fact that he's currently guarding the thermostat with his life.

"You're insufferable," I hiss, stepping closer to him. "If we can't even agree on the temperature, how are we supposed to write sketches together?"

"This has nothing to do with sketch writing," he shrugs, still not moving.

"You're really not going to budge?"

"Nope," Chris says, the corners of his mouth quirking up in a self-satisfied smile. "Not on this."

Not on anything, if our writing progress—or rather, lack thereof—is any indication.

"Then you leave me no choice," I reply solemnly, and then, to both his horror and utter confusion, I stick my hands under his armpits and start to tickle him.

"Stop it," Chris exclaims through giggles he flinches out of the way. "This is inappropriate!"

"The thermostat is mine," I cheer, moving to lower the temperature now that he's out of the way. But then his hand closes over my wrist just as I lift it, pinning my arm against the wall.

I lift my head, and realize how close he is to me. His body is inches away, practically pressing me up against the wall.

He exhales, and I feel the warmth of his breath against my face as he glowers at me. Gooseflesh erupts over my arms, and it takes everything in me not to shiver under the intensity of his gaze. It's transformed from a glare into something else altogether. Something full of heat and urgency.

"Perhaps," Chris says, his voice soft and low, "We can reach a temperature compromise."

"How about we set it to 69°F?" I ask, keeping my face blank. I'm rewarded with a bark of laughter. My heart pounds, the sound of his throaty chuckle making my knees feel slightly wobbly. This is wrong. Chris isn't for me. He belongs to someone else, and even if he didn't, I find him insufferable. It's just that when he's standing this close to me, his body towering over mine, I find it hard to remember exactly why. "What was that I heard?" I cup my hand around my ear. "Did you find something that *I* said...funny?"

"I can appreciate a good sixty-nine joke when it's in the right context." His tone is flippant, but he fails to hide his smile. Should it really be this fun, finding new ways to drive him insane? Maybe not. But he makes it so entertaining. *What would it be like to watch buttoned-up Chris Galloway lose control?*

That thought fills my brain with images that are absolutely not workplace appropriate, ones I quickly shove aside. Yes, Chris is objectively attractive. Yes, I enjoy pushing his buttons, and I suspect that he enjoys pushing mine. But that doesn't matter. It *can't* matter. We're supposed to be acting as head writers and co-hosting the *Update* together. I need to write material about him, not fantasize about getting him naked.

Because that's all it is. A fantasy. He's with someone else, and I need to remember that before I really get myself in trouble.

And I will get myself in trouble, because his hand is still on mine, and I like that feeling way, *way* too much.

"Um." I move my wrist slightly, trying to wriggle out of his grasp. "So, are we good on temperature?"

He drops my hand as if it's scalded him, stepping back until he bumps into the front of his desk. Chris winces, looking as if he's forgotten himself. "I think 69°F will satisfy us both."

Our eyes meet, widening slightly as we both hear the innuendo. And then, I can't help it. I laugh. I start and then I can't stop, and after a few moments I hear Chris join in.

~

Unfortunately, our ability to compromise about the thermostat doesn't mean we're ready to do the same with our ideas for the *Weekend Update*.

"I think this is a one-off joke, not a recurring character," Chris frowns at my latest proposal.

"Why?"

"Because, it's over the top."

"That's kind of the point. She's a drag queen." I frown, leaning back in my desk chair and taking a long sip of coffee.

"Can I come in now?" someone calls from behind the door.

Chris's eyes widen. "Is that Riley?"

"Who's Riley?" The voice has transformed to something deep and sexy "He sounds like a dish."

"Please tell me this isn't what I think it is," Chris moans.

"It's Jennifer Coolest, bitches!" Riley pushes the door open, dressed in full drag. I actually came up with the idea when I was writing with him and Mandy on Tuesday, and Riley mentioned that he used to do drag in college. He didn't mention that his character involved a Jennifer Coolidge impersonation, but that's just an added bonus.

"Did you make him do this?" Chris looks simultaneously delighted and horrified, even as his tone is accusatory.

"She did not, sweet face." Riley sashays towards him, hips swishing with every movement. He's wearing a wig from a Dolly Parton costume—actually, I think the dress is also from a Dolly Parton costume—and giant silver heels. We even got makeup to do a full face for him. Riley doesn't do drag anymore, largely because, in his own words, "He can't dance or contour for shit," but he loved the idea of making a drag queen persona a regular *Weekend Update* character.

"Miss Jennifer Coolest," I smile, even as Chris shakes his head.

"The name was a stretch," Riley admits, dropping the persona and flopping onto one of the couches. "I just wanted to honor the queen."

"You can really walk in those things," Chris sighs. "I'll admit, I'm impressed. And glad that Beckerman didn't browbeat you into this."

"We thought it would be fun to have Jennifer come and do a segment discussing the laws that have passed in some states restricting drag shows, saying that they're harmful to minors. This character comes on as a special guest to discuss and pokes holes in that logic, in a funny way," I smile.

"Yeah, like why lawmakers think drag queens are dangerous but guns are perfectly safe," Riley adds.

"I just don't see where the joke is with that," Chris scratches his chin thoughtfully. "I think we need to make this less straightforward if it's going to work. Now it kind of just seems like an educational statement with a funny character."

Riley and I swap glances. We anticipated this. The only question is if Chris will be on board. "We were thinking," I hedge, tapping my fingers anxiously against my desk, "It might be funny if this drag queen character was actually just coming on the show to hit on you."

"She says she's not political. There can be these offhanded moments making jokes about why conservatives are so freaked out by drag queens, but the joke is that she's hitting on you in a super aggressive way and you're forced to play the straight man, and sort of bring her character back down to earth," Riley continues.

Chris swings his gaze around to me, looking thoughtful. "But what about you, Beckerman?"

"What do you mean?" I ask, confused.

"There's not really anything for you to do with this."

"I think Emily can just be there, enjoying the show," Riley suggests. "She can join in with this character and gang up on you sometimes, but mostly it's just about you being embarrassed. You're trying to steer things back to the subject at hand as this character goes off the rails."

"Do you really think that many people are going to like watching me be embarrassed?"

"Yes," Riley and I say at the same time.

"Then, let's write it and see if it works,

That ends up being the only relatively easy thing to write all week. It's great. In fact, it might just be the only good part of this week's *Update*. And we can't even use it, because Riley is in full makeup for a different sketch right before the *Update*, so he won't have time to get ready to do the bit. We fell back on one of the characters Chris created with Alex a few seasons ago, Girl Who's Allergic to Everything, but I don't feel good about it.

I can tell Chris doesn't, either. But we have no choice.

It's how we find ourselves sitting behind the desk again, ten minutes before the *Update*, both of us silently wondering whether we've made a huge mistake. Are we about to humiliate ourselves on national television? Was Jessica wrong about our writing styles working well together? It's hard to know for sure, considering how little writing we actually got done. Most of our time was occupied with bickering. And now we've run out of it.

"Was it like this when you wrote with Alex?"

Chris's entire body jolts, one of his knees smacking into the *Update* desk with a thunk that makes me wince. I'm just as surprised by the question as he is, even though I'm the one who asked it. I wanted to break the silence, but my mouth opened before my brain had a chance to catch up.

"I gave in. Whatever Alex argued for, we kept." Anger and regret seep into his expression. I don't know what inspires the sudden bout of honesty; if it's the adrenaline of how close we are to showtime, the desperate knowledge that neither of us is happy with the material we're about to read, or something bigger. That little seed of hope, that we might have finally started breaking down each other's walls and building trust.

"So, just do the same for me," I suggest. He rolls his eyes, but I smile when I notice some of the tightly coiled tension leave his body.

"We both know that's now how this works."

"Is it supposed to be this hard?" I ask.

Chris frowns, looking as if he's seriously contemplating the question. "I don't know."

I sigh. "That's not particularly helpful."

"I know. But it's just so different. Alex and I were writing partners for so long. We knew each other."

"And we don't," I frown. "But we're starting to."

"Is that enough?"

"We're on in five," someone warns us.

"I don't know. I can't talk about this right now. I need to focus," he says, pushing me away.

For a moment, I hate the nature of this show that I love so much. We will be on in five minutes. Nothing short of the end of the world could stop that. And even then, I think Jessica Braugher would find some way for the show to go on. It doesn't matter if I might be close to a breakthrough with Chris. It's too late, anyway. At least for what's about to happen now, the heavy burden that we both carry. We're inching towards the guillotine. Towards the fear that keeps me up at night, that I suspect haunts him just as much: failure.

"See you on the other side," I say quietly, as the lights come up and we paste on our smiles.

I hope we at least look like we know what we're doing.

13

There is no feeling as exhilarating as killing it on live television. I'm glad I got to experience that at least once, because there is a strong chance that after tonight's show I will never be allowed on *Live From New York* again.

We bomb. We bomb so hard that even our camera operators are giving us sympathetic looks by the end of the *Update*, perhaps wondering if it would be a greater mercy to kill us then to let us walk away from this.

We both knew it was coming. Our feeble attempts at partnership left us with half-baked, weak jokes, the artifacts of what happens when you try to fake a compromise: meaningless words, fiddled with to the point that they're falling apart, clumsy and sad. Not just because they aren't funny, or interesting, but because I know in my bones that if we had trusted each other enough to try, it might have been different.

Two shows. Two failures, for different reasons. I strongly suspect that we're running out of chances if we haven't already. Jessica Braugher does not enjoy failure. The only glimmer of hope I can hold onto is the knowledge that the only thing she hates as much as failure is being wrong.

But it won't matter if Chris and I can't figure this out.

We say our goodbyes on autopilot, slumping with defeat the moment the cameras cut out. There's an awkward silence, uncomfortable enough for a usually bustling television set and doubly so because it seems that not only does no one know what to say to us, they're actively trying to avoid the subject. To avoid *us*. I can't blame them. Failure feels contagious.

I turn to Chris, about to offer him a word of reassurance, but he's already standing. He stalks off without so much as a word, and I take a deep breath to steel myself before I follow.

I trail him through backstage, not even needing to dodge the usual mayhem and foot traffic of everyone rushing around to get ready for the next sketch. No, everyone gives Chris a wide berth, as if the anger radiating off him repels them. Or maybe it's out of embarrassment on our behalf, no one wanting to make accidental eye contact and be forced to offer the uncomfortable words of condolence for this unmitigated disaster.

I wonder how many times we're going to do this little dance, me chasing after Chris as he tries to avoid the conversation that I know we need to have.

When Chris reaches the door that separates the offices from the backstage area, he shoulders it open only to nearly let it slam in my face. I stick my arm out to stop it, pushing through.

"Hey." I call. He ignores me, and I hurry after him, cursing his annoyingly long legs for covering so much distance in each step.

"Stop following me," Chris pauses with a hand on the door to our office, his back still to me.

"It's my office too."

His hand tightens on the handle, every inch of his body going taut with tension, as if he's trying so hard not to let me push him over the edge. But I want to. And I think…I think he might need me to.

I think we need to be fully honest with each other, air out everything we've been holding back, so that we can truly move forward.

"I'd like to be alone."

"Too bad. We need to talk."

"No, we don't." He wrenches open the office door, storming in, and I follow.

"I think we can both agree that that sucked," I pause, watching him pace back and forth across the meager bit of foot space in our office. "Maybe they give out an award for worst *Weekend Update* Ever?"

Chris turns around, still rooted in place with this distance between us. He clenches his fists, his green eyes practically molten with rage. "I'm glad you think this is funny, at least. You forced me to write with you, and we bombed. We failed. It's over,"

"It's not over."

"Are you conveniently forgetting that we're in danger of being canceled?"

"Of course not. But we've only been working together for a week. Things aren't going to go smoothly right away. We're figuring it out."

"That's the problem," he shouts. "We. You and I are tied together now. And I don't want to be. You don't deserve to be here. You're dragging me down."

"Excuse me?" I recoil. "I'm not the one who got hired because his writing partner's uncle is on some corporate board!"

"This is all your fault. If you hadn't convinced me that we should write together—"

"We would have had another show like last week's," I challenge him.

"Last week's show wasn't as bad as this one."

"It wasn't as hard to watch, but it wasn't what we were supposed to be doing. At least this week, we tried!"

"We don't have time to try," Chris says harshly. "I should never have listened to you."

"No. You should never have listened to Alex." I shake my head at him. "Give up the ghost, Galloway. Stop being a coward. If you wanted Alex gone so you could be in charge, why are you just doing exactly what he did now that you got your wish? You're better than this!"

"And what if I'm not?" Chris takes a step closer to me, before faltering, his hands clenching and unclenching at his sides. He heaves out a wrenching breath, turning to face his desk. Turning away from me. Trying to hide this part of himself, but that's not going to work. Slowly, I walk around, coming to the other side of his desk. "Alex told me I was nothing without him. What if he was right?"

A tear slips down his cheek, and the sight of him crying rips open a part of me that I didn't even know existed. "He wasn't," I say fiercely.

"This show is all I have," he says quietly. "And if it doesn't exist anymore, I don't know what I'm going to do."

I reach for the box of tissues on my desk and hand him one. He accepts gratefully, wiping his cheeks before loudly blowing his nose.

And I know then that I'm in deep trouble, because even as Chris stuffs the dirty tissue in his pocket, he's so handsome that it steals my breath. Even with redness around his nose and eyes from crying, he's perfect. It actually makes him even more beautiful. I wonder how many people have seen this part of him. How many people he's let see this part of him.

Has Zoe? It's ugly, the jealousy I feel, how badly I want for her not to have witnessed Chris at his most vulnerable when I have. His solid facade has cracked open, revealing the man underneath. Someone tender, and vulnerable, and brave. Someone trying his best, just like the rest of us.

That is the Chris I want to know. The Chris I can see myself being partners with. And for the sake of that partnership, I will banish all of these despicable feelings surfacing inside me. I'm not going to wreck this entire show and any chance we have of establishing ourselves as *Weekend Update* partners over a little crush.

Even if part of me suspects that this is much, much deeper than that.

It doesn't matter. I'll never know. That question will always go unanswered. He's taken, and he's not for me, and we have a show to save. And if I have to carry that tenderness, that hurt of knowing that this could have been something that I only thought possible on the pages of a romance novel, I'll do it. I'll live with that.

"I'm sorry," Chris mumbles. "I don't usually cry in front of people."

"I get it. We're under a lot of pressure."

"Decades of comedy history, to be precise," he says, sniffling a bit even as he laughs. "I should apologize for what I said earlier, though. I was...I was projecting. You deserve to be here, Emily."

"Do I, though? Do any of us?"

"Don't get existential on me now, Beckerman." I wonder if he knows how beautiful that crooked half-smile of his is.

"Imposter syndrome, party of two." I give him a little grin, and his own widens, pure sunshine. As if it could drive out all of my darkest thoughts. "I can't ever know, objectively, if I deserve this. If you do. There's so many other factors at play. What matters is that we're here, and that we try our best to do something with this opportunity we've been given."

"I don't know if I can handle going through *that* again," Chris shudders.

"I can't, either. That's why we'll make sure next week is better. It can't be worse."

"You never know."

"I do. Did you really think it was going to go perfectly right away? This was the jumping off point. And now, we learn from our mistakes, and we keep getting better."

"How do you know?"

"How do I know what?"

"That it's going to get better between us."

"Because I believe in you," I say quietly. "And I believe in myself.

Because we're too stubborn not to figure this out. We're going to save this show. Together." *At least for now.* Because if we do succeed, if we do save *Live From New York* from cancellation...then we're back to competing.

He exhales, rubbing a hand over his face. "I've wanted to write for *Live From New York* since I was ten years old. This show, its legacy...it means everything to me."

"I feel the same way."

"I know that, now. And I know we're different, but maybe Jessica was right. Maybe if we keep trying, we can use those differences to our advantage. We can save this show together."

"Then we have to forget about the competition. No more trying to one-up each other. *Live From New York* needs to be the most important thing to both of us," I insist, the words for my benefit as much as his. Whatever weird fetish my body seems to be developing for his disgustingly sexy emotional vulnerability, I need to shove down deep, deep inside of me.

Because even in another universe where the future of the show didn't rest on our shoulders, nothing would ever happen between us. A man who could have his pick of famous actresses and models would never want to be with a sharp-edged, insecure comedy writer.

"Okay." Chris holds out his hand, sticking out his pinky finger. "Let's swear it. From this moment forward, we're a team. We're not going to try to make the other person look bad. We're going to work together and make this show great, as a team, because the show comes first. And then once that's settled, we can think about our own careers."

"Deal," I agree, locking my pinky around his.

We're not really solving the problem so much as delaying it. But out of sight, out of mind, as they say.

"We're still going to fight," I warn him. "Probably more."

"As long as we make sure we pick our battles, and only fight about the things that matter."

"Fair enough," I grin up at him. "Wow, look at this. Are we actually becoming friends?"

He grimaces. "I wouldn't go that far. I still find you annoying."

"And I still find you insufferable. But here we are, sticking it out."

Suddenly, both of our phones buzz. I look down at mine and see a text from Jessica.

"Fuck."

"Fuck," Chris agrees.

"Should we read it at the same time?" I suggest, biting my lip. "We did what she asked. How mad can she be?"

"Very mad," Chris tenses. "Alright. At the same time."

It takes only a few seconds to read. I look up from my phone, meeting his eyes, seeing my own relief reflected back at them. "That was not what I was expecting."

Jessica only said that she was glad we were working together and to make sure next week went better. It could have been worse. So much worse.

"She must know that we fought." I frown down at my phone. "Or she would have been harsher."

"Probably."

Our phones buzz again. Her second text simply reads:

JESSICA

You know what to do. Get your shit together.

I laugh. "That's more like it." Jessica is a master of tough love. "Besides, she put us together for a reason. This was all her idea. Questioning our ability to succeed would mean she was questioning her own judgment."

Chris gives me a crooked grin. "That is an excellent point, Beckerman."

"Why, thank you, Galloway," I smile back, enjoying the seed of hopefulness sprouting in my chest. We can do this.

"We should get back to the stage," Chris suggests. "The show's almost over."

"Good idea. Do you need me to touch up your makeup?" I ask. He gives me an exasperated look.

"I should have known that even with our truce, you were never going to give me a moment's peace."

"Where would be the fun in that?" I ask brightly.

"As long as you remember that the teasing extends both ways. You mess with me, I mess right back."

"I'm so scared."

We continue our playful bickering as we walk back through the halls of the office, making our way to the side of the stage to get ready to walk back on for the final goodbye. And I wonder if Chris knows that I just told him the truth. I am scared.

Not of him messing with me. But of how much I'm starting to like it.

14

Now that we're tentatively friends, I know a lot of things about Chris. Like the fact that he can't start work until he's completed the New York Times crossword, and he refuses to cheat. I know that he loves running and cheesy 2000's club music. I even know his coffee order.

When I bring him coffee Thursday morning, his eyes widen with surprise. "How did you know?"

"Riley cracks under torture," I reply. "Seriously, he could never be a spy. After thirty seconds of waterboarding, I learned all your darkest secrets."

"Like my highly classified and extremely shameful coffee order?"

"Who knew you had such a sweet tooth?" I almost didn't believe Riley when he told me that Chris's fall drink of choice is a pumpkin latte, but the expression of utter delight on Chris's face as he sips it was worth the gamble.

"I'm a sweet guy, Beckerman," he teases. He pushes his chair back and stretches his legs out. I pointedly ignore the way it makes his entire body seem long and sinuous.

I've been pointedly ignoring a lot of things about him. The more time we spend together, the more I realize that the flutter of attraction I feel whenever his infuriatingly beautiful green eyes meet mine isn't going to go away. So, I try to keep things strictly business. But that's easier said than done when our business involves coming up with jokes together.

Sense of humor is more personal than people think. And the more time I spend thinking about it, the more I realize that ours aren't as opposite as I thought they were. Chris is different around me now. He's sillier, more playful. And I like that I've brought out this side of him. That he feels like he can be his authentic self when I'm with him.

"Emily?" Case in point. My spiraling thoughts are interrupted when a paper airplane whizzes past me.

"What's next, spitballs? Are you twelve?"

"Men mature more slowly than women, you know." He crosses his arms and leans back, kicking his feet up on his desk. I made fun of him once for his tendency to manspread and now he does it all the time. I've come to find it slightly adorable, not that I'd ever admit it. It gives me a warm and fuzzy feeling somewhere lower than my stomach, the idea that he's comfortable enough with me to spread his legs—er, sprawl his body. *I need to get my mind out of the gutter.*

"Anyway, do you want me?"

"What?" I do a literal mini spit-take, releasing hot coffee onto my light gray T-shirt. "Oh, fuck."

"Do you want me to get you anything from the kitchen?" There's a teasing flicker in his eyes that suggests he picked that very specific phrasing on purpose. Maybe I'm not the only one whose mind is in the gutter.

"No, I'm okay." I clear my throat. "Are you sure you don't want to just have one of the *interns* grab it for you?"

"I'm perfectly capable of going to the kitchen myself." He gives me a confused look.

When the door closes behind him, I sigh dramatically. I should have brought up Zoe directly, but I chickened out. He has a girlfriend.

I keep trying to remind myself—to remind both of us—of that. To him, our flirty teasing is completely innocent. It's just banter, the kind of thing that's helped us build up our chemistry during the actual show.

Which we have. We've gotten our *Update* rhythm down. It's similar to our dynamic offscreen, full of teasing and trying to make the other person uncomfortable, but in a playful way. It's exactly what we wanted, the reason why we agreed to work together, and yet every day it gets harder for me to remember that line between what's real and what's for the show.

Especially when we're spending more time together than ever. Chris and I work constantly to ensure that the jokes for each week's *Update* are as close to perfect as they could possibly be.

If we're not working on the *Update*, our time is consumed by working together as head writers. Chris and I spend hours helping the other writers refine sketches, debating which ones we want to keep in the weekly post-table meeting with Jessica, a few producers, and that week's host.

The process is lengthier and more exhausting than I would have imagined, but neither of us is willing to give up. I've come to appreciate our mutual stubbornness and how it helps us push each other. Now, with only two shows left until our winter hiatus, I can appreciate how much progress we've made.

I've also spent more time collaborating with some of the other writers.

"I think we should do this as an infomercial," Faith suggests after her, Mandy and I have spent the better part of an hour trying to figure out the setup for our latest sketch idea.

"Oh, I like that." Mandy sits up on the couch in her and Faith's office. "Should we start with a Dracula talking head?"

"What if we start and play it as a generic diet commercial?" I suggest, tapping my pen against my knee. "Like, it starts out with rolling fields and happy, laughing white people. And then we cut to Dracula."

"'Turning into a vampire is a surefire way to drop those nagging pounds and slim down,'" Faith ad-libs.

"'Other liquid diets don't provide you the nutrients you need. With vampirism, your human body and its pesky need for food will be as dead as you are,'" Mandy joins in.

"'It's all-natural, with thousands of years of ancient tradition behind the process. Especially because the original founders are still alive today. That is, depending on what your definition of alive is,'" I add.

"'Sign up today and receive your first gallon on us,'" Faith suggests through honking laughter.

"'With vampirism, you'll look and feel your best, and you never have to go to church again.'"

"We can do a big side effects disclaimer at the end," I add. "Inability to walk in daylight, garlic allergy, turning into a bat, and murderous impulses."

"'Do not combine vampirism with holy water.'"

"'If you want to look young and beautiful forever, skip the Botox. Try becoming a vampire today!'"

"Yes!" Mandy starts typing furiously. "I love all of this."

"We can even get some talking heads doing testimonials," I suggest. "Maybe one woman who's like 'I haven't seen my family in ten years, but if I could, they'd tell me I've never looked better.'"

"Oh, that's perfect," Faith agrees. "It's perfect, and Nicholas Cage is hosting. He'll be perfect. He's actually played Dracula."

"Should we have him wear a costume or regular clothes?" I wonder. "Is he Dracula pretending to be human, or should it just be him as a full-blown ancient vampire promoting this?"

"Hmmm," Mandy frowns, bouncing her knee up and down as she thinks. "I think we should go for the cheesy vampire outfit. And a horrible Eastern European accent. The contrast of that after the generic diet commercial opening would work well."

"I agree. And we can always change it if other people think regular clothes work better."

Faith and Mandy exchange conspiratorial glances. "By other people, you mean Chris, right?"

"Well, he's the other head writer, so his opinion is important." They do it again. "Is there something I'm missing here?"

"Do you read stuff people say online about you?" Mandy asks.

I make a face. "No. Do you?"

"I don't read about *myself*, but I have seen some interesting theories about you. And Chris," Faith replies mysteriously.

"The internet thinks you're fucking," Mandy, always with the direct approach.

"Well, dating," Faith clarifies at my flabbergasted expression. "Look at the comments on last week's *Update*,"

She stands up, moving from her desk to sit next to me on the couch. Faith opens the YouTube app on her phone, pulling up the clip. It's from Riley's drag queen guest appearance.

"That did so well. Riley is amazing," I smile, taking a moment to watch.

"If we're passing laws about things that are harmful to minors, let's start with things that actually kill minors," Riley drawls in his drag persona. We decided to give her a Southern twist, since so many of the states passing anti-drag laws are in the South. And because Riley does a fabulous drawl. "Chris, what's the difference between me and a semi-automatic weapon?"

"I don't know," Chris replies, his face already red.

"I need more than a finger to find my release," Riley laughs, and I join in, as Chris goes even redder, emitting a few choked sounds. "I'm just kidding, handsome. The difference is that I've never killed anybody." Riley bats his fake eyelashes at Chris, one of his hands snaking under the table to grab Chris's thigh. Of course, the camera can't see that, but they do see Chris jump nearly a foot in the air as he and I dissolve into laughter.

"Thank you, Jennifer Coolest!"

"I love you all. Come find me after the show, Chris," Riley shouts.

"Always a treat," Chris jokes, our eyes meeting. I remember that

moment so clearly—the electricity of it, the high of a great Update combined with the high of him looking at me.

"Someone's got a fan," I smirk at him.

"Don't get jealous," Chris replies.

He's smiling at me like...well, like he's seen me naked. Which he hasn't. But that expression is full of playful intimacy, the teasing of two people who know each other...intimately.

And we didn't see it. I haven't watched any of our other *Update* segments. I'm still getting comfortable with the idea of being on camera, and I knew it would only lead to me picking myself apart.

But right now, watching us, I'm not thinking about how my body looks, my joke delivery, or if I look like I belong.

I'm wondering if this is all part of the show, or if Chris looks at me that way when the cameras aren't rolling.

I scroll down to the comments section, doing my best to avoid reading the creepy, offensive, and/or antisemitic comments. There are plenty of those, but there are also plenty of positive ones.

- When your love language is negging.
- OBSESSED. Finally watching *LFNY* again bc I need to see what these two get up to.
- Guys, they're the head writers too-so cute. R they dating in real life? Can we find out?
- If Chris Galloway looked at me that way, I would simply explode.

There are comments celebrating Riley, too, and more about how much people have been enjoying the show. I knew the ratings were going up, but seeing the excited responses fills me with pride. We're doing it. *I'm* doing it.

I didn't realize how that voice in my head had still lingered, whispering poison in my ear, trying to convince me that even though the writing felt like it was going better, it was all a lie. Telling me I'd never be enough, that I wasn't worthy, that I was going to mess everything up.

That's the hardest thing about comedy. I can think something's funny, the rest of the writers and cast members of *Live From New York* could enjoy it, but I'm not writing for just us. If other people don't laugh, it's not working. And even hearing the reaction from the studio audience doesn't compare to this. That's a microcosm. *This* is the truth. And as much as I've been relieved to see our numbers improving, nothing compares to this. To see the reactions, knowing that I've made people feel the way I once felt when I first discovered this show.

"This is incredible," I whisper reverently. "People like it!" I'm practically vibrating with joy.

"And what about the other comments? The ones not about your writing?" Mandy presses.

"I guess we have good chemistry," I shrug, desperately trying to convey nonchalance.

"You're not an actor for a reason, Beckerman." Mandy narrows her eyes at me. "Is this a thing?"

"What?" I look between them. "Are you two serious? You actually think..." I can't even bring myself to say the words.

"That there's something going on between you and Chris?" Faith supplies.

"Of course not. That's ridiculous. We hated each other a few weeks ago."

"But you don't anymore," Mandy points out.

"It doesn't matter," I say harshly. "We're still competing for the same job. And even if we weren't, guys like Chris don't date girls like me."

I've spent enough time googling him to know his exes: models, actresses, musicians. Tall, svelte, glamorous women who walk through life knowing that everyone wants to be them or be with them. Not anxious, curvy comedy writers who he barely even liked a few months ago.

"Why the hell not?" Mandy demands. "What's so bad about you?"

"Nothing. But I just know that he's not interested."

"How? Have you asked?" Riley raises his eyebrows at me.

"No. And I'm not going to, because it always ends badly," I snap. "I'm sorry. I didn't mean to lose my temper," I add, seeing the shocked expressions on their faces. "But just…I had this guy friend in college, like Chris. He was handsome, smart, and funny, and I thought he was way out of my league. But sometimes, when we would banter and joke, it felt flirty. And so one night, I got drunk and I asked him out," I pause, staring down at my hands. Not wanting to see the pity in their faces. "I asked him out, and he said no."

"Is that it?" Faith sounds underwhelmed. "*That*'s why you're so sure Chris isn't into you? Because some random other guy wasn't?"

When she puts it that way, it sounds ridiculous. But I can't get that memory out of my head. The moment that I thought I had found something incredible, the kind of connection I always dreamed about, only to learn that it was one sided. All in my head. That I might have wanted him, but he didn't want me.

"You need rejection therapy."

"*Mandy*," Faith hisses.

"What?" Mandy crosses her long legs, leaning back against the couch. "I'm just saying. You got turned down once, it's not the end of the world. I get rejected all the time. Last week I asked Harry Styles out, and he said no."

"Doesn't he have a girlfriend? I thought I saw that on DeuxMoi."

"Maybe," Mandy shrugs. "All he said when I asked was thanks, but no thanks. Except in a British accent."

"It would have been weird if he did an American one," Faith says dryly.

I look at Mandy like she's sprouted a second head. "You met Harry Styles, asked him out, he said no, and you didn't immediately die from embarrassment?"

"Nope," Mandy grins at me. "I mean, it didn't feel great, but the world didn't end. It's not about me. There are billions of people out there. The way I see it, you just need one yes. I'm always gonna shoot my shot because even if I hear no 99 percent of the time, that one yes could be the person who changes my entire life."

"Wow," Faith shakes her head. "Mandy, that was beautiful."

"I want to be you," I say reverently.

"No, you don't," Mandy insists. "You want to be *you*, Emily. The best, most badass version of you. And that's going to be exactly who the right person wants."

"Okay, okay" I hold up my hands in surrender. "Yes. You're right. I love that philosophy."

"So…" Faith hedges. "Are you going to use it on Chris?"

"No," They look disappointed. "No. I'm going to use it on someone else, but I just don't see Chris that way."

"Liar," Mandy coughs.

"You think he's hot, or you would have just said you didn't to begin with and we wouldn't be having this conversation," Faith points out.

"Fine. Fine. Chris is a good-looking guy. I find him…objectively attractive." They both look far too delighted, so I quickly clarify, "If he were just some guy I'd met, I would do it. But we have to work together for the rest of the season. I basically spend all my time with him."

"You're assuming he doesn't feel the same way," Mandy says.

"It doesn't matter. We have the future of this entire show resting on our shoulders. *Live From New York* is more important."

It has to be. I see the skepticism on their faces, but they aren't going to change my mind. Yes, Chris is handsome. Yes, I'm attracted to him, against my better judgment. But that doesn't mean I need to act on it. There are bigger things at stake here.

It's just physical. It'll pass. And I'll be glad that I stopped myself from doing something stupid.

"Fair enough," Faith concedes.

Mandy looks ready to argue, but I change the subject before she can. There's no point in talking about this more. "Should we do another quick pass on the sketch before the table read tomorrow?"

We spend another half an hour polishing the sketch. They don't bring up Chris again, but I can't get him out of my head. Reading those comments, seeing that other people noticed our chemistry...it makes me want to believe that it's real.

And that makes it that much harder to ignore.

15

"Well, what did you think?" I ask, leaning forward on the couch in our office. Chris is sitting on the one across from me, looking thoughtfully down at the pages of the "Vampirism Diet" sketch I wrote with Faith, Mandy, and Riley.

"It certainly fits the host."

"But do you think it's funny?" I press.

"*I* laughed. A lot. I like the setup, and I think a corny Dracula character is really funny. I'm worried that it's trying to do too much, with the silliness and the social commentary."

My initial impulse is to jump down his throat, to tell him why it's so important that the sketch parodies society's desperation for thinness at any cost. But I force myself to stop, to consider what Chris is actually saying instead of assuming that he's trying to silence me. And he has a point—the sketch does dip into heavy-handed messaging in certain moments. "What if we made Dracula ugly?"

Chris looks intrigued. "What would that do?"

"We play up the scariness of the character. Make the vampires more Buffy and less Twilight."

He pretends to pout. "But I wanted to put Nicholas Cage in full body glitter."

I ignore him. "I think if we make the vampires more grotesque, we could tie it into the side effects part at the end. The desire for food is gone, but you're a bloodsucking immortal who looks like a half-melted candle."

"That's better," Chris nods thoughtfully. "It gets the message across without being preachy. We could even lean into the idea that it's branded as just another diet, and then suddenly you can't go to church or go outside in daylight."

"I love that." I try not to shiver when his hand brushes mine as he passes over his copy of the sketch. I check my phone, realizing it's almost 10. Rachel complains that she never sees me anymore, and she's kind of right. Being head writer and doing the *Update* is time consuming. Chris and I are usually working twelve-hour days, minimum. But the time passes quickly with him, and I don't feel lonely like I did before when I needed to work late to pull a sketch together. Probably because now, I'm not alone. I'm working with Chris. If not him, then I'm usually doing something with Faith, Mandy, and/or Riley.

I don't mind spending most of my time here because it finally feels like the *Live From New York* experience that I dreamed of when I first started. Working tirelessly, writing with friends, grinding to create something that I'm proud of. That *we're* proud of.

"I should probably head out."

"Yeah, me too. I just need to—"

Chris is interrupted by his phone ringing. He looks down at it for a second before his face pales.

"Shit," Chris shoots up from the couch, racing for the door to the hallway. He slams it shut behind him. When he comes back into the room a moment later, there's a resigned expression on his face.

"I have to go." Chris stares down at his phone screen distractedly, his entire body taut with tension.

"Is everything okay?"

"Yes," he pauses, reconsidering. "Actually, no. It's not. But it's personal stuff. Nothing with the show. Nothing you need to worry about."

And he's right. I don't need to worry about him. But that doesn't stop me from doing it.

Chris strides over to his desk, reaching for his wallet. "Are you leaving?" I ask.

"I'm sorry. I wouldn't bail if it wasn't an emergency." He rifles through his desk drawers, his movements growing increasingly erratic. "Shit. Shit! Where are my keys?"

"Pocket," I supply, the memory of him slipping them in this morning still fresh in my mind. And definitely not because the motion drew my attention to his butt.

Chris doesn't hear, continuing to paw at the contents of his desk frantically. He slams a drawer shut, raising his head, and suddenly I'm standing too, walking over to him, placing my hand on his arm.

"Your keys are in your pocket, Chris," I repeat softly.

"Right." He sighs, dragging his other hand down his face. "Thank you."

"Are you okay to go alone?"

"Of course I am." He shrugs out of my grasp and turns towards the door. "Who else would come with me?"

"I would."

Chris turns back around to face me, his eyes full of regret, and something harder to identify. Something that looks a lot like longing.

I've faced hard things in my life, but I've never had to be alone. And I don't want him to be, either. I want someone to be there for him.

No, that's not entirely true. What I want is to be the someone who's there for him.

He's silent for several moments, for long enough that I'm not sure if he's going to answer my question. He inhales sharply, looking away from me again. As if he's trying to hide.

"It's my sister," he says, and I say nothing, waiting for him to continue. "She's a sophomore at NYU. Her friend just called me. She's drunk, and she was asking for me. I have to go pick her up. She needs me. She doesn't...I'm all she has." And she's all he has.

"The sister who taught you how to do makeup?"

"Yeah." He laughs bitterly, turning back to face me. "All grown up and causing trouble." He sounds angry, but there's pain in his expression, too.

"I could help," I offer.

"If you're trying to get a look at my dirty laundry to use it against me, don't bother," Chris snaps.

I reel back. "Of course I'm not. We don't do that anymore."

"Shit. Emily, I'm sorry. It's just...I appreciate the offer. But I don't want to burden you when I don't even know how I'm going to handle this."

"We could work together. Good cop, bad cop?" I suggest. "We make a surprisingly good team." Even if it's only for the year.

"We kind of do, don't we?" He laughs to himself. "I never thought I'd say it, but... you helped me, Emily. I'm green lighting crazy sketches left and right now."

"And I'm curbing my impulses to go big and weird," I smile up at him. "We're good partners. We balance each other out."

"I guess Jessica was right," he replies softly, leaning a little closer to me. And for a moment I forget all about his crisis, and I think he might too. But then his phone buzzes again and he pulls away. "I need to go," he repeats.

"I meant what I said before. About going with you." And I realize I'm not offering only because I want to help, but because I want to stay with him.

"You don't need to do that, Beckerman. I don't want to ruin your night."

"It's ten o'clock. The rest of my night involved reading in bed. You're not ruining anything."

"I'd be taking you away from a good book. I couldn't live with that."

"It'll be there tomorrow."

"Emily..." I can't pretend that my heart doesn't leap at the way he says my name. And I know the smart thing would be to let him go, and tell him I'll see him tomorrow. To keep our relationship strictly within the confines of *Live From New York* and this building.

But I don't want that.

"Do you want me to?" I ask.

His eyes widen. I'm about to apologize for overstepping, for reading too much into all the time we've spent together and thinking it meant closeness when it was just professional collaboration, but then he speaks.

"Yes," he breathes, looking slightly surprised at his own answer, as if he didn't realize it was the truth until he spoke it into existence.

"Then I'm coming."

We leave the office quickly and get on the subway, exiting near NYU's campus and walking a few blocks before he stops in front of a nondescript building. The garden of plastic cups littering the pavement out front and music loud enough to be heard from the street indicate that we're at a college party, if the drunk co-eds stumbling in and out weren't proof enough.

"So, your sister goes to NYU?" I ask him, but he's on the phone, so he only nods. I hope for both of their sakes that she doesn't know his girlfriend. That would be another level of weird.

"You remember our intern, Zoe?" Chris asks.

"Please don't tell me you met her through your sister," I blurt.

"What?" He looks at me like I'm insane. "Zoe *is* my sister."

"Oh. *Oh!*" I laugh, hoping I don't sound relieved. But...fuck. I am. Not just that he isn't dating a college student, but also that he's not dating *anyone*. "So, she's not your girlfriend."

"You thought we were dating?" Chris looks horrified.

"You didn't deny it when I asked you."

"I didn't think I had to. I don't date college girls. I mean, I did when I was in college, but not *now*." He shoves his phone back in his pocket. "You really thought I was that much of a creep."

"You do have a certain...image." Or at least, he used to. The empty-headed charmer persona hasn't come out in weeks. And now I can recognize it for what it was: a defense mechanism, a way to defuse the tension that Alex always caused.

"I haven't dated anyone in two years."

"Seriously?" I blink at him. "But..."

"Photographs aren't dating," Chris shrugs. "It's not as bad for me, because I'm nowhere near as famous as the people I've been photographed with, but...no. I haven't dated any of them. Mostly, we're just friends getting coffee and one photo turns into a whole false narrative."

"Well," I inhale. "I haven't dated anyone in longer, if that makes you feel any better."

"I didn't say I felt badly about it," he smirks, taking a step closer to me. "Do you?"

"Yes. I pity any woman who has to spend an extended amount of time with you, including myself."

"You sound like Zoe." I try not to die inside at being compared to his little sister. "She likes to give me shit, too."

"How come no one knows that you're related?" I ask.

"She insisted. She didn't want to just be seen as my sister." It makes sense. "She didn't even want to take the internship, but I pushed. I've been worried about her." He shoves his hands into the pockets of his sweatshirt, and I realize that he must be freezing. He didn't even get a coat before we left. Without thinking, I reach for him, slipping my hand into the pocket of his Harvard hoodie and squeezing his freezing fingers gently.

Chris melts into the touch, his hands capturing mine and holding on for dear life. Concern and fear are etched across his face, and yet some of the tension leaves his body at my touch. As if he's never had anyone to comfort him, to share his burdens.

Zoe spills out of the front door a moment later, and I quickly snatch my hand back as Chris surges forward to grab his sister. Her friend is practically supporting her with an arm around her waist, and every step she takes in her heels is wobblier than the next.

"Thanks for coming," her friend says, sagging with relief as she passes Zoe into her brother's arms.

"Why'd you call him?" Zoe slurs, even as her head slumps against Chris's shoulder. Delicately, he scoops her up in his arms. The sight nearly sends me to my knees as I wonder how it would feel if he carried me like that. I mentally scold myself, willing my horny brain to focus on the actual problem at hand instead of mooning over Chris when he's completely off-limits. Unfortunately, my brain struggles to obey.

"I hope she's not pissed at me," Zoe's friend says, bouncing nervously on the balls of her feet.

"She'll be fine," I assure her. "You did the right thing, finding someone who could make sure she was safe."

"Can you let me know if she's okay?" she asks, and I nod. The friend darts back inside the party after waving a quick goodbye at us, one that Zoe doesn't notice, having immediately fallen asleep on her brother's shoulder.

"My apartment is a block from here," Chris tells me. We must make a strange sight, but that's one of the great things about living in New York. People see weird things on the street all the time, and no one pays you any attention.

"A convenient location for someone who doesn't date college girls," I mutter.

"A convenient location to keep an eye on her," Chris dips his chin. Zoe chooses that moment to snore theatrically.

"Hmmm."

"What?"

"Nothing."

"No, it's not nothing," Chris grunts slightly, shifting Zoe in his arms. We've stopped in front of a cozy-looking apartment building that I assume is his, but he makes no move to start heading up the front steps. "Tell me what you were going to say."

"I just didn't realize you were the overprotective brother type," I shrug, a coy smile spreading across my face.

"Is that a bad thing?"

Is it a bad thing, he asks, as he literally carries his younger sister in his arms. It's bad for the odds of my attraction to him disappearing. It's bad because it makes him look like some kind of hero. And to her, he is.

But he's also the man standing between me and my future on *Live From New York* when this season ends. Lusting after him won't change that. Seeing the way he cares for someone he loves won't change that. So I can't let it change me.

Except that I'm here, in front of his apartment. So maybe it already has.

"No," I admit, hoping he can't see me blush in the dark. "It's sweet, honestly. As much as it pains me to admit it, you're not a bad person."

I wait for his taunting response, but he just continues looking at me. And even though it's dark, I almost think the look on his face right now is him realizing that something has changed for him, too.

"Can you get my key from my pocket?"

"What?" I stare at him incredulously. "You want me to...get your key... from your pocket?"

"That's what I just said," He sounds almost playful.

"Which pocket?"

"I don't know. Just keep checking until you find it."

I gulp. "Are you sure you can't just check yourself?" I scramble for any excuse, any reason to avoid touching him. Not because I don't want to. Because I want to so badly. Because I know it's going to be exquisite torture, being so close to parts of him that I should not under any circumstances be thinking about. "I can hold Zoe."

"No, you can't. She's taller than you. And I can't put her down," he pauses. "What's the big deal?" There's a challenge in his voice, one that I can't walk away from.

Is he doing this on purpose? Is he playing with me the way I play with him, taking our teasing and sparring one step further? I dismiss the thought as quickly as it arrives. That's not what this is. That would mean Chris feels something for me, too, and I can't let myself wonder about that. Not just because it might snap the last threads of my restraint, but because it would mean letting myself hope.

I can survive the wondering, the fantasizing, the sneaky glances and the knowledge that I've come very close to memorizing every detail of him that he's given me a glimpse of.

What I can't survive is the day that hope is crushed.

Because I'm me, and he's Chris, and the only place something romantic will ever happen between us is inside my head.

"Nope. No big deal," I reply, my voice sounding strangled even to my own ears.

"Great."

I don't move.

"Can you hurry up? My arms are getting tired." And I know then that he's lying, because I've seen his arms. But calling him out would mean admitting that I've been ogling his muscles. It would mean losing.

"God, give me strength," I mutter under my breath, steeling myself for the ultimate test of my willpower: groping Chris. Well, groping with consent, and with the purpose of locating his keys, but right now I'm pretty much unable to think about any of that.

I step forward, gently sliding my hand into the front left pocket of his jeans. I bite my tongue to keep myself from doing anything humiliating like moaning, my hand uncomfortably prodding the depths of his pocket, careful to explore only as much as necessary and avoid the obvious elephant in the room. Or, more aptly, the snake in his pants.

"I don't think it's in there." Oh, he's definitely laughing at me. At least one of us is enjoying this.

"Just making sure." I move on to the other pocket, squeezing my eyes shut. As if that will help. As if anything will help. Oh, god. It's not in this one, either. I am well and truly fucked, and not in a good way.

I slip my hand into Chris's back pocket.

Life is truly, desperately unfair. Why else would someone whose literal job is to be funny also be blessed with such an undeniably luscious ass? It's the kind of butt a girl could sink her teeth into. I was never much of an ass woman, but now? I'm a this-ass woman. Which is a huge fucking problem, considering who this ass belongs to.

"Not in that one, either." Chris turns his head slightly so that his breath tickles the side of my neck. I nearly jump out of my skin. Did I skip too many High Holidays? Is this cosmic punishment for being a bad Jew? Or do I just have the worst luck in the world, that the key is in the very last pocket I searched?

"Definitely this one, then!" I carefully use my index finger to take the key ring out of his other pocket. I try not to audibly exhale as I follow him up the front steps. I did it. My hand was mere millimeters away from Chris's crotch, and I didn't melt into a pile of woman-shaped goo.

"It's the green one," Chris supplies. My hands are shaking so badly that I'm having difficulty fitting it into the lock, but eventually I do. I hold it open for him.

"You know, I heard what you said before," Chris says quietly, pausing in the doorway. It feels as if his eyes see right through me, directly into all of the parts of myself that I usually try to hide. In the dim light of this building's foyer, they look impossibly deep. As if they contain all the secrets of the universe.

"W-what?" My heart races in my chest.

"Did you get what you asked for?" is all he says before he heads inside, leaving me with no choice but to follow.

16

No, I did not get what I asked for. Otherwise, I wouldn't still be panting after you like this. I don't answer Chris's question out loud. I don't know how to. I just trudge after him, wondering what it all means. I asked for strength, and yet I feel weaker by the second.

I told myself I would keep things professional, and here I am, walking into Chris's apartment. Chris sets Zoe down on his worn leather couch as I nudge his door shut behind me.

Zoe wakes up, shaking her feet out of her heels. They go flying across the room, nearly hitting his framed *Trading Places* poster. Chris winces.

"Sorry," Zoe mumbles, pushing herself up to sit. "Are we at your apartment? Why didn't you just drop me at my dorm?"

"Probably because you were passed out," Chris replies shortly.

"Well, I'm fine now." Zoe moves to stand, smoothing down the hem of her tight black dress. She wobbles slightly, placing a hand on his coffee table for support.

"Watch the puzzle." Chris yelps, and Zoe rolls her eyes.

"I didn't touch it." She yawns, stretching, and then her gaze lands on me standing in front of the door. "Emily?"

"Hey," I wave awkwardly. "Uh, how's it going?"

"I need to shower," Zoe mumbles.

"Drink this first," Chris hands her a glass of water. She chugs it, moving to set it down on the coffee table.

"What did I just say about the puzzle?"

"Sorry, sorry." Zoe rolls her eyes, handing the glass back to him. "You're almost done anyway."

"Almost isn't done."

"He's so weird about his puzzles. He has his favorite ones framed," Zoe gestures to a few completed puzzles hanging from the walls. "He doesn't even let me help with them because I lost one piece one time—"

"Twice," Chris mutters. "Go shower. You smell like jungle juice."

"I do not," Zoe pauses, sniffing herself. "Oh, shit. I do. But I'll be back in a minute. Don't leave, Emily." Apparently, her surprise at my presence has transformed to delight. I can't help but be flattered, considering that Zoe is infinitely cooler than I am.

"I won't," I promise, hiding my laughter behind my hand as she bounds off towards what I assume is the bathroom door.

Chris stalks over to the coffee table, pausing over his puzzle as he double checks each piece. I follow, peering around his shoulder.

"What is it?"

"Fenway Park," He replies, frowning as his eyes scrutinize every inch until he's satisfied that nothing is out of place. I wonder what it would be like to be that puzzle, to have Chris's eyes rove over every inch of me as if trying to memorize it.

"So. You're a puzzler."

Chris swivels to face me, the corner of his mouth twitching in amusement. "I don't know if that's the technical term, but yes. I like puzzles."

"I've never seen them in our office."

"I do the crossword."

"But not your puzzles."

"I don't like doing them at work. It's how I switch my brain off when I get home."

"I've never liked puzzles," I admit.

"Yeah? Why's that?" Chris leans in slightly, his breath ghosting against my face.

"I don't know. It's just so…uncreative. Black and white. There's no room for interpretation. Every piece, in one specific place…it's so rigid."

"That's exactly why I like them." He steps back, coming to sit on the couch. "In a puzzle, there's always a right answer."

"Ah," I sit down on the other side and curl my legs underneath me, careful to leave a full leather cushion between us. "Unlike in life."

"I suppose, if you're being psychoanalytical about it." He steals a glance at me. "So. If it's not a puzzle, what do you do to relax?"

"Are you saying I'm high-strung?"

Chris gives me an exasperated look. "I'm not saying that, because we both know it's true. *Live From New York* is demanding. Don't you need something to distract you when you're done for the day?"

"I read," I say casually.

"What do you read?"

"Romance novels," I pause, waiting to see what he says. It's always been a little test for me, telling men that I read romance novels and seeing how they react. Are they open-minded, or insulting? Do they write me off as a delusional, clingy hopeless romantic or a crazed sex maniac?

Chris does none of that. "Why romance?" he asks curiously, without even a hint of judgment.

"I like knowing that there's going to be a happy ending." I pick at a loose thread on my sweater. "And…I've never been in love. I sometimes worry if I'm too much. If my body, or my sense of humor, or my ridiculous family, or my job, or any number of intense things about me is going to drive someone off."

"You don't really believe that, do you?" He sounds surprised.

"I don't know," I shrug, still playing with the thread, unable to look at him. "I've never been in love before, or been loved romantically. But when I'm reading romance, it reminds me that everyone has their own baggage. We're all crazy, in our own ways. And someday there's going to be someone who sees all of me and loves me for it. Exactly as I am."

"Your own personal Mark Darcy." This is definitely some kind of cruel joke from the universe. I've found a gorgeous, funny guy who can quote Bridget Jones's Diary, and under no circumstances can I even think about pursuing him.

I laugh, finally lifting my head. His eyes sparkle with mischief, and my heart physically aches from how badly I want him. "I'm actually more of a Hugh Grant girl. But, yes, that's the idea. I like romance because it takes you on a journey of two people falling in love. And even though it's the same basic story, no two are the same, because every person is different. Every love story is different."

"But they all end the same."

"Well, technically. It's always a happy ending, but that's something different in every book."

"I've never read a romance before."

"You want recommendations?" I ask eagerly, the wheels in my mind already turning as I try to come up with titles Chris might like. There's nothing I love more than suggesting books to people.

"I don't know if I'm the right audience," he admits.

"Why?" I lean forward, resting my hands against the soft leather of the couch cushion between us. "Because you're a guy?"

"Because I don't really believe in all that."

"In...in all what?" I look at him in confusion, until it dawns on me, the knowledge forming a pit in my stomach. "You don't...you don't believe in love?"

"I believe it exists." He shrugs, running a hand through his soft brown hair. "I'm just not sure I believe in it ending happily."

"Ever?" My jaw drops. "For anyone?"

"Well, I guess I can't speak for others. But not for me."

"Why not?" I blurt. His eyebrows shoot up, and I realize a moment too late how invasive and personal of a question that is to ask someone. "I'm sorry. I shouldn't...it's not my business."

The shower turns on, dragging both of our eyes towards the bathroom door where his sister, Zoe, is. We look back at each other, another inappropriate question that I can't ask beginning to form on my lips.

"I guess you want me to tell you the whole story," Chris says quietly. "About me and Zoe,"

"You don't have to."

"I dragged you out here. I feel like I owe you an explanation, at least."

"You don't owe me anything," I reply softly. "But if you want to talk about it, I want to listen."

Chris takes a deep, shuddering breath. His hand slides across the couch, onto the leather cushion between us. I stop breathing when he reaches my fingertips.

I look down at his hand, just barely touching mine, and then back up at Chris. There's a plea on his face that he can't vocalize. And I can't refuse him. I don't want to. I move my hand closer, just slightly. He quickly takes my hand in his, squeezing tightly, and I try to remind myself that this is a touch of comfort, not romance. And yet I know too well just how much those feelings are intertwined.

My heart pounds loudly in my chest as I try to quiet the giddy voice inside my head that's practically jumping up and down with glee because I'm holding Chris Galloway's hand. It feels so fucking nice. Better than nice.

It feels like I never want to let him go, and from the way he's holding onto me, I want to think that he might be feeling the same.

He takes a deep breath and squeezes my hand tighter before he begins. "I didn't know Zoe existed until I was twenty. That year, her mom passed away. She didn't have any other family, so she came to live with us. My dad..." He trails off, bitterness seeping into his voice. "My dad told me the day before. He didn't even say the words, that he'd had an affair. Just expected me to put two and two together, I guess. My parents were—are—obsessed with image. Growing up, all they cared about was other people's opinions. And then, suddenly, we had this thirteen-year-old girl living in our house."

"My mom just shut down completely. She hired a nanny for Zoe. Didn't so much as speak to her, or acknowledge her. My mom had been a big drinker before, but...it got bad. I didn't realize how much until I came home from college for the first time since Zoe moved in. I pleaded with her to get help, but she didn't want to. She didn't want to get better. She didn't want to face the truth." His face crumples, and I scoot closer, my shoulder brushing his.

"My parents told people that Zoe was a distant relative, but everyone knew. They'd never had a healthy marriage, if it wasn't obvious from the whole secret child thing. But they just stopped speaking to each other behind closed doors. They might have been living in the same house, but Zoe was alone."

"It wasn't your responsibility to take care of her," I say quietly.

"Maybe not. It's not like she was starving or neglected or anything, but my mom wouldn't even look at her. And my dad wasn't an affectionate person to begin with. He didn't know what to do with a teenage girl who hated him. And she did. He barely spoke to her mom, and had met Zoe twice since she was born. Didn't even go to the funeral when her mom died. And he just expected Zoe to be grateful for the roof over her head, when they couldn't even be bothered to try to love her."

"That's horrible," I murmur.

"I just felt so powerless," Chris continues, the hand that isn't holding mine curling into a tight fist. "Watching my family treat her like some dirty little secret instead of a person. As if it was her fault for existing instead of my dad's for cheating and lying and never even telling me I had a sister until he had no other choice."

"How did you and Zoe come to be so close?"

"I came home every weekend. I packed my schedule so I didn't have Friday classes, and took a step back on the Lampoon," Chris winces. "It's why I always felt so loyal to Alex. Because without him, I might not have gotten anywhere. He made sure I kept writing when I fell behind. But all that time away…it took me too long to realize what kind of person he was around other people."

"That's not your fault either, Chris. Alex always knew how to play people."

He sighs. "He helped us get hired on *Live From New York* right out of college. I felt guilty, not seeing Zoe as much, but she wouldn't let me turn it down."

"That sounds like Zoe," I smile.

"Yeah," Chris smiles back. "But then, when Zoe was applying to college, my dad told her he wouldn't help her pay for it. He said it wasn't his problem that her mom didn't bother to leave Zoe any money for college," Chris's face darkens. "As if she'd had any to spare."

"What did you do?" I ask, trying to keep my expression neutral even as fury threatens to rise to the surface. To think that anyone could be so entitled, could deny their own child…my heart breaks for the both of them.

"I told them if they wouldn't pay for Zoe's college, I was done with them. They didn't budge. And neither did I. Zoe and I haven't spoken to them since."

"I'm so sorry, Chris," I say, my throat tightening. "I can't even imagine."

"It ended up working out okay. I was making enough at *Live From New York* to cosign her loans. But if I didn't have that job…"

I exhale sharply. "You would both be screwed."

All this time, I thought Chris was privileged. And in many ways, he is. But he never had the luxury of taking risks the way I did. If I had lost my job, I would have been devastated emotionally, but I wouldn't have been on the street. I was financially independent, but I had a safety net.

Chris doesn't. Instead, he has to be one.

"Well. Now you know all my secrets," Chris says teasingly,

quickly changing the subject. Steering us towards safer, less emotionally vulnerable waters.

"You can expect my blackmail note on Monday."

"Oh, yeah?" He leans closer, and suddenly our thighs are touching, and things feel decidedly unsafe. "What are you trying to get me to do? Quit?"

"Nah," I bump him playfully with my shoulder. "As much as I hate to admit it, I'd miss you."

"You would?" He leans in closer, and I'm suddenly hyper aware of every place where our bodies are touching. His face is close enough to mine that it would take only a small movement from either of us to close the distance. "I would miss you, too."

Something about hearing those words from his lips lights every nerve in my body on fire, until I'm pulsing with energy. With wanting him. I look into his emerald eyes and try to memorize every detail of his face: the spray of boyish freckles across his nose and cheeks, his full lips, the flutter of his golden-brown eyelashes.

I can feel the thundering of my heart in my chest. He must know. He must feel it too. And yet, he doesn't pull back.

He's going to kiss me. Or I'm going to kiss him. It's going to happen, and I can't fight it. I can't stop it. I don't want to. He's my *Update* co-host, my writing partner, and my competition. There are a thousand reasons why this shouldn't be happening. And yet none of them are enough to stop me.

"I'm sorry." The words hit me like a rush of cold water as Chris pulls away. "I—I'm gonna go check on Zoe." He leaps up, racing for her door. With every step he takes away from me, I wonder what he's thinking. What made him change his mind.

Was any of this even real? Was it innocent flirting, and he let himself get carried away? Chris just poured his heart out to me. He showed me pieces of himself that he keeps locked inside. Did that all mean nothing?

It's as good a reminder as any. This closeness is an illusion, created from all the time we're spending together. He probably just remembered what I shouldn't have let myself forget. Our truce is temporary.

Chris Galloway is never going to be my friend. And he's definitely never going to be anything more.

I'm tempted to slip away while he's gone, but I owe it to Zoe to stay. They re-emerge a few minutes later as I'm flipping through Chris's bookshelf.

"Hey, Emily." Zoe is clutching a bottle of water, looking decidedly more sober. "I'm really sorry about all this." The way she looks back at Chris tells me everything that I need to know.

"Please. I was a hot mess in college." I give her a knowing smile. "I once got so drunk that I threw up in a photo booth. And then I texted the guy I had a crush on sixty-seven times in a row. With no response."

Zoe laughs, and something in my chest loosens. After everything I learned from Chris about their family tonight, I want Zoe to know that I'm not another person in her life who will judge her.

"Not to be rude, but what are you doing here?" Zoe asks. "Because Chris hasn't told *anyone* at work I'm his sister."

"Because you told me not to," he interjects, looking every bit the beleaguered older brother.

"We were writing, and he got your friend's call. He looked worried, and I had nothing better to do, so...here I am," I shrug.

"Uh huh." Zoe glances between us, clearly not convinced. "Is this, like, a really bad date? Because I love my brother, but if his idea of romance was rescuing his drunk sister from a college party, I may need to stage an intervention."

"Not a date." *He made sure of that.*

Chris clears his throat, looking a little bit uncomfortable. His phone dings, breaking the tension. "Oh! Freddie's back. I'll go get him."

Chris disappears into the hallway. "Who's Freddie?" I ask Zoe.

"You don't know Freddie?" Zoe's eyes widen, just as Chris walks back in, a fluffy dachshund in his arms.

"Freddie, you were such a good boy for the dog walker, weren't you?" he coos.

He has a *dog*. I need to get out of here before I fall hopelessly in love with this man. Chris puts Freddie down, and he immediately jumps on me, showering me with kisses.

"Freddie! Don't be aggressive." Zoe scolds.

"Sorry. Down, boy." Chris calls, although his dog ignores the command. Luckily, Freddie is small enough that his enthusiastic greeting doesn't do any damage to me.

"Oh. My. Goodness." I kneel and immediately begin showering the good boy with kisses. "How did a sweet boy like you end up with this grumpy man?"

"That's a question I've been asking myself for months," Zoe quips.

"Hey." Chris protests, but he doesn't have a comeback. Freddie licks my face enthusiastically. "Oh, he likes you."

"Does he like everyone?" I ask with a laugh, scratching his ears before my allure as a new person to sniff fades and he moves on to his dinner.

"He hated Alex," Zoe says.

"He has good taste in people," Chris replies, and his sister snickers.

I wonder if Chris knows how much character it shows, for him to have chosen Zoe even when his parents didn't. For standing by her side despite what other people thought, what his own family thought, even if it came at the expense of the two people whose approval probably used to matter the most to him.

"I have a great idea. Let's watch the last few episodes of *Live From New York* and I can tell you what you could've done better." Zoe says.

"Don't you have class tomorrow?"

"Not till eleven." she protests.

"I should go," I say quickly, sensing a fight brewing. "I'll see you tomorrow, Chris?"

"Stay here until your car gets here, at least."

"It was super quick. It's already outside," I lie. "Zoe, text your friend and tell her you made it home safely, okay?"

"For sure. Night, Emily. Thanks for taking care of my brother." She's still drunk. The words don't mean anything, and yet...

"Thank you," Chris says, more quietly, striding away from the couch to hold the door open for me.

"Anytime." I mean it. Even if, when I stand outside in the bracing November midnight cold, I wonder if I'll be able to keep my word without risking an entirely different part of myself. Specifically, my heart.

"Tonight marks the first night of Hanukkah!"

"And Emily and I have decided that our gifts to each other this year will be jokes," Chris says.

"We're making each other read jokes live on air that the other person has never seen before."

"Here goes nothing." The audience cheers loudly as we prepare ourselves.

"A recent survey by the Anti-Defamation League found that 70% of Americans believe Jews stick together more than other Americans," Chris says. "They have to, because separating would make it much harder to coordinate controlling the Jewish space lasers."

"Wow, Chris," I feign shock, shaking my head at the roaring audience. "News outlets have warned about an upcoming shortage of triple A batteries due to issues with the supply chain. I am unconcerned, because my vibrator uses double A."

I shake my head at Chris, who continues with the next joke I've written for him. "A robot in Oregon beat a high school student by finishing the hundred-meter dash in 9.98 seconds, which is .02 seconds faster than I finish."

The audience shrieks with laughter as Chris gives me a put-upon look, although it doesn't quite hide the smile on his face. When I first suggested this joke swap, I expected Chris to say no. It wasn't something any other *Weekend Update* anchors had ever done before. But he was open to it, and now, I think he might even be having fun. The opportunity to make me read embarrassing jokes that he wrote for me on live television probably didn't hurt.

The idea was inspired by my prank on Alex at the end of last season. I kept finding myself rewatching that *Update* segment. Not just because it was so entertaining to see Alex Nabakov humiliate himself—although that never failed to bring a smile to my face—but because there was so much humor in the unscripted reaction to the joke.

"The growing popularity of AI chatbots has many writers concerned that the service could one day replace us. I'm not worried, because most of my jokes already come from the internet and no one seems to have figured that out yet," Chris snickers, and I playfully roll my eyes.

"Alright, thank you and have a good night, everyone! This has been the *Weekend Update*. I'm Chris Galloway."

"And I'm Emily Beckerman. Thank you, and goodnight!"

"I can't believe we're almost done," Riley says later as we're celebrating at the afterparty. It's on the *Live From New York* soundstage tonight, because the restaurant we originally booked had a last-minute rodent infestation.

"Are you doing anything exciting over hiatus?" I ask.

"I plan on hibernating until New Year's," Riley answers as Mandy walks over to join us, followed by Faith.

"That reminds me. I have a Netflix special coming out January first, and they're throwing a New Year's Eve party to celebrate. You should come," Faith suggests.

"Are you sure?"

Faith raises an eyebrow at me. "If I wasn't, I wouldn't have invited you. No one was more surprised than me by this development, but I think I might just be your friend, Beckerman."

I beam. She gives me an exaggerated eye roll, one I know that she doesn't mean because of the wide smile accompanying it. "You like me."

"We do." Mandy appears, carrying a full bottle of champagne that she extends to me. I take a decidedly un-ladylike swig from it. "You've wormed your way into our hearts."

"Gross analogy." Riley wrinkles his nose, then sticks his hand out to me, gesturing for the bottle. I hold up a finger, taking one more gulp before I give it to him.

We chat for a few more minutes before I spot Zoe on the side of the stage, and excuse myself to go talk to her.

"Hey! How are you doing?" I ask. I haven't seen her much since the night I picked her up with Chris.

"I'm excited for a break," Zoe sighs theatrically. "This schedule is exhausting."

"Tell me about it," I agree. "It's even worse when it's your full-time job."

"Well, at least you're making more than minimum wage."

"Point taken," The internship system is so fucked up. "But having *Live From New York* on your resume will make it much easier to get a job in comedy once you graduate."

"Except, I don't think I want to work in comedy," she admits.

"What? Then why are you here?"

"Chris," Zoe looks at me guiltily. "I don't mean to sound ungrateful. I know I'm lucky to be here. But...whenever I try to tell him that I don't want to work in comedy, it's like he doesn't even hear me. He thinks that he's doing me this huge favor, making things so easy for me when they weren't for him."

"I'm sorry, Zoe." I don't even know what to say. Being somewhere like *Live From New York* is intense, even for those of us who live and breathe the show. If Zoe doesn't, she must be exhausted. "I'm sure he'll come around."

"Maybe you could talk to him?" she asks hopefully.

I let out a nervous laugh. "I think you're overestimating my influence on your brother."

"Oh, trust me. I'm not." Her expression turns conspiratorial. "Even when he was complaining, Chris talked about you all the time."

"Only because I'm part of *Live From New York.*"

Zoe rolls her eyes. "Emily. Are you really this hardheaded? He's into you. It's disgustingly obvious to everyone. Everyone but you, I guess."

"That's ridiculous," I laugh nervously. "He's not."

"So you're telling me that nothing has happened between the two of you?" She looks at me skeptically.

"Well…" I hesitate. "We may or may not have almost kissed that night he picked you up from the party. While you were in the shower. But then he stopped it. He pulled away."

"What?" She frowns. "Why would he do that?"

"I don't know," I shrug, trying to act nonchalant. Trying not to let her know how much it hurt me. "He didn't say. And it doesn't matter. If he wanted to, he would."

"It's not always that simple," she protests.

"No, of course not," I reply. "But it's probably for the best. We spend all our time together. If something happened, if it didn't work out, we'd be risking what we have now," Partnership. Albeit, one with an expiration date.

"Right." Her face falls. "I guess it would be weird. And maybe not kosher with company policy."

"As long as the relationship is properly disclosed to HR, nothing in this show's bylaws prevents us from engaging in a consensual, appropriate romantic relationship with each other," I reply quickly. Zoe smirks, and I realize I've been tricked.

"Someone knows her bylaws."

"I was curious," I reply defensively. "I really enjoy reading workplace conduct manuals. I find it very helpful to be well-informed."

"By all means, keep defending yourself. That makes it sound less suspicious," she teases, sounding so much like her brother.

"It doesn't matter. Chris and I aren't a good fit."

"I just want him to be happy," Zoe says. "He's always taking care of me. He should have someone to take care of him, too."

"He should." And whoever she is, I'll hate her. It will be my selfish, closely guarded secret, as I watch her make him happy in ways that I probably never could. I'll hate her because she gets to have him.

"I just wonder..." Zoe trails off. "Never mind. At least I know, now."

"Know what?" Chris materializes in front of us, carrying two plates of cake. He hands one to me, and I eagerly accept.

"Hi," she squeaks.

"Know what?" he repeats, his gaze darting suspiciously between us.

"The best tampon brand," I say, much louder than necessary. "You know. Just girl stuff. That girls talk about."

"Don't you have an IUD?" he asks Zoe. She looks horrified. "What? You're on my health insurance. And you're the one who brought up tampons," he pauses, taking another bite of cake. "I'm glad you're being safe."

"What was that?" Zoe cups a hand over her ear. "I think I heard someone say my name. I should go! Bye!" She speeds off, and Chris grins at me.

"It never gets old."

"You're the worst," I roll my eyes at him.

"See, you say that," Chris elbows me. "But the look on your face tells a different story. You find my brotherly teasing utterly charming."

"I..." Our eyes meet, and I forget what I was going to say. I forget everything that isn't him. I kick myself internally. This has to stop.

It's been over a week since our almost-kiss at his apartment, and Chris has yet to acknowledge what happened. In fairness, I haven't brought it up either, but what do I say? Hey, Chris, it was super weird how you were maybe about to kiss me and then completely changed your mind? No thanks. I got the message. We had a moment, but he didn't act on it. He's not into me. And no amount of flirty teasing will change that.

All it does is torture me with thoughts of what might have been.

"This cake is great." I say quickly, taking an enormous bite. I can't help but moan loudly, borderline obscenely, at the taste. It's that good.

"That sound should not be heard in a workplace." Chris side-eyes me.

"What? Of a woman eating? You think I should be seen and not heard?"

"I think if you want to make pornographic noises to your dessert, you should do it in private."

"*I* think if you're not moaning, you're not enjoying it." My face flushes when I realize my inadvertent innuendo. "Cake, I mean,"

"That's what I thought you meant." His eyes dance with amusement. Before Chris, I thought that was just something romance authors made up, like multiple orgasms. But Chris's eyes do things I've never seen eyes do before. Or maybe I've just never noticed anyone else's eyes the way I notice his.

"Yes, you did," I smile back. Chris's expression freezes as he stares at me, his eyes lingering. I self-consciously wipe my face with my hand. "Is there frosting on my face?"

"No. I just..." he trails off, rubbing his neck sheepishly.

"If I have food on my face, you have to tell me," I plead.

"You don't," His gaze trails across my face, and I feel my skin growing hot. "I just love it when you smile."

For a few moments, we only look at each other, as if each of us is trying to process in our own way what that admission means. We're interrupted by Mandy, who pulls us onto the makeshift dance floor, and soon the afterparty is in full swing.

After tonight, there's only one show left this year. The first half of the season has flown by, which is normal, even if nothing else is. I finally feel truly proud of my work on this show. Network executives and people that I consider my comedy heroes have been coming up to me all night, complimenting the *Update* and my work as head writer.

We haven't heard anything specific from Jessica on *Live From New York*'s fate, but our ratings are at a five-year high. After starting this season convinced that my tension with Chris would doom the entire show, it feels like we've done something incredible. We have.

Chris and I make a good team. We've worked tirelessly to combine our visions for *Live From New York*. Our styles of comedy seem like they wouldn't work, and yet they balance each other out perfectly. I push Chris to take risks, and he brings my ideas down to earth. When we overcame our personal grudges and petty squabbling, the result was something incredible.

And it's more than just our writing. Chris and I speak the same language. We spend hours sitting in our office, discussing our favorite sketches from past seasons of *Live From New York*. We're not just head writers for the show. We're superfans. And I don't know if we would have reached the point of being able to work together without that. If we weren't so deeply invested in *LFNY*, if we hadn't both spent our entire lives dreaming of working on this show, we wouldn't have had the incentive to overcome our differences.

By 3:00 a.m., my face hurts from smiling. I can't remember another time when I felt so at home, so *happy* here, instead of waiting for the other shoe to drop.

I feel like I belong.

"I'm gonna go pee," I announce to my dance partner, Riley. When I get out of the bathroom, Chris is waiting for me. "Oh. Hey."

"Hey," he says breathlessly. "I've been looking for you. Where have you been?"

"I was dancing," I reply casually. That's true, but I was also intentionally avoiding him. He's the person I should be celebrating with. We did this together. But after what happened at his apartment, interacting with Chris outside of our show responsibilities feels like dangerous territory.

"Can I show you something?" he asks. I hesitate, but then I see the eagerness in his face. The hope in his eyes.

It's a terrible idea to follow him back into the office area, but I'm unable to stop myself. We wander through the hallways until he pushes open the door to a random storage closet. Actually, not a random storage closet—at least not for me. This is where I hid when I eavesdropped on his conversation with Zoe.

"You wanted to show me a closet?" I ask skeptically, trying to distract myself from the anticipation thundering in my chest. The door snicks shut behind us, and I feel my palms grow sweaty.

"Can you please be patient for once?" He pulls out a random box from a high shelf. I try to ignore the way his shirt lifts slightly when he reaches for it, revealing a tantalizing strip of skin. I want to feel it with my hands. I can't be in this closet with him. It's driving me crazy. *He's* driving me crazy. I've never noticed someone the way I notice Chris. Every movement has me practically panting. I'm overcome with desire to touch every inch of him, slowly, methodically, until I have him memorized.

I shouldn't just stand here, letting him torture me. But even as I tell myself I'm going to leave, I'm going to walk away from him, my feet stay rooted to the spot.

I can't stay. But I can't go, either. Even though I know he doesn't want me, I can't break that habit of hoping. It will probably be the death of me.

Chris drops to the floor, kneeling in front of the box and gently taking the lid off. "Look at this."

I join him. The box is full of old *LFNY* cast photos, captured in candid moments: eating Chinese food backstage, sitting in makeup chairs, laughing behind the same *Weekend Update* desk that I laugh behind.

They were all where I once was. And maybe someday, someone will find pictures like this of me and my friends in this box. Maybe someday, someone will look up to me and dream of *LFNY* the way that I did for my entire life.

"How did you find these?" I ask, my voice full of wonder. I run my finger along the edge of one snapshot, featuring a young Jessica standing next to Billy Joel. "They're incredible."

"Zoe found them and told me."

"Your sister is awesome."

"She is," he agrees. We peruse the pictures in silence for a few minutes, before he adds, "I would have felt so guilty looking at these last season. But now…I feel like the people who came before us might be proud of what we're doing. Or at least, they wouldn't be ashamed."

"Yeah," I agree softly. "It kind of feels amazing, doesn't it?"

"It feels perfect." He's so close to me. I try not to breathe in the smell of him, the vaguely male scent of his deodorant. Nothing particularly unique to Chris, and yet it's so different then it would be on someone else.

Chris leans forward, just slightly. He tucks a lock of hair behind my ear, and I suddenly have the sickening suspicion that I'm being toyed with. Because why would he do this, now, when he stopped things between us the other night without so much as a word? Is he drunk, or lonely?

Does Chris want me? Or does he want someone, and I happen to be here?

The thought makes me go cold. I push to my feet, suddenly unable to stand being here for another second. "I need to go."

"Don't." The words are so quiet I can pretend that I don't hear them. My hand closes around the door handle, and I push, but nothing happens. It's…it's stuck. I jiggle the door handle furiously, but it doesn't budge.

"Oh, my god." I lean my head against the door. "This can't be happening."

"Let me try," Chris says impatiently, as if his man strength will fix everything. It does not. On his first attempt, he yanks the handle clean off. "Whoops," he says sheepishly, depositing the door handle on a shelf behind him.

"Help," I shout, pounding on the closet door with my fists until they sting. "*Help!*"

"No one's going to hear you," he murmurs.

"This is all your fault!" I whirl on him. He's standing so close to me that the movement puts my chest flush with his.

"You think I'm the reason the closet door is stuck?"

"I wouldn't be here if you hadn't brought me."

"Oh, I'm so sorry for showing you a bunch of cool photos that I knew you'd like!"

"We should be out there, *celebrating*, and instead—"

"You're stuck with me." His face is so close to mine that I can feel his breath on my skin. "And I'm stuck with you. And neither of us asked for it."

I can't tell if he's talking about this closet, or our partnership this season, or both.

"I didn't ask for any of this," Chris says, his eyes turning stormy, and then he kisses me.

18

Kissing Chris Galloway is everything I wanted it to be. No, it's better, because it's not happening in my imagination. It's real.

His mouth moves softly against mine, but it's not enough. I grab his shoulders, not roughly but desperately, pressing him against a shelf. His arms snake around my waist, holding me tightly against him. "Emily," he breathes, whispering my name against the sensitive skin of my neck, and I think that if he wasn't holding me up I might melt into the floor right then. The sound of my name in his mouth unravels me completely.

My fingers reach upwards to tangle in his hair, pulling him closer to me as our kisses grow more insistent. My mouth slides against his, savoring the taste of him. His tongue traces my bottom lip, teasing me until I open my mouth for him and it meets my own. Every stroke is perfect, raw and hungry and working me into a frenzy. I could kiss him for hours, and it would be time well spent.

His hands slide underneath my shirt, splaying against the small of my back. My hands drift down to fist his shirt, tightening against the fabric as if I could rip it open when he takes my earlobe and tugs it gently with his teeth. Chris kisses a path down the column of my throat. His tongue darts out when he reaches the hollow of my neck, tracing my pounding pulse as I writhe against him. He exhales sharply when I drag my hands down his back, gripping onto him greedily as if he'll disappear when I let go.

"Oh, god, *Chris*," I whimper when he nudges his knee between my thighs, exactly the place where I'm aching for him.

"Emily," he murmurs, lifting his mouth from my neck. One of his hands grips the flesh of my hips as the thumb of his other brushes the top of my jeans. I feel him smile against the curve my jaw before kissing it. He rocks into me. "I can't believe this is happening."

"Should we stop?" I whisper.

"No. Fuck, no. I want the opposite of that." He drags himself against me, and I inhale sharply at the exquisite friction. "I want you."

"I want you, too. Even when I hated you, I wanted you," I admit. "It was extremely inconvenient."

"Yeah?" Chris looks far too pleased by that information. He reaches one hand behind me, twining around the nape of my neck, as the other comes to my hip. "I guess you weren't immune to my flirting after all."

"Shut up," I growl, dragging my mouth to his again, and for once, he listens. I'm lost in the rhythm of our kisses, the feeling of his body against mine. Here, in the silence, we fit together perfectly. Like we were made for each other.

Loud Polish music suddenly blares out, interrupting us. I release Chris, staggering back, my hands on my chest as if to stop my heart from galloping right out of it.

"Shit," Chris mutters, adjusting himself in his jeans. His expression changes from one of bliss to panic, tinged with regret, and it douses my lust more than any interruption could.

"Is someone in there?" Doris, the night janitor, knocks loudly on the door.

"Yes," I call, wincing internally at the breathy state of my voice. I sound like someone moments away from orgasm. And I was. A few hurried kisses and gropes with Chris got me closer to release than some of the actual sex I've had in the past. Not just because he's good with his hands and mouth, although he definitely is. But because I could feel how desperate he was for me in every touch. Because I imagined what it would feel like with him, but the reality was ten thousand times better.

Before reality came crashing back in and that remorse on his face took it all away.

"The door is stuck," Chris calls.

"Just a second." The door swings open a moment later. "It wasn't stuck. It was locked from the outside."

"What?" Chris looks confused. "How would that have happened?"

"I don't know." Doris crosses her arms. "You two tell me."

"How could we have locked a door from the outside if we were stuck in here?" I question.

"I don't know what kind of shenanigans you get up to after these shows."

"It was probably just an accident," Chris says firmly. "So, no one needs to know that this happened."

Because the gossip that would cause...

Chris is doing the smart thing, keeping this under wraps, and yet I can't help but fixate on the way he said accident. As if he was closing a door.

"Uh, should I give this to you?" I pick up the door handle that fell off.

"Sure." She accepts it, dropping it onto her cart of cleaning supplies before she walks away.

"So—" I begin.

"We should—" Chris starts.

I blush as his ears turn red. *Please don't let this be the ending*, I want to say. Instead, I go with, "We should get back to the afterparty."

We walk back in silence, neither of us willing or able to acknowledge what just happened. I'm not sure what I could say. It feels like there's no going back, and yet I can't tell if anything has truly changed. Does he think this was a mistake? Are we going to keep pretending that we're just friends or finally acknowledge the truth that's been sitting between us?

Maybe if I were braver, I could ask him. But I would rather not know than be told he regrets it. That he didn't mean it.

That one of the most perfect moments of my life was a mistake to him.

When we get back to the stage, we split up immediately. I don't see Chris for the rest of the night.

I do, however, see Mandy and Faith not-so-subtly winking at me. And then Mandy reaches in her pocket, waving something at me before she puts it away again.

A key.

I get back to Josh and Rachel's place early Sunday morning, around five. I sleep until noon and then manage to drag myself out of bed.

"Hey, sleepyhead," Rachel smiles at me when I stumble into the kitchen. I nod blearily at her, going to turn on the coffee machine. She's used to this by now. The night after a show is always brutal. "How was last night?"

I pause with my hand on a mug, last night coming back to me in a rush. Chris. The closet. "Oh no." I put the mug back, sliding to the floor, my hands coming to cover my face. "Oh no."

"What the hell happened?" Rachel demands. "Are you okay?"

"Chris and I kissed."

"Oh, boy." She comes to sit next to me on the floor. "I think we need pancakes to dissect this."

She is, of course, right. Half an hour later, we're eating chocolate chip pancakes, eggs, and bacon at the diner around the corner from her apartment.

"So," she says, after I tell her the specifics of what happened. "Is this a good thing?"

"I don't know," I admit through a bite of pancake.

"Well, where did you leave things?"

"Um," I bite my lip, looking down at my lap. "We sort of just... walked off."

"And you haven't talked to him since?" Rachel looks chagrined.

"It's only been a few hours!" I may or may not have slept with my ringer on so that I could hear if a text or call came through. I risked my post-show sleep for him, and he still hasn't reached out.

"You could text him," Rachel suggests innocently. "Okay, don't look at me like I just said something insane. What I'm trying to say is that if you want answers, you can ask for them."

"I don't want to chase him," I mumble, twisting my napkin between my hands. "It's like they say. Don't chase anything but drinks and dreams."

"Who, exactly, is the 'they' you're referring to?" Rachel asks archly.

"A pillow my roommate freshman year had. But it's good advice," I reply defensively. "He kissed me. He should reach out."

"Maybe. But what are you going to do if you don't hear from him before work tomorrow?"

"Find a different job?" Rachel throws a packet of sugar at me. It hits me in the forehead. "Ow!"

"That did not hurt you."

"I still wish you hadn't thrown it," I grumble. "I'm not going to quit. I'll figure it out, I guess. We'll go back to the way it was before."

And I'll never kiss Chris Galloway again. The thought makes me want to curl up into a ball and cry.

"And is that what you want?" Rachel asks.

"No," I sigh. "But it's not just about what I want."

He told me that he wanted me. I believed him. Could he really kiss me like that if he didn't? But it doesn't just matter how he feels. It matters what he chooses.

I want him to choose me so fucking badly.

"What does Chris want?" Rachel asks.

"I suppose I'm going to have to find out."

When I walk into our office the next morning, Chris is already there. He looks up from his computer, and for a split second I hope that the answers to all my questions will be written on his face. But he just looks conflicted, and slightly tortured.

"Hey," he says awkwardly.

"Hey," I clear my throat. "How was your Sunday?"

"Good. Zoe and I took Freddie to the dog park."

"That's so fun." I wince internally at how high-pitched my voice just became. It always does that when I'm uncomfortable. I stand in the doorway for a few more moments, shifting my weight between my feet. Waiting for him to say something. But he just goes back to his typing.

The next few hours are business as usual, and yet there's a deep undercurrent of panic. We're like two people in a movie who found out the world is ending and are just pretending everything is fine, trying to go about their day to day, hoping that the meteor hurtling for Earth will disappear if they don't acknowledge it.

It's not until after dinner that I finally break. I didn't want to be the one to do this, but I can't leave the building without knowing what he's thinking.

"Chris," I say, breaking the silence, trying not to sound cryptic.

"What's up?" He's trying to sound casual, but Chris is no actor. We both know what I'm about to say.

"Stop it," I say tightly. "Don't pretend like you don't know exactly what's up. Not talking about it isn't going to make it go away."

"Is that what you want?" he asks tiredly. My eyes scan his face, noticing the dark circles under his eyes, the tension in his neck. And my heart sinks, because I don't think he would look so exhausted and unhappy if he didn't regret our kiss. "For it to go away?"

No. I want the opposite. I want it so much that my chest aches. But the thought of admitting that makes me break out in a cold sweat. "Is that possible?"

"Yeah." He rubs his jaw. "I should probably apologize."

"You didn't do anything that I didn't want you to." *That I didn't practically beg you for.* My face heats at the memory of his body pressed tightly against mine.

"I got carried away. You know how it is. The adrenaline of a really good show. We've been on this high, with everything going so well, and I lost my head."

In other words, he was happy and horny, and I was there.

And when he almost kissed me at his apartment, it was because he was emotionally vulnerable.

I'm such an idiot. All those years of reading romance novels had me making up a narrative in my own head that never existed. I blurred the lines because I wanted so badly to be wanted by someone like Chris: someone smart, funny, and handsome. Someone who saw me, and respected me.

My five minutes of fame on the *Update* have clearly gone to my head. A few months of appearing on television and I forget that Chris isn't for me. That I am not the girl he dates, the girl he falls in love with. I should be happy with what I have. We've accomplished exactly what I hoped we would. We found a way to work together. We're transforming *Live From New York* and the *Weekend Update* into something that I'm deeply proud of.

And that's enough. It has to be. Because I am not who he wants. And the sooner I can accept that and move on, the sooner I'll stop feeling like my heart went through a meat grinder.

"I feel the same way," I lie, hoping I sound even slightly convincing. "Laughter. It's a hell of a drug."

"It really is." He laughs, sounding relieved that I'm on the same page as him and he doesn't have to let me down gently. "Should we get back to writing?"

"I just have to run to the bathroom," I say. I speed out of our office and down the hallway, refusing to let the tears fall until the door is shut firmly behind me.

19

"I don't know about this," I mutter.

Mandy looks herself over, straightening the Santa hat on her head. "I look kinda good."

"Everyone loves Santa," Chris insists.

"Not the Jews," I say with a side-eye.

"Then explain why all the best Christmas songs are written by Jewish people." I don't have a comeback for that. When Chris suggested we have Mandy do a bit as Santa on the *Update*, I was hesitant. And by hesitant, I mean I said something along the lines of 'over my dead body'.

Unfortunately, as Chris reminded me, compromise isn't just about him agreeing to do things that I want to do. I have to be willing to compromise, too.

"God, forgive me," I sigh, adjusting my star of David necklace to make sure it's easily visible as Chris and I make our way over to the *Update* desk.

"I've seen you pound shrimp cocktail without batting an eye, and this is what you're worried about?" Chris quips as we sit down in our chairs and get last minute touch-ups.

"Don't tell me how to practice my Judaism."

"I wouldn't dream of it," He smiles, and something inside my gut twists.

Chris is devastating when he smiles. I try not to remember the feeling of that smile against my lips, but I can't help it.

～

We breeze through the first few *Weekend Update* jokes before I introduce Mandy.

"It's Christmastime in New York, and everywhere else. And who better to talk to us about Christmas than Santa herself!" I smile as Mandy joins us. She sits down, cracking open a Red Bull.

"Hi, yes, it's me, Santa," Mandy says sounding less than thrilled to be here. "Ho, ho, ho," she adds with zero enthusiasm.

"Santa, you seem a bit...stressed," Chis looks like he's trying very hard not to smile. "Do you have a lot on your plate?"

"Do you always ask dumb questions?" she retorts. "You people love Christmas. You call it the most wonderful time of the year. Meanwhile, I'm trying to out-deliver Amazon without violating elf labor laws."

"That does sound difficult," Chris swallows a laugh as Mandy takes an enormous swig of Red Bull.

"That sounds difficult," Mandy repeats in a singsong, mocking voice. "It's impossible! I haven't slept since Halloween."

"Are there any parts of Christmas that you do enjoy, Santa?" he asks.

"Let me see," Mandy says sarcastically. "Reading incoherent letters written by children? Shoveling reindeer poop? Living in the goddamn North Pole?"

"If you hate your job so much, why do you do it?"

"For the same reason you do. *Money.*"

"Is there a lot of money in being Santa?"

"Have you seen how big Christmas is? I'm a billionaire, Chris!

They keep it a secret, because no one wants to think that Santa is in it for the money. But when it's not Christmas season, I spend all my time on a private island that I bought from Jeffrey Epstein for *nothing*."

"But if you have so much money, doesn't that make the stress worth it? Wouldn't that be enough to make you happy?" Chris is struggling to speak through his laughter now. I'm dying next to him, thankful that I don't have to talk right now. We wrote this bit together, so nothing is a surprise to us, but I don't think either of us anticipated just how funny Mandy's delivery would be.

"Of course not. Didn't you watch Succession? Billionaires aren't happy," Mandy scoffs. "Otherwise we wouldn't keep doing such terrible things." She proceeds to chug the rest of her Red Bull, and tosses the empty can at Chris's head.

"All right, thank you, Santa," Chris says, pretending to shoo her off.

"Don't ask me about my taxes," Mandy calls as she leaves the stage.

"That went really well," I tell Chris once the *Update* ends.

"I knew it was going to. You wouldn't have been so worried if you believed in me from the start." His tone is light, but I sense an undercurrent of something more serious.

I bump my knee against his under the desk. Since the first show, that's become our little signal, a way we can connect with each other. "I do trust you." His words from the night we kissed echo in my mind. He said that I'd changed him. And he's changed me too.

Six months ago, I would have sneered at a sketch about a stressed-out Santa. I would have dismissed it as silly. And it is, but that doesn't mean it's bad.

Under Alex, I became so fixated on using my sketch writing to challenge societal norms that I forgot how much fun it was to write humor just for the purpose of being funny. Chris helped me find that part of myself again, even if it was against my will.

It's just as fun doing the *Update* with him as it is writing it. I love our easy banter, the way the audience reacts when we tease each other. Being in front of the camera instead of behind it terrified me, and now it might just be my favorite part of writing for *Live From New York.*

I love when people come up to me on the streets of New York and mention a sketch or an *Update* bit that they loved. Everywhere I go, even when no one acknowledges me—which is most of the time, because the majority of New Yorkers would rather die than admit they recognize someone famous to their face—I hear chatter about *Live From New York* in a way that I haven't since I started writing for the show. We're the thing that the city is talking about, the comeback kids. And it doesn't go unnoticed by the rest of the writers and cast members. Everyone is riding a high. Even Jessica seems like she's in a better mood, although we haven't gotten any specific updates on our potential cancellation.

Or which of us she's going to choose at the end of the season.

I can't think about that. I don't want to think about it, and not just because it's a reminder that any partnership Chris and I have built between us is only temporary.

It's because I no longer feel satisfaction at the idea of firing him or demoting him if I'm chosen to stay. I don't want to do this without him.

He's my favorite part.

"I trust you, too," Chris says quietly. His knee meets mine again, but this time it stays.

And even though I know it's all temporary, that it will die either by my hand or by his at the end of this year, I let myself appreciate that trust.

I had hoped that hiatus would make my feelings about Chris go away. Instead, they only intensify. I find myself missing him. I didn't realize how accustomed I was to seeing him every day and spending most of my time with him. I feel his absence in a way that I don't want to.

We text a little bit, but it's not the same. And it kills me, knowing that Chris doesn't miss me the way that I miss him. Even as a friend. He doesn't ask to see me, or try to make plans, and I don't know why I expected him to.

He doesn't belong to me. He doesn't owe me anything.

Tonight is the first time I'm seeing him since our last show of the year, at Faith's New Year's Eve party. I'm wearing a tight black dress, made of a stretchy material that hugs my curves like a second skin. It has a v-neck that shows off my cleavage and a slit on the left side.

It's the kind of dress designed to bring men to their knees. I should know better than to fantasize about Chris in that position, but I can't help it. Every night I fall asleep dreaming of the glide of his lips against mine, the perfect heat of his tongue in my mouth, the way his hands tightened around my waist as he pulled me closer... essentially, the type of late-night thoughts that lead to me opening the drawer of my nightstand and feeling very grateful for quiet vibrators.

He doesn't want me. But I can't stop wishing that he did.

Tonight is about Faith, I remind myself. It's hard to forget when I walk into the spectacular loft and am greeted by an enormous poster of her. The party is spectacular. Floor-to-ceiling windows offer incredible views of the city, and waiters in glittery unitards walk around carrying trays of appetizers and spicy pineapple mezcal margaritas, in addition to a full open bar and plenty of champagne.

I find the woman of the hour surrounded by a crowd of admirers and patiently wait my turn.

"Emily!" Faith grins, pulling me in for a tight hug. "It's so good to see you! Thank you for coming."

"I wouldn't miss it. This is insane," I squeeze her arm. "I can't wait to watch the special."

"It's fantastic. We were there for the taping this summer," Riley says as he and Mandy materialize from the crowd.

"To Faith, finally getting the spotlight she's always deserved," Mandy cheers. I snag a flute of champagne from a nearby waiter and join in the toast, lifting my glass to meet my friends'.

My friends. "I can't believe how much I missed you three." I take a sip of champagne, feeling it go straight to my head and yet not caring. I don't need the liquid courage to be honest, even if it helps. "Not to get cheesy, but this is the first season that I've actually had fun. And it's because of all of you."

"It's New Year's. Cheesiness is expected." Riley smiles at me. "And I missed you, too."

"So did I," Faith adds.

"I did, too." Mandy rolls her eyes. "Now, can we stop being maudlin and start getting drunk? I don't usually get this sentimental until I've had an entire bottle of champagne, and I haven't even finished my first glass."

I spend the next few hours schmoozing with various producers and Netflix executives, all of whom are much more interested in me now that I'm on the *Weekend Update*. It's both very flattering and deeply weird to see the kind of people who didn't bother giving me the time of day when I was a writer treat me like a celebrity now that I'm actually on the show.

As much as I'm indignant on behalf of the other overlooked writers, it's hard not to enjoy the attention. It's not just empty flattery, either. I feel like people in the comedy world have noticed the hard work Chris and I are putting in to make *Live From New York* an institution again.

"Guess who," someone whispers from behind me, covering my eyes with their hands.

"Ah!" I shriek, elbowing my attacker in the stomach.

"Damn, Emily," my attacker winces. It's Zoe. "I don't have abs, you can't do that to me."

"Sorry!" I hug her. "How are you?"

"Oh, *I'm* great," she says mischievously. "But am I really the sibling you want to know about?"

"I have no idea what you mean," I reply unconvincingly.

Zoe shakes her head at me sadly. "You two are so fucking stubborn. I really thought after the closet, you'd admit you were into each other."

"Excuse me?" My face turns bright red. "How do you know about the closet?"

"She may or may not have been on in the whole thing," Mandy says, coming to stand with us. "As in, it was her idea. All I did was lock you in."

"I'm sorry," Riley glances between us. "What the actual fuck are you talking about?"

"They locked me in a closet with Chris."

"And how, exactly, did you end up in the closet in the first place?" He arches an eyebrow at me.

My face heats. "He was showing me pictures!"

"It was all my idea," Zoe says smugly. "I found these awesome old pictures, and I told Chris about them, and very sneakily mentioned how much you would love them."

"Okay, so what happened in the closet?" Riley asks eagerly.

"It doesn't matter, because it's never going to happen again. Chris doesn't feel that way about me," I say firmly.

"Bullshit. I've seen the way he looks at you," Zoe replies, the ferocity in her voice surprising.

"Maybe we should give you two a moment alone?" Riley suggests.

"Let's take a lap," Mandy offers Riley her elbow, which he graciously accepts.

"Zoe, why are you so invested in this?" I ask.

"Because I've never seen him as happy as he looks when he's with you. He's taken on so much stress to make my life easier. I think you can make each other happy."

"He told me he wished it never happened," I say softly. "He's happy because the show is doing better. Chris and I were forced together. We're a temporary solution. Everything that's between us... it's not real."

"But what if it could be?" she insists. "What if you both stopped being afraid of what it would mean and just admit that you're falling for each other?"

"Because he doesn't feel that way," I say sadly.

"Hey."

My heart leaps into my throat as I hear a familiar voice behind us. Slowly, I turn around.

I feel Chris's gaze on me as mine rakes over him. He looks ridiculously handsome in a navy suit and dark gray tie. Our eyes meet, and the longing in his expression takes my breath away.

"Zoe," I exhale shakily. "Did you—"

"No. I had no idea." She looks between us. "At least, not this time."

"This time?" Chris's eyebrows shoot up.

"Zoe and Mandy conspired to lock us in the closet."

"Did they?" Chris narrows his eyes at his sister.

"Wow, look at the time! I should go. I have another party to get to. But you two, have fun!" She gives Chris a quick hug and then winks at me before disappearing.

"Do you want to dance?" Chris asks, extending his hand to me. The air between us crackles with anticipation.

"No, Chris. I don't." I can't stand the hurt in his eyes, but it needed to be said. "You were right. What we did—our kiss—it never should have happened. There's too much at stake for us to risk it for whatever this is," I gesture between us.

"Then why do you sound like you're trying to convince yourself?"

"Because I am," I snap. "So, don't make it harder for me, Chris. I can't keep getting my hopes up and having you take them away."

"Emily..." He looks at me pleadingly.

"I'm going to get some air," I don't wait for a reply. I walk quickly across the party. On the opposite end of the dance floor, I notice a doorway to a small balcony. It's completely empty, probably because there's another much bigger one with a better view of the city that most people willing to brave the cold have flocked to.

I step outside, feeling the freezing air against the champagne flush of my skin. It's bracing in the best way possible.

I'm doing the right thing, even if it hurts now. The only thing that's changed between now and when we last spoke is that he misses me. And maybe a few years ago, that would have been enough. That girl who didn't know what she was worth would have jumped at the chance to have someone like Chris want her, not caring that it was all on his terms, not caring that she was giving so much of herself and him so little.

But then the door slides open, and Chris joins me on the balcony.

"Go back inside, Galloway." I turn away from him, propping my forearms on the balcony.

"Can I say something first?" He moves to stand next to me. His hand falls next to mine on the railing, just barely grazing the edge of it, and I shudder. I wish he didn't have this kind of power over me, to make me react with the barest hint of touch.

"I don't know what else there is to say," I exhale, my breath clouding in front of me.

"Please, just hear me out, Emily." The desperation in his voice has me turning to face him.

"Fine. Talk."

"I'm sorry."

"I know." My chest tightens as I take a step back, unwilling to subject myself to another second of this. "You made it clear how sorry you are that you kissed me."

"No." He catches my elbow. "I'm not sorry that I kissed you. I'm sorry that I lied to you about why I did it." He drops my elbow, leaning forward to grip the balcony railing. "You snuck up on me, Beckerman." Chris looks at me, his eyes full of intensity. "I hate not talking to you every day. You're the first person I want to tell things to. When I see something that I know would make you laugh, or something that pisses me off, or makes me smile. I want you to be at the desk next to mine so that I can tell you everything. Since hiatus, I haven't been able to think about anything except how much I miss you. How much it sucks, not talking to you every day."

"You made me feel like you didn't want me," I say quietly. "You said it was just the adrenaline of the show. That it made you lose your head,"

He inhales deeply. "That was a lie. *You* make me lose my head, Beckerman. Ever since we kissed—before that—I've been losing my mind because I want you so badly."

Chris takes my hand, lifting it towards him and then looking at me as if for permission. To touch me. To free him from his torment. I nod, just barely. He lowers his mouth, flipping my hand so that the inside of my wrist faces him and pressing a reverent kiss to the inside of it.

"You want me?" I whisper into the night. I let him place my palm on his chest, just above his racing heart. Our gazes lock as he places his other hand over mine, intertwining our fingers before resting them against his chest again.

"So much. But I have one condition." His breath hitches, and my heart aches at the raw vulnerability in his eyes. The man behind the confident facade. "I think...I think for this to work, we have to be all in."

"All in?" My eyes widen. "What do you mean?"

"I mean when this season ends, we both stay. I don't want to do the *Weekend Update* or be head writer with anyone but you, Beckerman."

I throw my arms around his neck. He lets out a surprised oof even as his arms twist around my back, pulling me tightly against him. "I'm all in, Chris."

"Thank god," he murmurs against my hair. "It would have been so embarrassing if you said no."

I lean back, resting my forehead against his. "Aren't you scared?"

"Fuck being afraid," Chris laughs. "I don't want to live like that anymore. I don't want to assume that things won't work. You make me want to believe, Emily."

He says it so casually, as if he hasn't just laid his heart at my feet.

"You make me want to believe, too," I reply fiercely. "No more fighting."

"We're probably still going to fight," he says, his hand coming to cup my cheek.

"Okay. No more working against each other," I amend. "Or trying to make things harder."

"Speaking of hard…" Chris says, and I groan, my forehead falling against his chest.

"I changed my mind."

"What do you want me to say? Of all the ways you've tried to drive me insane, this is the most effective one by far," He drags his hands down my body, his fingers gripping the material of my dress.

"So I should have worn this instead of lighting a bunch of candles?"

"I would have thrown myself at your feet and begged for mercy," he murmurs.

My mouth curves up in a wicked grin. "I think we can make that happen."

"You devious woman." Chris drags his gaze down the column of my throat, drinking in every inch of me until I'm tempted to rip his clothes off on this balcony.

As if he can sense my growing desperation, he slowly removes his hands from my body. I nearly drag them back, but stop when he takes both of my hands in his. His thumbs trace a featherlight pattern across the backs of my hands, leaving a trail of sparks in their wake.

"Why do you think I wore this dress?" I whisper in his ear. "Because I wanted you to take it off me."

Chris looks like someone just hit him with an anvil. "Can we please, please get out of here?"

I drop his hands and slowly saunter toward the balcony door, giving him what I hope is a sultry look over my shoulder. "Meet me downstairs in five minutes. I'll call a car for us around the corner."

"I'll be down in three," he replies breathlessly.

20

When we get to Chris's apartment, he takes my hand in his as he pays for the cab. He doesn't let go as we get out, his skin warm against mine as he practically drags me up the stairs to his apartment.

"Where's Freddie?" I ask breathlessly after Chris unlocks his front door. "I want to say hi."

"He's not here." He raises an eyebrow at my disappointed expression. "Is that a dealbreaker?"

"It's not *ideal*."

Chris laughs lowly, the sound sending shivers down my spine as reaches behind me to shut the door. "He's with his dog-sitter."

"Is he?"

The tips of his ears go slightly red. "I kind of hoped you would end up coming over tonight."

"I see how it is. You wanted to have the place to yourself so you can have your wicked way with me without any distractions," I tease. He *blushes*. And it's really fucking adorable.

"Stop smiling at me like that." Chris leans forward, tucking a strand of my hair behind my ear. "I don't like how much you enjoy my embarrassment."

"It's cute," I defend myself. "And so is that," I laugh as I catch him in the act of rubbing the back of his neck.

"You noticed?" He looks a little surprised.

"Mhmmm," I reply, looping my arms around his neck. He's so tall I have to stand on my tiptoes to do it even though I'm wearing heels. "I'm not too proud to admit that I've spent a lot of time looking at you,"

"I'm not too proud to admit the same." My face tilts upwards, practically begging for his kiss, but he resists, staring at me instead, his gaze full of awe. I'm sure he sees the same reflected back at him. He's here, and he's mine, and I want to learn every inch of him.

I raise my lips to his face, kissing the freckles scattered across it. My mouth brushes his forehead, his cheeks, his chin. Chris closes his eyes, and the only sign of his wavering patience is the pulse bobbing in his throat. I press a softer, more lingering kiss against the underside of his jaw, and he inhales deeply. When I brush the shell of his ear with my lips, his breath turns sharp and ragged. I grin up at him, loving just how much he enjoys the way I tease his body like I've always teased his mind.

Chris makes a low sound in his throat as his hands wrap tightly around my waist, pulling me flush against his body.

"I'm not done yet," I protest, my mouth against his neck.

But then his palm squeezes my hip, and I lose the ability to form words as his lips meet mine. He kisses me tenderly but with abandon, as if he's unleashed himself. His tongue slides into my mouth as his teeth scrape delicately across my bottom lip. We find a rhythm in our kissing, our tongues meeting stroke for stroke. I lose myself completely in the feel of his mouth on mine as our bodies mold together, letting go of everything but this moment with him.

"*Emily*," Chris moans hoarsely, and the sound of my name rasping from his lips sends a rush of heat straight to the center of me.

He kisses down the side of my neck and I tilt my head back to grant him full access. His lips trail down the column of my throat, tracing the tops of my shoulders and my collarbone. He lightly exhales, his breath leaving goosebumps in its wake as he kisses the tops of my breasts and the space between them. I grip his shoulders tightly when his mouth moves further down, tracing one nipple and then the other over my dress in tantalizingly slow, indulgent circles.

Unwilling to let him have all the fun, I reach for his shirt. I take my time undoing the top few buttons, running my hands along the planes of his broad chest before exchanging them for my lips. I savor the prickle of the light hair against my face and the moan that reverberates through his skin as I explore his body with my hands. I finish unbuttoning his shirt, dropping open-mouthed kisses along his neck and shoulders before depositing it behind us.

I stare at him for a few moments, his chest rising and falling with excited breaths, the perfect combination of strength and softness. Perfect not because it lives up to some bullshit societal idea of the male body but because it's *him*, and I want him so badly that I feel like I might fly out of my skin if I stop touching him.

I want to feel him. All of him. I want to give him pleasure and see him come apart because of me, to make him feel so good that he can't see straight.

Chris's breath catches as I reach for the top of his pants. "What are you—" he starts, unable to finish his sentence when I unzip them and slip my hand inside, palming him over his boxers. His jeans slide to the floor, and he kicks them across the room. "Jesus Christ, Emily," he says raggedly when I tug his boxers down his hips.

And then, I sink to my knees before him. I raise my gaze to look at his face as my tongue flicks gently against the tip of his dick.

"Are you trying to kill me?" he moans, his hands coming to rest alongside the back of my head. His fingers tangle in my hair, gentle even as every part of his body goes taut with lust. The touch is light enough that I'm still very much in control while allowing me to feel his desperation, how close he is to completely coming undone, all because of me.

"You like that?" I ask, pulling back slightly.

"I'm not sure," he pants. "Maybe you should do it again, so I can find out."

I sweep my tongue down each side of his length, tasting him, and he moans. I take him into my mouth, and he gasps, his breath hitching with every movement of my tongue as I finally taste him.

"I can't..." He inhales sharply. I lean back, releasing him.

"Everything good?"

"Very good. *Too* good." He shakes his head. "I don't want to...," he trails off, looking slightly sheepish.

"What?" I look up at him, the picture of innocence as my fingers trace patterns along the backs of his thighs. "Use your words, Galloway."

"Fine," He hauls me to my feet. "I finally found a use for your mouth that I actually enjoy."

"Asshole," I murmur against his chest.

One of his hands comes to rest on my thigh. "I was trying to charm your pants off. Is it working?"

"I'm not wearing pants."

"That's convenient." He presses a kiss to my bare shoulder as his hand slides up my dress, coming to rest on my thigh.

"A little higher."

He chuckles softly. "Are you still trying to tell me what to do?" One knuckle skims along the center of me, and I hiss. Even through the fabric of my shapewear, his touch is perfection.

"Please."

"Please, what?"

"Please touch me, or I'm going to—"

He kisses me fiercely, cutting me off. "Fuck. I don't know what it says about me that I find your threats so sexy."

"Terrible taste in women?"

His hand drifts upwards, palming my stomach. It's ordinarily a part of myself that I don't love, but right now, I'm too turned on to be self-conscious about the roundness there. And then his thumb traces the curve of my stomach, the touch leaving fire in its wake, and I exhale sharply. "I only have a taste for you right now,"

"You are so cheesy." I laugh as his hands reach underneath my dress, sliding my shapewear down my thighs. He discards it somewhere on the floor without comment. And before I have time to wonder if the other women he's been with had to wear shapewear, one of his hands moves to the small of my back to pull me flush against him as the other reaches back underneath my dress. Chris hisses when he reaches the space between my thighs.

"You seem to like it," he says as his fingers stroke gently, exploring the wet heat there. His thumb presses down on my clit, and I moan into his shoulder, my lips slick against his skin as pleasure pulses between my legs. I grip his arms as he kisses my neck. He slides a gentle finger inside me as his thumb continues swirling against the bundle of nerves. Bringing me closer and closer, but with agonizing slowness.

"Fuck me, I do," I mutter.

He smirks, sliding another finger inside me. I moan, lifting my head to brush my lips against his. I deepen the kiss as he pumps in and out of me, the pace increasing until I'm putty in his hands. I fall forward onto him to support myself as the orgasm I was already chasing when I was on my knees before him crests through me. I try to catch my breath with my cheek pressed against the slightly sweaty skin of his bare chest as his hands wrap around my lower back, holding me tightly against him.

"I think both of us need to be naked. Now," I insist. Sliding out of his arms, I quickly unzip my dress so that I can step out of it. I gently fold it and place it on the couch, his eyes never moving from my body. "What?" I ask, a little self-conscious in just my thong.

He walks over to me, wrapping his arms around my middle and pulling me close against him. Chris brushes my hair out of the way so that he can kiss the space where my shoulder meets my neck. "You're so beautiful," he says quietly.

Somehow, when he says it, it doesn't sound corny or fake. It doesn't sound like the compliments from other guys I've hooked up with that felt obligatory or rushed, something said just because they thought it was what they were supposed to or what would make me want to sleep with them. Chris calls me beautiful in a way that makes me feel beautiful.

"When you say it, I'm convinced."

He tenses behind me. "Were you not before?"

Suddenly, I'm glad to be facing away from him, even as he buries his face in the crook of my neck. I'm glad I don't have to look at him when I admit this ugly part of myself. "I don't look like the other girls you've dated."

"I told you, most of those were rumors."

"I just...for a long time, I didn't believe that someone like you could want someone like me."

His hands find my stomach, and I hold my breath. Slowly, they trace along the rounded curve of it, around my hips, and down my thighs.

"What are you doing?"

"Touching you."

"You don't have to touch those parts of me. If you don't want to."

His hands tighten around me, pinning me to his chest. "I want to touch every part of you with my hands, and then my mouth. And if you don't fucking believe me, I'm going to show you," he pauses, his lips pressing against the pulse fluttering in my throat. "Actually, I'm going to show you either way."

I melt against him, thankful that he can't see my face, which I'm sure is giving away every tender gooey feeling rising inside of me at his perfect words. "Well. When you put it like that."

"Finally admitting I've won an argument?" He lets me go, and I turn to face him.

"I let you win, because we have better things to do than argue."

"That's true," he murmurs. "But just so you never have any doubts, I love your body because you live in it."

I try not to latch onto that word, even as his head falls forward. He bends down, his mouth hovering in front of my breasts. My nipples tighten as he moves his hands up to grip my waist, tugging me against him. I arch toward him as his mouth finds my breast.

"Can we please go into the bedroom?" I ask, barely able to string words together as his tongue teases my nipple. I grip his shoulders, digging my fingers into his strong back as he gently nudges his knee between my thighs and traces my other nipple with his finger before replacing that finger with his mouth.

"God, yes." He smiles wickedly and takes my hand, leading me into his bedroom. It's perfectly him, decorated with vintage Red Sox posters, pictures of him and Zoe, some of him with Faith, Riley, and Mandy, and even...

"No way," I whisper, making a beeline for his bedside table when I notice the photo booth strip.

"Wait!" Chris leaps forward, catching me around the waist, but he's too late. I've already grabbed it. He pulls us both down onto his bed, banding his arms around my stomach as he settles me onto his lap.

"You kept it," I marvel. The pictures of us are from the photo booth at Riley's birthday party a month and half ago. I was admittedly drunk enough that night that I didn't consider where the actual pictures had gone. But here they are. On his bedside table. "You have a picture of me next to your bed."

"Strictly for masturbation purposes." I swat him. "Okay, fine, it's not for that. Well, not *just* for that."

"Good. Because if I found out you jerked off to pictures of yourself, that might be a dealbreaker."

Chris laughs. "I might as well not be in it. I only ever look at you." He runs his hands along my thighs as I lean into him, my back coming to rest against his chest as I examine the images. The first shows us grinning with our arms around each other. In the second one, he's pinching my side, and his arm is snaked around my waist. And the third...

It's a simple enough photo. I'm laughing as I push him away, my gaze to the floor. And he's...he's looking at me. Looking at me in a way that no one has ever looked at me before. Like he never wants to stop.

Chris takes the pictures out of my hand and sets them back on his nightstand. I scoot out of his lap, falling back onto his comforter in a motion that I wish had been more elegant. But then he moves, hands bracketing my body on either side as he hovers over me, and I stop caring about anything but the carnal promise in his eyes.

"I kept that picture because I thought I couldn't have you," he murmurs.

"You have me." I kiss him hard.

He breaks the kiss, trailing his mouth down my neck and beneath my breasts. He moves down my stomach, discarding my lacy thong with ease. My heart nearly stops as his gaze drifts over my stretch marks. My chest squeezes, hating how vulnerable I feel to show him the parts of my body that feel less than perfect, even after his beautiful words in the living room.

But then Chris drags his tongue along each red sliver, tracing the stretch marks with passion and precision until I know I'll never be able to think about them again without thinking of his tongue. Until I'm squirming with need beneath him, desperate for him to go lower.

"Chris," I whimper, lifting my hips in silent plea.

He doesn't make me beg. His hands press against my inner thighs, spreading my legs wide as he licks a searing path up the center of me. I hear strangled sounds escape my throat, but I can't even bring myself to be embarrassed, because his tongue is devouring me in precise, perfect strokes that set my entire body on fire. All I can do is grip his comforter, holding on for dear life as his hands tighten against my thighs.

The world narrows until it's only us, in this room. One of his hands reaches up, and I grab it, twining our fingers together and pressing our clasped hands against my chest. He takes my clit into his mouth, sucking with expert precision, and I surrender myself to this moment. To him.

The orgasm hits me hard and fast. I squeeze his hand tighter, my back arching off the bed as waves of pleasure ripple through me. I'm destroyed. Utterly ruined. And I still need more.

Chris lifts his head. And I know that as long as I live, I'll never forget this image of him grinning up at me from between my legs, his hair mussed from my fingers and my thighs.

He licks the taste of me off of his lips, and I'm fucking gone.

I surge forward, capturing his mouth with mine as my hands squeeze and knead his butt.

"So, you're an ass woman." He says. "Good to know."

I want to tell him that I've never been one before, but his drives me insane. "Do you have a condom?" I ask instead.

"One sec." He shimmies out of his boxers, and I have to hide my giggle behind my hand at the less-than-graceful motions of his hips as he reaches into his bedside table to grab one. I snatch the condom out of his hands and rip it open. Carefully, I slide it onto his dick, not breaking eye contact the entire time.

"You're perfect." I grip the base of his shaft as his eyes meet mine. "Fucking perfect, Chris."

He sits up and wraps one arm around my waist, lifting me so that I can sink onto him. I do so with agonizing slowness. He groans, his eyes squeezing shut as his head falls back. "Fuck, Emily. You feel incredible."

He lets me set the pace until he's completely inside me. My knees come to either side of his hips as I adjust to the sensation of fullness. He shifts under me and I moan, my forehead coming to rest against his as our ragged breaths intermingle. I move my hands to grip the strong muscles of his back, feeling them ripple beneath my palms as he fucks me.

"Shit, Chris," I pant, my fingers tightening against his skin as the pleasure builds. I hope I leave a mark. I hope every time he sees his naked back he thinks of me and the promises he made.

"Are you close?" he asks, the question gritted between heaving breaths as our movements become faster, sloppier, and more urgent.

"Yes—*yes*," I practically whimper as his hand reaches between us to find my clit. He presses the pad of this thumb against it, and I can't hold out any longer. I break apart, the climax ripping through me in heaving breaths, and his follows moments after.

I bury my face in his neck as he presses his lips to the top of my head, still buried inside me. His fingers trace patterns across my lower back as we catch our respective breaths, neither of us wanting to break apart.

We finally do, mostly out of necessity: I need to go to the bathroom, because UTIs are not cute, and Chris has to throw the condom away. I may or may not spend several minutes on the toilet staring at my knees and smiling like an idiot after I pee. Despite the physical realness of tonight, some part of it still seems too good to be true.

"Are you okay in there?" Chris calls. "I could hear you pee. I know you're done."

"It's not sexy to tell someone you were listening to them pee," I call through the door.

"Everything I do is sexy."

"Not *everything*." Slowly, I exit, feeling slightly shy in my naked body now that we're not actively hooking up.

"Some things, at least?" he asks hopefully, flopping down onto his bed and gesturing to the empty space beside him.

"Don't fish for compliments," I concede, my body curling into his under the covers. I rest my head against his chest.

"I don't need to. I remember you moaning several of them at me a few minutes ago." He kisses my jaw.

"Next time, I'm keeping my mouth shut so I don't inflate your ego." I snuggle against his chest.

"You can try."

I'm wrung out from three orgasms, but the sensual promise in his tone still has my toes curling. He wraps his arms around me, pulling me close.

"Tomorrow," I say, yawning.

"Tomorrow," he agrees, brushing his lips against the top of my head.

And even as he says it, I can't help hearing something else echoing inside my heart. Something that sounds suspiciously like forever.

21

When my eyes blink open the next morning, the first thing that I notice is that I'm not in my bedroom. The second thing I notice is the warm, naked body next to mine.

My eyes fly open as the events of last night flood my memories: the party, leaving with Chris, mind-blowing sex with Chris…

I peek over at him, snoring quietly on the other side of the bed. He rolls over, falling onto his back. I take advantage of his sleeping state to stare, trying to memorize every detail. The faint line on his left cheek from where he slept on it, the freckles covering his arms, the rise and fall of his chest as he breathes. It feels so intimate, even with everything we did last night.

I fell asleep in Chris's arms. I learned that he hogs the covers, and that he doesn't wake up when I have to pee in the middle of the night. I learned that when I fall asleep tucked against his naked chest, I can feel his inhales and exhales.

He's not the first man I've slept next to. But he's the first one I've wanted to watch sleep. The first one to put a hand on my stomach that made me feel safe instead of judged.

Safe. I tuck my knees up against my chest, shivering slightly. We both fell asleep naked. I've never done that before, either. I've never finished hooking up with someone and not instinctively wanted to put clothes back on, to cover myself back up.

He makes me feel things that I thought didn't exist in real life, at least for me. The kind of things that I told myself would never happen because I was tired of being disappointed.

I scoot closer, hovering over him, having a reverse Little Mermaid moment as I gently brush his hair back from his face.

"What are you doing?" he asks.

"Ah!" I reel back, instinctively drawing the covers over my naked chest. "I didn't realize you were awake."

"I wasn't, until I felt you breathing on me." He sits up. "How'd you sleep?"

"How—how did I sleep?" I can't see my face, but I'm sure my eyes are bulging out of their sockets. How can he be so normal? I feel changed. My world has been rocked, shifted on its axis, and he's concerned with how I slept?

"Yeah." Chris yawns, stretching his arms above his head, the movement causing the muscles in his chest to shift enticingly. Everything he does is enticing. I'm officially so far gone that I think this man *yawning* is hot. It's fucking adorable. Bleary, first-thing-in-the-morning Chris, grinning up at me lazily like he wants to stay in bed with me all day.

"How did you sleep?"

"I asked you first, Beckerman."

"Surprisingly great," I say, my fingers curling around the bedsheets.

"Surprisingly?" He shifts closer to me, his shoulder brushing mine. "Do I really snore that loudly?"

"No," I chuckle. "I'm just...I'm freaking out a little." I turn to face him. "Are you freaking out?"

"A little." He presses his knee against mine under the covers, like we always do under the *Update* desk. "It's never going to be the same between us now."

He's right. We've crossed a line. I don't regret it, but it still terrifies me. He's seen every part of me now. He licked my stretch marks, for fuck's sake. I've never had a guy do anything like that. They either ignore them entirely or, in the case of one guy in college, ask me if they're cat scratches—which was especially weird, because I didn't own a cat.

I've made peace with the parts of my body that I used to try so hard to erase, but I never imagined that someone could find them worthy of such worship. I never imagined that the flesh of my stomach and hips and every other part of my body that I've worked so hard to appreciate myself could be appreciated by someone else.

"No, it's not," I pause, resting my head against his chest. "It's going to be better."

"I don't know how it could get better than this." His thumb strokes the flesh of my hip. His arms wrap around my back as our legs tangle together. All of us intertwined, and it feels so perfect—so right.

"Neither do I," I whisper into his skin.

"Do you want to get dressed? I could leave, make some coffee, get us bagels if you want to shower—not that I think you smell bad or need to shower or anything—" he stops, catching the smile spreading across my face.

"You're nervous."

"And of course, you're enjoying that," he frowns playfully.

"I'm not enjoying it," I protest. "I'm surprised that I can make you nervous."

"When are you going to get it through that thick skull of yours, Emily?" He bites my shoulder playfully, and I yelp, falling back onto the pillows. He flops down next to me, turning onto his side to face me as his arm falls across my stomach. "You make me feel everything."

"How did this even happen?" I wonder. I press a kiss to his chest, right above his heart. "When did we become—this?"

"I don't know. Somewhere between you driving me crazy and handing my ass to me every week, you became the person whose opinion I cared about the most. We were spending so much time together, and then suddenly I just...I needed you," he murmurs into my hair. "Without even realizing anything had changed."

"I need you, too." I arch up to kiss him as his hands snake around the back of my neck. He lowers his body over mine, my legs wrapping around the backs of his knees. I moan against his mouth, my nipples tightening at the delicious friction of his chest pressed against them.

"How are we supposed to spend all day in our office without doing this?" I whisper against his neck.

"Well," he pretends to think about it. "I suppose we'll have to try really, really hard to get as much of it out of our systems as possible before hiatus is over."

"We should talk about what to do, once we're back at work," I say. "How we're going to act around each other."

"We should," he groans. "We need to get out of bed to do that."

"We don't *need* to."

"*I* need to."

I sit up, baring my chest to him.

He swears under his breath. "If you're trying to get me to stop touching you, it's not working." He stares hungrily at my breasts.

"You saw them last night!"

"That was different. It was dark out," he pauses, stroking his chin thoughtfully. "Come to think of it, I'd like to see the rest of you in daylight." Chris reaches forward, slowly peeling the duvet back to reveal the rest of my naked body. His throat bobs. "Wow."

"I want to see you too." I shift the sheet off of him, letting it fall to the floor.

"What happened to talking?" he asks, his legs swinging off the bed. He stands, giving me a full view of his perfect ass.

"Talk later," I decide.

Chris turns around to face me, and my mouth dries out. He's unbearably sexy in the watery morning light. "And what, exactly, do you suggest we do instead?" His dick is straining against his stomach. He knows *exactly* what we should do. He just wants to make me say it.

"Get back in this bed, right now," I demand.

I don't need to tell him twice.

Some time later, we resurface. I shower while Chris goes to get us bagels and coffee. When I emerge, wearing one of his Red Sox t-shirts that hits me mid-thigh, I expect a bit of appreciation for the sexy sight of me in his shirt.

"What is on your head?" he squawks when I sit down, even as he passes me my toasted everything bagel and a coffee.

"A towel?"

"For your head?"

"For my hair," I roll my eyes playfully. "I hope it doesn't dry weirdly. I usually use a special microfiber hair towel on it."

"A special microfiber hair towel," Chris repeats.

"If you think the hair towel is weird, you're going to lose your mind when you see how many products I have on my bathroom counter," I tease him.

"Is that an invitation to your bedroom?" he asks, raising an eyebrow at me as he sips his coffee.

"To my bathroom. Which technically isn't even mine. I live with my cousin Rachel and her family," I explain. "I bought a condo. It's a whole thing."

"Post-promotion impulse purchase?"

"Sort of a fuck-you to my mom, who told me it was a bad idea. She was right, of course. She usually is." I take a sip of coffee. "Except when she wanted me to quit the show."

"What? You weren't considering it, were you?"

"No. No," I shake my head. "I was too stubborn to quit. But before this year, it wasn't exactly a fun environment for me. I killed myself writing *Update* jokes that never got picked, I didn't have any friends, and Alex did his best to sabotage my career because he didn't agree with my style of comedy."

"Right." He sets his coffee down, a muscle in his jaw feathering. "Fuck. I'm sorry, Emily. I never realized...I was so worried about keeping myself safe that I never thought about any of that. About how my behavior might have made you feel."

"Well, you weren't obligated to look out for me. I didn't need your protection," I bristle.

"That's not what I'm saying." He swallows. "I just hate that I ever did anything that made you unhappy."

"Are you forgetting the first two months of us working together this season?" I try to lighten the mood. "We both made each other miserable. But that's the past. Now, we're a team. Right?"

"We're a team," he agrees. "But...I do think we should keep all of this," he gestures between us, "Between us, for now."

"We're allowed to date. Nothing in the employee handbook bylaws prevents it, as long as the relationship is properly disclosed to human resources."

"Did your research?" Chris smirks at me.

"Maybe," I flush.

"I still think it's a bad idea to tell people at work that we're together." *We're together.* Hearing those words out of Chris's mouth... I can't contain the fluttering in my chest, even if I don't agree with his desire to keep it a secret.

But things are new between us. They're delicate. Fighting him on this could scare him off and make him change his mind.

I could lose him.

It's that fear that has me nodding in agreement with him, even as the idea of pretending that he's not mine kills me.

Because there's an us now. And I'll do anything to protect it.

"And when it's just us?" I ask hesitantly.

"I want to be with you, Emily. But only if that's what you want, too. If you need more time—"

"I don't," I interrupt. "I want to be with you, too, Chris."

Chris's answering smile is nothing short of spectacular.

22

The first few weeks after Christmas hiatus fly by in a blissful blur. Chris and I keep our distance in front of everyone else, but behind closed doors, we're a couple. I spend most nights at his place, to the point where we've had to stagger our entrances to work so that it doesn't seem like we get in at the same time every single morning. Rachel has been dropping not-so-subtle hints that she wants to meet him, ones that I avoid by making excuses about how busy we are. And we are busy. Between the *Weekend Update* and our head writer responsibilities, the only time we really get to spend together outside of work happens when we fall into bed at his apartment.

One morning, the Monday after our second show back, I wake up to find Chris scrolling on his phone with a familiar angry expression on his handsome face.

"I know that look." I sit up, the folds of his oversized T-shirt cascading around me and pooling over my thighs. "Are you reading internet comments?"

He doesn't say anything in response. That pinched expression doesn't move. After a few more moments of scrolling, it tightens, and I see him start typing.

"That's a terrible idea." I reach for his phone, but Chris twists out of reach, causing me to fall across his lap. "Hey, not fair. You have a height advantage."

"I have to say *something*. This is disgusting." I peer over his shoulder to look at the screen of his iPhone. Just as I suspected, Chris is deep in the comments section. Of a video of us, I realize, from this Saturday's *Weekend Update.*

"Chris," I say quietly, my voice full of warning. "The people who write nasty comments on YouTube videos and Instagram posts are the scum of the earth. They're freaky incels who are so full of anger that they feel the need to spew hate towards other people. Engaging with them is pointless."

"How can you just ignore this? People are saying terrible things about you."

"Well, for starters, I'm used to it." I pluck the phone out of his hands, and he sighs, slumping against his headboard and burying his head in his hands. I deposit Chris's phone on my side of the bed, out of his reach, and then gently place a hand on the nape of his neck. I stroke it lightly, and feel him relax beneath my fingers. "I'm Jewish, and a woman. Those are two categories that are historically very unpopular with people. If I read everything a crazy person on the internet said, I would lose my mind."

"So what do you do? Ignore it?" He lifts his head.

"You fill your time with other more important things." I lean forward to kiss him, and he playfully growls against my lips, dragging me into his lap. "For example, instead of scrolling through Instagram comments, you could have woken me up so that we can do this."

"You're right." He murmurs against my mouth. Chris kisses me deeply, his hands tightening against my back and pulling me closer.

"It's so hot when you say that." I lean forward to kiss him, and he playfully growls against my lips, dragging me into his lap. "What, specifically, am I right about this time?"

"Not engaging with psychotic, misogynistic, racist and anti-semitic internet trolls."

"So true. And what else?"

"Putting all that wasted time to better use." He kisses the base of my neck. "As much as it pains me to just let people speak about you that way."

"If someone says that to my face, you have my permission to punch them in the jaw," I promise.

"Punch them?" Chris's green eyes widen in surprise. "I was thinking more along the lines of a stern-dressing down. Or public humiliation."

"Public humiliation." I move to kiss him again, but he pulls back.

"That gives me an idea," Chris says.

"Is it to have sex?"

"No. I mean, yes, but not right now. I have a writing idea."

"Fine. But I still want sex."

"Hello, welcome to the *Weekend Update*! I'm Emily Beckerman."

"And I'm Chris Galloway."

"First Lady Jill Biden announced that she will be serving American wine and cheese to the French Prime Minister and his wife at an upcoming dinner celebrating their diplomatic visit. In other news, the draft has been reinstated in anticipation of France's forthcoming declaration of war." I smile, relishing the applause that follows my delivery. I'm more than just comfortable on camera now. I love it. There is no greater rush than the response from a crowd after a perfectly written joke. It feels *right*. I could never imagine going back to being behind the scenes after this.

"Ye, formerly known as talented rapper Kanye West, said in an interview with Sandy Hook conspiracy theorist Alex Jones—" Chris pauses, letting the crowd laugh. "Yeah, nothing good was gonna come of that," he ad-libs, throwing the audience a charming grin. "Ye said, 'I love Jewish people, but I also love Nazis'. Which is sort of like saying, I love small woodland creatures, but I also love hunting."

"Ye also praised Hitler's 'cool outfit' during the interview. It's always a bad sign when the least offensive thing someone says is that they think Hitler was well dressed," I add.

"This week, we're introducing a new segment on the *Weekend Update* that we are calling, 'Who's got it worse?' Myself and another cast member will read hate Tweets or comments, and we'll decide who has it worse. My co-host Emily has graciously agreed to be the first victim of this idea!"

"Happy to be here." I wink at the camera once the applause dies down. "Chris, why don't you go first?"

"Of course. Someone commented on a clip from last week's *Weekend Update* saying, 'Chris Galloway? No thank you!'"

"Ouch," I smirk at him.

"Yeah, I found it very hurtful," he smirks back, a hint of sarcasm flavoring his tone, not enough to be heavy-handed but just the right amount indicating that Chris is in on the joke.

"A comment directed at me was, 'I used to be against murder, until I heard Emily Beckerman's annoying high-pitched Jew shriek. Not funny.'"

"You do have a very high-pitched voice," Chris muses, and I kick him under the table.

"You love it," I retort.

"I do," he replies, the sharp confidence of his *Update* persona melting away into something sweeter. I freeze, our eyes meeting, forgetting for a moment where I am and what I'm doing.

"Well, I think the death threat might be the winner here," Chris says, recovering first.

Hearing his *Update* voice is enough to snap me back into action. "I'd say you're right."

"Well, there's a first time for everything," He says, smiling at the camera. "Thank you, this has been the *Weekend Update*. I'm Chris Galloway."

"And I'm Emily Beckerman. Have a great night, everyone!" I say as we smile into the camera before it cuts out.

"That was amazing." We high five, a juvenile gesture but pretty much the only one we can engage in that doesn't end with us falling all over each other. Even the short and arguably very platonic contact of our palms smacking together sends tingles throughout my entire body. It's just *him*, overriding my usual ability to think and distracting me.

"That was a fun one," I grin as we walk backstage. "Your bit went perfectly. Can you imagine if I showed a clip of that to the Chris of six months ago?"

"He would be shocked. And not just because of the time travel," Chris nudges my shoulder. "Thank you for helping me refine it. I was a little nervous."

"I'm always happy to mentor promising young writers. Boost their confidence, make them feel better—anything for a newbie," I tease.

"If you really want to make me feel better, I can think of a few ideas," he lowers his voice slightly so that no one will hear us. Not that anyone is paying attention—the people backstage are much too busy.

"You're a cad," I playfully shove him with my shoulder.

"A cad?" Chris's eyebrows shoot upwards. "What does that even mean?"

"A man who behaves dishonorably toward a woman." I shake my head at him in faux disappointment. "I've got to get you to read historical romance. Your vocabulary is severely lacking."

"When this season is over, I'll read whatever books you want me to," he promises.

"That is literally the sexiest thing you've ever said to me."

"Of course it is," he snorts. "So, are you excited to see your parents?"

I'm so busy making a mental list of all the historicals I need to force Chris to read that it takes me a moment to register what he said.

"Shit." I stop in my tracks. Chris takes several more steps before he realizes that I'm not following him. "I forgot they were coming tonight!"

"You forgot?"

"You distracted me," I hiss, jabbing a finger at his chest.

"How, exactly, is this my fault?"

"You know how," I whisper-yell, as he gives me a shit-eating grin, likely remembering *exactly* how he decided to take my mind off my pre-show nerves. If we fail and the show gets canceled, I'll have to find a way to keep the couch from my side of our office. It's ours now.

"You didn't mind," he says lowly, leaning down to deliver the words into my ear. The suggestive tone makes my toes curl. "In fact, I distinctly remember you begging by the end."

"It'll be you next. I'll have my revenge," I promise.

"If your revenge involves getting me off, I'm okay with that," he replies. I'm half-tempted to drag him back to our office to do just that. My family can wait. "But later. We have to get onstage."

"We do," I gulp, following him into the wings. We wait for the last sketch to finish up, and Chris takes my hand in the dark, squeezing gently. That reminder that he's there with me, just like before our first *Update* together. The sketch ends, and he quickly drops my hand so that we can head onstage to wave with the rest of the cast, the host, and the musical guest as the end credits of *Live From New York* roll.

"I don't understand why you're so nervous. You love your fami-ly," Chris says out of the corner of his mouth.

"I do. But they can be...opinionated," I reply as the cameras cut out. The regular audience leaves, with only the personal guests of staff remaining. Including Rachel, Josh, and both of my parents.

"You don't say," he responds dryly.

My family rushes the stage as soon as they're able and descend on me.

"Oh, sweetie, you were wonderful! I was so nervous for you," my mother exclaims, pulling me in for a tight hug. "You look tired. Are you tired?"

"We had a late night last night," I say. Behind my mom, Rachel waggles her eyebrows at me, and I quickly add, "With work." Not only with work. But Tracey Beckerman certainly doesn't need to know about that.

Suddenly, I feel a solid presence behind me. I don't even have to turn to know that it's Chris. We were separated in the initial flood of people coming onstage, but he found his way back to me.

"And you must be Chris," Mom smiles warmly. "I'm Emily's mother, and this is her father. We're so thankful that you've been taking care of our daughter onstage. We were so worried when we found out she'd be doing the *Update*."

"Mom," I hiss.

"It's so nice to meet you both, after hearing so many wonderful things from Emily," Chris interjects smoothly. "And really, she's been taking care of me. It's been a pleasure working with her."

"I bet," Rachel mutters.

"Being on camera would be stressful for anyone, but Emily handles it like a pro. I feel more relaxed just knowing she's there with me. And she's made me braver. I used to be so afraid of making a mistake. We had to fail to figure out how to succeed, but Emily also helped me see that failure isn't the ending point. What matters is how you go on after it."

Warmth suffuses my chest, and I wish we weren't in public surrounded by my entire family right now so that I could embrace him. I've never told Chris the source of the tension between me and my mother, that lingering lack of faith in me that she has after years of helping me through my anxiety. I'm grateful for it, but it's hard for her to see me as someone capable of fighting my own battles.

Chris knows my strength because he tested it, just as I tested his. Until we realized that we were that much stronger together.

"Well said," my father chimes in. "Tracey, didn't you want to meet the other writers?"

"I can introduce you," Chris offers.

"Thank you, sweetheart," my mother says. "Emily, I'll be right over there if you need me." She leans in for another hug. "He's very handsome," she whispers in my ear.

Oh, god. That's the last thing I need. Tracey Beckerman would scare Chris away in an instant if she knew what was happening between us. She once reduced my high school situationship to tears after questioning why he wouldn't date me for real. It was humiliating, especially because *I* was the one who didn't want to date *him*—if memory serves, because of his utter lack of a personality.

Chris and I are in a good place, but that's because we've been careful. We're in a bubble, and the slightest pinprick from outside could shatter everything.

"Does she have to treat me like a child all the time?" I moan to my dad when my mother and Chris are out of earshot.

"Well, you are *her* child," he unhelpfully points out.

"She doesn't need to worry about me. I'm not the same person I was back then."

"She's always going to worry about you. That's how being a parent works." He wraps an arm around my shoulders. "Did I ever tell you that we couldn't sleep the night before your first show?"

"This year?"

"No, your first show as a writer. We were so nervous. Happy for you, but scared, too. This place doesn't have a stellar reputation for prioritizing mental health."

"Fair enough," I acquiesce. "But you've always known that I wanted this."

"We have. But I think your mother and I worried that it would come at the expense of something more important."

I resist the temptation to defend myself, thinking of the years before this one. The loneliness and uncertainty that accompanied my job. The isolation that I felt, despite my success. I brushed off those feelings, because I'd felt worse. But just because it wasn't the worst I've ever felt in my life didn't mean it was bad. My parents saw that, and they saw me keep going anyway. It must have hurt them.

"It's better now," I tell him quietly. "It feels more...more like home here, I guess. I'm friends with Chris, and the other writers. It's easier, not doing everything on my own."

"You know, I've been telling you that for years," he replies dryly. "But I'm glad you're happy. That's all your mother and I want. Speaking of, I should track her down."

"I love you, Dad."

"I love you too, Emily." He walks off to find my mom, leaving me alone with Rachel.

"Em, that was amazing! I can't believe you do that every week." She tackles me in a bear hug. "And the jokes are so good. They really feel like *you*. I never used to be able to tell what you wrote, but now I always know."

"Love you, Rachey."

"I love *you*. I haven't felt this cool in a long time," she jokes. "Josh is convinced he saw Steph Curry and disappeared five minutes ago trying to find out."

"I've never been the cool cousin before." As soon as those words are out of my mouth, I hear Chris laugh. Not his usual laugh, but a deep belly cackle that only emerges on the rarest of occasions.

I have a sinking feeling that I already know what he's laughing at. Sure enough, my mother has her enormous iPhone open and is without a doubt showing him a highlight reel of my most embarrassing childhood moments.

"This is when she spilled all of her animal crackers in her crib," my mother says loudly.

"Is that Barbara Streisand?" I exclaim, attempting to distract her.

"If she's here, I'm sure I'll see her," my mother replies. She's shockingly jaded from her first brush with celebrity. "Chris, your family must be so proud of you."

He tenses, and I brush my arm against his in a gesture meant to look accidental while still reminding me that he's right there with me.

"I'm close with my sister, but I don't speak to my parents," he says simply.

"Oh, you poor thing," She squeezes his arm. "That must be so difficult. All alone, in a city like this."

"It was," Chris says, and I turn to look up at him, surprised by his honesty. He's looking back at me. His eyes soften. "But not anymore."

"You look like you could use a home-cooked meal," my mother declares.

"He's an adult, Mom. He knows how to cook," I protest. "Don't infantilize him."

"I would *love* a home-cooked meal," Chris says, his expression shifting to one of mischief. "Emily is exaggerating my capabilities. I can barely make pasta."

"Then it's settled," Mom beams. "Whenever you two have your next off week, you'll join us for Shabbat dinner on Friday, Chris."

"I can't wait." He smiles.

And there it is again, blooming in my chest, even though I know it's dangerous to indulge it. Hope.

23

"Hey, Emily!" I'm a little surprised when I open the door to Rachel's apartment and see Zoe outside, standing next to Chris and carrying an enormous box of black and white cookies.

"Zoe! I didn't know you were coming."

"Is that okay? She found out about this and insisted." Chris pops up behind her, looking absolutely adorable in a dark green sweater.

"Of course," I smile, melting a little bit at how Chris is so incapable of denying his sister's wishes. As promised, he's here for Shabbat dinner with my family. Rachel offered to host since my parents still live in the suburbs.

"Is your family at all involved in the mafia?" Chris asks, his eyes widening at the sprawling (for New York, at least) apartment. "There's a *dining room* in here."

"Josh's grandma bought it in the '40s," I explain.

"It's sick," Zoe declares. "Where should I put these?"

"Oh, I'll take those." My mother bursts in from the kitchen. "You must be Chris's sister. I'm so glad you could make it."

"When did my mom invite Zoe?" I whisper to Chris.

"She texted me."

"How did she get your number?"

"I still have access to all of your contacts," Mom answers.

"But not my texts, right?" I say, ice shooting through my veins as I start mentally cataloging all of the deeply inappropriate things I've said to Chris that I would probably die if my mother read.

"Of course not. I would never invade your privacy that way," she says defensively. "Zoe, it's so lovely to meet you."

"You too, Mrs. Beckerman." There's a shyness in her tone, and it tugs at my heartstrings. Zoe has always struck me as fearless, but it makes sense that this would be the thing to make her nervous.

"And aren't you just darling, bringing us dessert. I want to hear everything about you." My mother takes the cookies from Zoe and gestures for her to follow into the kitchen. "Let me get you a glass of wine. Red, white, rose? Or something stronger?"

"She's twenty," I call after them.

"Oh, and you never drank before you were twenty-one? Do you want me to start sharing stories?" I blanch, remembering several nights in high school and on breaks from college that I've tried very hard to erase from my memory. "That's what I thought," Mom says triumphantly.

"I need something stronger," I sigh, taking advantage of the empty hallway to rest my head against Chris's chest.

"Yeah. Must be hard, dealing with the burdens of a close-knit and loving family." There's a bitter edge to his words.

"Is something the matter?" I ask, trying not to let the hurt seep into my voice.

"I'm sorry," Chris pulls me close to him again, a hand rubbing up and down my back. "I shouldn't put my shit on you."

"I want to hear about it," I say softly.

"Can I see your room?" he asks, quickly changing the subject. Part of me is frustrated that he won't let me in when he's obviously struggling, but I don't want to push him.

"Fine. But no funny business."

"That wasn't really my intention, considering your entire family is in the vicinity."

"Just making sure you behave," I say, heading down the hall, stopping in front of the door to Josh and Rachel's guest room that I've been staying in.

"I thought you liked a bad boy." Chris's breath tickles my ear as he leans over me to open the door.

"Do you know of any who might want to go out with me?" I ask, gently closing the door behind us. I'm an adult who is very much allowed to have anyone in her room if she so chooses, but I also don't really want to answer questions about why, exactly, Chris and I might have been in my room with the door shut.

Chris dives forward, hoisting me into his arms. "Put me down," I protest halfheartedly, banging on his shoulders.

He does, my back hitting the bed with a soft thud. Chris braces his hands on either side of my head, hovering over me. "You're taken," he says, his breath warm against my face.

Something inside my chest cracks open at his possessiveness, the way he looks at me as if I'm his.

"Don't worry. You're the only bad boy I need," I press a featherlight kiss to his mouth. "And that sweater is cute."

"Zoe got this for me." He rolls over, moving to sit on the bed. I sit up next to him, placing my hand on top of his. "Speaking of cute..." he trails off, his eyes drifting to my stuffed polar bear. "Who's this?"

"That's Popsicle."

"Nice to meet you, Popsicle." His eyes scan the rest of the room as if he's trying to memorize every detail. It's largely generic, but I added little touches to make it my own once it became clear that I wasn't moving back into my condo within the year: my purple duvet, Popsicle, and a decent amount of photos and posters. A lot of them are *Live From New York*, and some of my favorite shows and movies that alumni have done. He pores over the pictures of me with my parents, Rachel, and her kids.

"You were a cute kid." He picks up a framed picture of me and Rachel that was sitting on the bedside table.

"That was taken at the Hannah Montana and Miley Cyrus: Best of Both Worlds tour," I say wistfully. "The Jonas Brothers opened for her. It was iconic."

"I can imagine."

"Which Jonas brother is your favorite?"

"Joe," he answers automatically. "Camp Rock era Joe."

"Ah. Angsty and misunderstood?"

His mouth twists into a crooked smile. "That's me. Without the brothers."

"I've always been a Nick girl, myself. I like a cinnamon roll."

"Yeah?" Chris shifts his weight, leaning against me. "Then why do you like me?"

I raise an eyebrow at him. "You don't think you're a cinnamon roll?"

"I'm not entirely sure what that means, but I wasn't warm and gooey towards you when we first started working together."

"True. But we didn't know each other then." I press a gentle kiss to the side of his neck.

"And now?" He meets my gaze, a question flickering behind his eyes.

"I've never brought anyone home to meet my family before. I wouldn't do that if you weren't special."

"But it's not like that."

"Like what?" My stomach twists.

"I'm not here as—" His throat bobs, as if he can't physically make himself say it. "Your family just thinks we're coworkers. Right?"

"Right," I confirm, even as the word tastes like poison. "But eventually, we'll tell them."

His jaw tightens, and for the first time since New Year's, I wonder if I'm being foolish. If I've trusted him with my heart when he had no intention of keeping it.

"Chris, Emily," my mom calls from down the hall. "Dinner's ready!"

And just like that, the conversation is over, as quickly as it began.

"Zoe, darling, what do you study at NYU?" my mother asks, passing her the plate of potatoes. Mom has found a new favorite Galloway. Zoe's enthusiastic offer to lead all of the prayers (she attends Shabbat dinners at NYU's Chabad house at least twice a month with her friends, because they have "the best food—but not as good as yours, Mrs. Beckerman") and her willingness to look at the many pictures of Amy and Alex that my mother has on her phone have turned Chris into an afterthought. I don't know whether to be relieved or disappointed.

"I swear, she has more pictures of my kids than I do." Rachel shakes her head, but her small smile betrays her happiness. Rachel's parents retired to Florida a few years ago, and having my mother around has been a blessing for her, Josh, and the kids. For my mother, too, since I'm not remotely close to giving her grandchildren of her own.

"I'm studying English literature and political science," Zoe replies.

"Emily was an English major, too," my father exclaims. "Do you also want to be a writer?"

"No, my plan is actually to go to law school."

"Law school?" Chris looks shocked. "I didn't know that."

"Well, it's a recent decision," Zoe twists her napkin in her lap. "I told you about that social work class I was taking, about the foster care system? Well, I was talking to my professor, and she thought it might be interesting for me to look into custody law."

"It's a difficult field, but really rewarding," Rachel says encouragingly. "I'm a lawyer. I do corporate law, so it's different and much less noble. But if you do decide to apply to law school, I'm happy to answer any questions you might have."

"Thank you. I really appreciate it." She turns her gaze to Chris, slightly hesitant. "What do you think?"

"I think law school is expensive," he answers.

I can practically see him doing calculations in his head.

"There are scholarships. And student loans, if I need them."

"You're not taking out student loans," Chris snaps. "I'm sure you can find a way to do what you want without going to law school, if it comes to that."

"Last time I checked, it was my life, not yours," Zoe retorts.

"We'll talk about this later," Chris says quickly. Zoe nods, although her expression is still stormy.

"So, Chris, you seem like such a lovely gentleman," my mom interjects, deftly changing the subject.

"That's very kind of you to say,'" he says with a tight smile. I take a long sip of my wine, knowing exactly what my mom is leading to. Tracey Beckerman is a hopeless romantic and a Jewish mother. And I know better than anyone that Chris is a total catch.

"Are you seeing anyone?" she presses.

"I'm not,"

His lie shouldn't devastate me. We agreed to keep our relationship secret, knowing how delicate the situation with *Live From New York* is. I assumed that wouldn't be forever, but after our conversation in my bedroom, I'm not so sure.

"How can that be?" my mother gasps theatrically. I roll my eyes as Rachel hides her snicker behind her napkin. "You're so wonderful!"

"Tragically, Chris has a micropenis," I explain. He kicks me under the table.

"Well, that's not such a deal breaker. You can work around that. Your father and I—"

"What does everyone think of our new mayor?" Josh asks loudly, earning grateful glances from everyone at the table with no desire to hear about my parents' sex life. Which is all of us, except for my mother.

"I liked that sketch about him on the show," Rachel says. "It seems like things are going well at *Live From New York*."

"We've been trying," Chris replies diplomatically. "There's a lot at stake, but Emily and I are doing our best to steer things back in the right direction."

"What do you mean?" Mom asks. I turn my head to Chris, trying to send him a silent signal to shut up.

Unfortunately, he doesn't see my panicked expression. "That was why Emily was promoted and brought onto the *Weekend Update*. *Live From New York*'s ratings have been dropping, and the network threatened us with cancellation if we didn't turn things around. But we have," he trails off, noticing how my mother has gone white as a sheet. "I'm sorry. I thought you knew."

"We should have," Mom snaps. "Emily, how could you not tell us that you might not have a job at the end of the year?"

"Because, it's none of your business," I reply tightly. "I'm an adult. I can take care of myself."

"And what if this puts you over the edge again?"

"The last time my anxiety left me unable to function was ten years ago," I snap. "And the show is doing much better. Chris and I have turned things around this season. You should be proud of me, not worried."

"I'm your mother. I can be both."

"Well, I'm telling you not to. It's not your problem." I regret the words as soon as they come out of my mouth.

"Not my problem?" She looks chagrined. "You're my only child! Don't you understand that if you're not doing well, I'm not doing well? I know you think you can handle yourself, but what if you can't?"

"Then I know I'll have you if I need you. And I'm grateful for that, but I'm tired of you treating me like I'm still a child! Everything is going to be fine."

"Really? So you've both gotten verbal confirmation that *Live From New York* won't be canceled?" she demands. Chris and I exchange a look, and my mother shakes her head. "That's what I thought. Emily, this is too much for you. You never should have taken this on. The weight of the entire show, on your shoulders?"

"On mine, too," Chris interjects. "And Emily has done a great job. I couldn't do this without her."

"You don't know what she's been through."

"Yes, he does, Mom. And he doesn't think I'm incapable of doing hard things just because I have anxiety."

"I don't think you're incapable. I think you're choosing a path that's going to hurt you."

I can't help but flinch, thinking of how her words apply not only to the show but also to my relationship with Chris.

"Maybe I am. But it's my choice to make."

"We should go," Chris says, standing.

"Please, don't," I say quietly, but he doesn't respond.

"It was nice meeting you all. Thank you so much for having me," Zoe says politely.

"I'm leaving, too." I move to get up, but Chris stops me.

"Don't. I have an early morning tomorrow, we won't get any writing done tonight." Dread pools in my stomach. A moment ago, he was defending me, and now he's leaving? "This isn't our business. It's personal. I don't want to overstep."

I inhale sharply, the words a stark reminder that there are boundaries to our relationship that I apparently didn't know about. And now I'm left sitting here like a fool, expecting him to stand by me when he did the exact opposite.

He told me he was all in. Does he not realize that this is a part of that? Or did he simply have a different definition?

They walk out, and it's not until the door closes behind them that I let my tears fall.

"Emily." Rachel moves across the table, taking me in her arms. "It's okay."

"I'm sorry, my love." My mom comes to sit on my other side. "I didn't mean to upset you."

"It's okay." I swallow against the lump in my throat. "I'll be okay, even if I get upset. I'm not the same person I used to be, Mom. I can handle my anxiety without letting it break me."

"You're right." She sniffles. "But it's hard for me, too. Your father and I were terrified for you when you first started college. We couldn't sleep, I was so worried about you."

"And I love you for that. You helped me so much." I squeeze her hand. "I still need my mom. Just not in the same way. I'm a big girl now. I have to make mistakes and take risks sometimes, even if I get hurt. That's how I learn."

"And do you think it was a mistake, accepting the promotion?" she asks.

"No." Even if it all blows up in my face, with *Live From New York* and with Chris, it will all have been worth it. "I wanted this for so long, and I didn't think it was possible. Even if this season is the last one, I'm glad I got to live my dream."

"Then I'm glad, too." My mom hugs me. "So why do you still look sad?"

"I can't believe he left," I choke.

"Ah." Tracey nods in understanding. "I take it that means there's no micropenis?"

"No. It's perfect," I say, as my dad and Josh take that cue to excuse themselves and start the dishes.

"Oh, Em," Rachel squeezes my hand. "You've got it bad."

"I think I love him," I admit.

"Love?" Mom asks, and I nod, burying my face in her shoulder. "Does he know that you feel that way?"

"No." I shake my head. "I can't tell him. It would make things too complicated."

"Emily." My mom sighs. "Love doesn't complicate things. It simplifies them. And if you do love him, things are already complicated enough. Being dishonest and hiding your feelings will only make everything worse."

"I can't," I repeat. "He's not ready."

"Still, you have to go after him."

"What?" I jerk back in surprise. "He should be going after *me*. He was the one who walked out."

"Are you really going to hold it against him if he got uncomfortable when the first time he met your family, things turned into a full-blown fight?"

"I guess you have a point," I grumble.

"Go." She practically shoves me out of her arms, shooing me. "Make it right. And once you save your show, then you'll tell him how you feel."

"I love you, Mom."

"I love you too, darling. And I'm saying this with love—get out!"

24

"I asked you not to come."

Not exactly the response a girl hopes for when knocking on the door to her maybe-boyfriend's apartment, even if it is the truth.

"I know," I steel myself. "But I wanted to apologize."

He clenches his jaw. "You don't have anything to apologize for. You didn't do anything wrong."

"It was rude of me to fight with my mom in front of you like that."

"Fine. I'll see you tomorrow."

"Seriously? You're not going to invite me in?"

From behind Chris, Freddie barks loudly. Chris looks between us, his brow crinkling. "Fine. Or my neighbors will complain about this one."

"Okay." Not exactly a win, but at least I'm here. Freddie greets me enthusiastically, and I bend down to scratch his head. "Hi, buddy," I whisper. My dad is allergic to dogs, so I've never had one of my own. It was easy to fall in love with Freddie.

Almost as easy as it was to fall in love with Chris.

I still mid-pet. Freddie whines, bumping his head against my hand, but then Chris tosses him a treat. He grabs it excitedly and takes it back to his crate.

"You should go, Emily." He sounds tired.

I love you. The words are on the tip of my tongue, but I can't say them. Not now. "Tell me what's wrong."

"Nothing."

"That's obviously not true, or you wouldn't have told me to leave."

"Like I said, I'm tired."

"We work in late night television. We're always tired. That's not the reason."

"Why can't you just leave it alone?" he snaps.

"Because you said we were all in!" My throat clenches, emotion causing it to tighten. "And then you left. I asked you to stay, and you left. That hurt me."

"I thought this was about you apologizing to me."

"It's about you pushing me away," I retort. "If we're doing this, you can't put up walls. You have to let me in, or it's never going to work."

"It didn't seem like you needed me."

"Maybe I didn't," I whisper. "But I still wanted you."

"To do what, exactly? Defend you for lying to the people who love you?" He stalks over to the couch, straightening the cushions. "Jesus, Emily. It's like you don't even know how lucky you are."

"I know that I'm lucky."

"Do you? Because you have all of the support a person could want, and you just ignore it," he says. "Do you know how much I wish I could tell someone about all the pressure of the show? Someone who wants to take care of me, and make my life easy?"

"I could be that person for you."

"It's not the same."

"Why not?" I ask.

"Because I could lose you," he exhales raggedly. "Because family is supposed to be there for you, no matter what. And I hate it when you take that for granted, because families don't always act the way they're supposed to."

"Just because your family sucked doesn't mean you can tell me how to deal with mine."

We stare at each other, chests heaving, poisonous words hanging between us. "I feel so alone sometimes," he says quietly. "I have Zoe, but it's different. I can't let myself go with her. I have to be strong, because I'm the one taking care of her. And I get so tired, Emily. I'm so tired of being on my own."

"And I'm telling you that you don't have to be anymore."

"I want to," he says quietly, reaching for me. "All of this is new to me. I've never been vulnerable like this, with anyone."

And I know that I should ask him when we're going to tell everyone the truth. I should force him to tear down that final wall, even knowing that it might be the thing that breaks us.

But I can't. I won't risk blowing everything up for my own sense of security, because I can't bear the thought of having to leave him tonight. Of being another person who he trusted who walked away from him.

Gently, I lift my hand to his face, tracing the pad of my thumb down his cheek. "Neither have I." I've opened up to my family, but this...this is different. I've never handed someone my body and my soul.

"I'm so happy that I chose you." His hands clutch mine, squeezing tightly, and in that moment I know that I never stood a chance.

"I'm happy that I chose you, too," I say thickly.

His hands come to cup my face, and the raw emotion in his green eyes takes my breath away. I lean in, pressing my mouth to his, kissing him so deeply that we forget anything but our mouths moving together. I put every ounce of the feelings I am too afraid to voice into every movement of my lips. *I'm yours, and you're mine*, I say, not with words but with my tongue. Chris captures my bottom lip with his teeth and tugs gently, and I melt into his embrace. My fingers trace a slow, tantalizing path down his chest, until I reach the hem of his sweater.

"Careful," Chris complains against my mouth when I yank it over his head. "I like that sweater."

"I didn't *rip* it," I protest. "I just wanted to see the goods." My lips trace his left nipple, and his laugh turns to a quiet groan as I lick it. He tightens his grip on my lower back.

"Am I just a piece of meat to you?" he murmurs, his hands slipping under my shirt.

"A very skilled hunk of muscle. That's how I'd describe you." I yelp when his hands tickle the sides of my ribcage.

"Well, you don't want to know how I'd describe you, then." Chris's hands skate forward, palming my breasts over the thin fabric of my bra. His hiss of pleasure as he traces my peaked nipples with the pads of his thumb has me moaning. I love how much he reacts to touching me, how good it makes him feel.

"No, tell me," I beg, my voice raw. "Tell me how I make you feel. And be honest." Maybe it's hypocritical to ask him for honesty when I'm holding part of myself back. But I can't tell him I love him and risk scaring him away.

"I'd say you're beautiful." He kisses the side of my neck, and I arch up into him. "And that you taste amazing," he adds, dragging his tongue against the hollow of my neck, right where my pulse is fluttering. "That you drove me to distraction, even before I knew how badly I wanted you."

"Because of how beautiful I am?" I ask hopefully

"Because you are impossible to ignore, Emily Beckerman."

"That works, too." I lean back, dragging my shirt over my head. I slowly unbutton my jeans, my eyes meeting his as I drag the material down my legs. I've never been the kind of person who felt certain in the power my physical appearance had over others. But Chris looks at me as if he's physically unable to tear his gaze from my body. I come alive under that stare, not just because of how much he wants me, but because he makes sure I know how desired I am.

I slip out of my underwear and unclasp my bra, completely bare before him.

"You're perfect," he whispers hoarsely.

To my eternal embarrassment, I feel myself begin to cry. I start to turn away from him, but he doesn't allow it, closing the distance between us and pulling me against him so that my back is flush with his chest.

"No one has ever said that to me before," I admit. "And even if they had…I wouldn't have believed it." Because no one else has ever held my heart so easily in their hands.

"Do you know the definition of the word perfect?" he whispers against my ear.

"I know that you're about to tell me." I yelp when he slides one hand up my chest to lightly pinch my nipple.

"Smart ass," he answers. I can't see him smiling so much as I can feel it as he dips his head to kiss the side of my neck. A noise that I can't even begin to identify escapes my throat as I stretch myself up to give him full access. "It means having all the desirable elements, qualities or characteristics. As good as it is possible to be."

"So, you don't wish I were less of a smart ass?"

"Not for a second." He lifts one hand to my face, gently brushing away the tears that leak down. "Before you, Emily, I was lost, and I was unhappy. And I thought I would always be that way. I didn't think I deserved better."

My heart breaks, thinking of how this man standing in front of me never even knew how much love that he had to give.

"You deserve everything," I tell him.

"You are everything. You see all of me, the good and the bad, and you still want me." His voice breaks. And I know then that even if he can't say it, Chris is in love with me. "So, you're perfect to me. You're perfect for me. Every part of you."

I love him.

I can't run or hide from the truth of it. I love him, even if I'm afraid. Afraid that if this ends badly, it might break our dynamic on the show. That it might break me. But my fears are small obstacles compared to the reassuring presence of this man before me. They are not silent, but grow quieter every time he touches me. Reminding me that he is real, and the worries of my anxious mind are not.

I can't say the words to him tonight. But I can show him. I can make sure that he feels how much I love him when I touch him, the way that he deserves to be touched. I can keep doing that until he's ready to believe that we have a future outside of the shadows. Emily and Chris, partners not just on the *Update* desk and as head writers, but in life.

I kiss him, deeply, laughing against his mouth as we make our way into the bedroom. He places me gently on his bed, his eyes glued to my body as if he's trying to memorize me.

"You're wearing too much clothing." I reach forward, unbuttoning his pants. He lays down, crossing his arms behind his head in a way that he's done countless times in our office. He's the picture of languid, lazy grace, watching me inch his boxers down as if he hasn't a care in the world. I shove them aside and sit back on my heels.

"What are you doing?" Chris asks, looking slightly less devil-may-care now that I'm further away from him.

"Looking," I reply, drinking in the crisp hair on his chest, the freckles scattered across his skin, the corded muscle of his thighs and best of all, his straining erection, the evidence of how much I affect him. How deeply he wants me. He notices where my gaze has drifted and drags his hand along the length of his dick in a slow pump.

My mouth dries out.

"See something you like?" he asks, all drawling charm.

"You tell me." I take his hand, dragging him up my inner thigh with torturous slowness until we reach the slick wetness between my thighs.

"I want you to say it."

"I'm yours, Chris. Tonight and always." The words fall out of my mouth before I can consider the weight of them, but his only response is to flip us so that my back is on the mattress. His hands press my legs apart, spreading me widely. He kisses the soft inside of my knee, sending a rush of warmth through me.

Our eyes meet, and I don't think I've ever felt more turned on than I am right now at the sight of his face peering up at me from between my legs. And then he dips his head down, his tongue tracing a pattern across my clit that has me seeing sparks. His strokes are precise but unhurried, and as I bury my fingers in his hair, the message is clear: there is no rush. He isn't going anywhere.

"God, the taste of you, Emily," he moans against the inside of my thigh, one finger sliding inside me.

I can only moan back in response, one foot sliding up the comforter as the other lands on his shoulder. The feel of his muscles working beneath me makes me gasp, as does the second finger he adds, reaching the exact spot where I crave his touch the most. He devours me. The brushes of his tongue grow faster and heavier, and the orgasm overtakes me as I shout his name.

I greedily pull him up into my arms, not even wanting to catch my breath before I crush my mouth against his. My arms slide around his neck and pull him tightly to me, craving the touch of his skin against my own.

"You feel so good," he murmurs into my shoulder, sweeping my hair aside to drag the flat of his tongue across one of my breasts, and then the other.

"I will never have enough of you," I say. *I love you*, is what I mean.

My mouth slides over his as I grip his face with my hands and kiss him deeply. I softly drag my lips down his jawline and over his throat, savoring the feel of his pulse racing beneath his skin when I kiss him. I run my hands and lips across his chest. I take my time tasting him, my lisp finding every crevice of his body and marking them. *Mine,* I mouth against his chest, tugging his nipple into my mouth. Maybe Chris's body is some kind of wishing well. Maybe if I whisper my heart's desires against his skin, they'll come true.

"Emily," he groans, and it's the sexiest thing I've ever heard, hearing him say my name like it's the only word he's capable of forming. He shudders as I move my mouth against his, his strong arms wrapping tighter around me and reaching down to cup my ass. He lifts it, twisting us so that I'm on top of him. "I need you."

"Take me," I reply. "I'm yours."

Chris retrieves a condom from the pocket of his discarded pants and puts it on. He reaches forward to grip my hips, and I sink down onto him slowly. He makes a strangled sound, his eyes fluttering shut as he enters me. "You're perfect," he rasps.

I brace my hands on his chest, adjusting to the fullness before I lift up and then sink down again. I repeat the movement, pleasure building. Chris throws his head back, a strangled moan escaping his throat, and I run a finger down the side of his neck.

If only I could memorize every part of this moment: the heavy warmth of him beneath me, the pads of his fingers gripping my skin, the way his eyelashes flutter as he groans in ecstasy.

I increase the pace of my movements as one of his hands reaches between my legs. His fingers circle my clit, the strokes growing faster in time with the rhythm of my body. My orgasm hits me fast and hard as I pant his name through strangled breaths, and Chris climaxes a moment later, shouting mine.

He leaves me only long enough to dispose of the condom, and I crawl eagerly back into his arms. I lay my head against his chest, nuzzling into the feeling of the hairs there scratching my skin and listening to his still-racing heart. I did that. I made him feel that.

He falls asleep first, his eyes fluttering shut peacefully. I stare at the ceiling, wondering how my heart can feel so full. I curl myself back over him, tucking my head against his chest.

We fit so perfectly; it feels like he was made for me.

Maybe he was. My perfect foil, the person who pulled things out of me as a comedian, a woman, and a person that I didn't know I was capable of. The one who challenged me to become the best version of myself, who worked with me to rebuild the show we both love so much into something we're proud of.

There's no going back. Not for me.

"I love you," I whisper into his skin, and I fall asleep dreaming of the day when I'll be able to say it to his face.

Imagining how Chris will feel knowing that he'll never be alone again, because now he has me.

25

The weeks fly by, full of Chris and writing, until it's somehow the Friday before our last show of the season. We still haven't heard anything from Jessica about the fate of *Live From New York*. It feels like a guillotine hanging above us, but as my mom loves to remind me, worrying doesn't help. So we try to concentrate on what we can control, instead of what we can't.

These days, the list of things I can't control feels like it's a CVS receipt wrapping around my neck and choking me to death. I spend most nights at Chris's apartment, and almost all of my days with him. Part of me worried that we would be sick of each other by now, but it's the opposite.

The more I have of him, the more I want.

"Fuck. I forgot my toothbrush," I say, rooting around in my backpack as if it'll appear out of thin air.

"Just use mine," He calls from the bathroom.

"Ugh. Okay. Fine." I walk over to join him, taking extra time to enjoy the sight of Chris shaving while wearing only a towel wrapped around his hips.

"You have no problem kissing me first thing in the morning, but the thought of using my toothbrush grosses you out?" Chris says.

"A toothbrush is not the same as a kiss."

"Fair enough." He finishes shaving and rinses off his face. "You could keep your own toothbrush here. If you wanted to."

"Just a toothbrush?" I ask hesitantly.

"And other things," he pauses, suddenly looking nervous. "Maybe some clothes. And your skin stuff. So you wouldn't have to haul everything back and forth."

"Yeah?"

"Yeah. And then you could spend the night here whenever you wanted." Gently, he tucks a strand of my auburn hair behind my ear. "I've suddenly found myself deeply regretting every second I spend away from you." I blink up at him, floored. He rubs the back of his neck. "Was that too much?"

"No," I breathe. "It was pretty much perfect."

It's moments like this that remind me I don't need anyone else to know that I'm Chris's girlfriend. I don't need him to tell me that he loves me, even if I'm dying to say it back.

I trust that just because he's on a different timeline than I am when it comes to his feelings doesn't mean that his aren't valid. I trust *him*. And I won't let my anxious, overthinking brain ruin something perfect.

I brush my teeth and then throw on leggings and one of Chris's sweatshirts before we leave to get coffee. He drapes his arm over my shoulder as we exit his apartment. We reach the lobby of his building only to find that it's pouring rain.

"Back upstairs we go," I chirp.

"I don't want to make coffee. *Someone* woke me up too early this morning. I'm tired," Chris whines.

"If I remember correctly, you were an active participant."

"I was seduced."

"Barely."

"You were naked." He pulls me into the warmth of his body. "I couldn't resist." He casts his gaze around the foyer, making sure we're still alone, and presses his lips against the base of my throat.

"Are you sure you don't just want to go back upstairs? Coffee isn't the only thing that energizes me," I ask breathlessly, and he laughs.

"As much as I do, we have to be at work in a few hours, and if we get back in bed there's no guarantee I'll ever leave." The words turn my insides to liquid. "The coffee shop is down the street. Let's just make a run for it. It'll be fun."

He extends his hand. Years of listening to Taylor Swift have taught me that when someone offers you the chance for a romantic moment in the rain, you don't say no. So, I place my hand in his. His fingers interlace with mine, and he looks down at me with excitement dancing in those perfect eyes.

We sprint down the street until we reach the coffee shop. Chris holds the door open for me as we duck under its awning, both of us decidedly wet. Kissing in the rain is more romantic in theory than in practice. But then he takes a moment to move the soggy hair off of my face and brush his lips against mine, and I understand the hype. With the water rushing down around us, it feels like we're the only two people in the world. In our perfect bubble where nothing will ever hurt us.

I thread my hands through his damp hair and pull him down to me when he tries to break the kiss, deepening it instead, kissing him in the rain like a goddamned romance heroine until someone clears their throat behind us. I'm not sure whether it's in response to the PDA or because we're blocking the door, but either way, we get the message and duck inside.

I try to stay present in the perfection of these moments. The feeling of his hand firm in mine as he rattles off my coffee order without having to ask. The casual intimacy of his touch against the small of my back. I'm on cloud nine as we sit in that coffee shop, brainstorming sketch ideas and sipping our drinks like we're going to do it for the rest of our lives.

When we get off at our subway stop near the building, I notice two missed calls from Faith.

"Everything okay?" Chris asks.

"Faith called me." We make our way through the throngs of tourists, stopping in front of the building. "Let me call her back before we go up."

"Emily." My stomach drops when I hear the note of worry in her voice. "Are you okay?"

"Should I not be?" Chris's hand comes to my arm, touching it briefly. No one has noticed us yet, but if we were going to get recognized, this would be the place for it to happen.

"Have you checked your phone recently?"

"No, I've been...distracted." Chris smiles smugly, and I give him the finger. "Why?"

"Someone posted pictures of you and Chris together."

"Oh. Weird." Maybe I'm unobservant, but I haven't picked up on anyone sneaking pictures of me when I'm out by myself or with Chris. We're not even relevant enough to warrant a Deuxmoi submission. At least, we weren't. "Nice to know we're famous now, I guess?"

"No, Emily," Faith says gently. "They posted pictures of you kissing."

"Shit." I suck in a sharp breath. I open my phone and instantly find a barrage of texts and links to articles, all of them confirming that our on-air chemistry wasn't just part of the show. Including one from my mom, simply saying, 'I knew it'.

"Emily?" Chris says from behind me.

"I have to go," I tell Faith. When I look up from my phone, it feels like every eye in the crowd is on me. On *us*. And I'm not imagining it, either—several people have their phones out, snapping pictures without our consent, as if we're zoo animals.

"I fucking knew it," someone whispers.

"Didn't he date that model?"

"He dates *everyone*. She's just the flavor of the month."

"It's gonna be so awkward when they break up."

"Yeah, but how funny will it be to watch?"

I'm frozen, my limbs rooted to the ground as I listen to the strangers around me speculate about my life.

"Emily." Chris's hand grips my elbow. "We have to get inside." I don't move, and he gently tugs me through the doors and towards the elevators. We pause in front of them, and he puts his hands on my shoulders. Out of habit, I look around, not wanting to get caught.

But we already have been. Laughter bubbles up inside me, bordering on hysterical.

"I need you to breathe," Chris instructs, and I do. I breathe even though it doesn't feel like it's doing anything as anxiety closes up my throat. The words of the crowd drift back to me. *Flavor of the month.* It shouldn't matter what other people think of us, but I can't get it out of my head.

"Did you see?" I ask quietly.

"I saw," he confirms, his jaw clenching. He looks furious. "There's nothing we can do about it now."

"Right." I scan his face for any sign of what he's thinking. But he's closed himself off to me. "Is this—what does this mean? For us?"

"We have to talk to Jessica. Do damage control."

"Damage?" I repeat faintly. "Is this...bad?"

"I just wanted to do this on my terms. The focus shouldn't be on our personal relationship. It should be on the show, and we don't even know what the fuck is going on with the next season yet."

"Do you really think our personal relationship would be the reason we don't get renewed?"

"I don't know what to think," he pauses, taking in the panic that I'm sure is written all over my face. "I'm sorry. I'm not trying to freak you out. I just need to figure out what the fuck is going on."

"Okay. We'll talk to Jessica."

I expected a lecture, but when we get to Jessica's office, she's doing something I've only seen her do a handful of times: smiling. If I wasn't so relieved, it would almost be unsettling.

"I haven't heard anything official about our future yet, but this only helps."

"How? If people are only watching because they want to psycho-analyze our body language, what's the fucking point? This is a comedy show, not a dating show," Chris snaps.

Jessica raises her eyebrows at him. "You should know better than anyone that it doesn't matter why people are watching." They exchange a look that I don't understand. Probably something to do with Alex. "Eyeballs are the only things that matter. And who knows? Those people might end up actually enjoying it."

"It compromises our integrity," Chris says.

Jessica's eyes narrow. "I don't give a shit about your integrity being compromised if it means that I get to tell everyone here that they're keeping their jobs."

Chris slumps back in his chair, looking appropriately chastised.

"And I should remind you both that you were more than willing to be underhanded when it came to getting rid of each other," she adds. "I'm assuming that's off the table now?"

"Yes. We're both staying," I confirm. I look to Chris.

"If there's a show to stay for, I guess."

I blink, trying not to let the hurt show on my face. Where the fuck is the man who promised me we were in this together on a balcony on New Year's Eve? Maybe he's just rattled. It's been a weird morning.

But I can't shake my growing unease, that sense that there's something happening inside his head that I don't understand. That he doesn't want me to know about.

This is our first test, and he's shutting me out. Even when we hated each other, I knew how he felt. Now, I'm not so sure. And it's fucking terrifying.

"Leave that to me," Jessica says firmly. "Now, I know it's a busy week. I'll let you both get back to writing."

We walk back to our office in silence. I wait until the door closes behind us before I open my mouth. "Are you okay?"

"I'm fine," Chris replies tightly, sitting down at his desk. "Are you?"

"Yeah," I lie, wishing I could bridge this distance between us. But there's no use. He's retreated into himself, and I can't get him out.

We spend the next few hours writing. The rest of the day is filled with our usual pre-show preparations. By midnight, I'm practically dead on my feet.

"You should go home, Beckerman," Chris suggests.

"I'm not tired," I protest.

"You've yawned eight times in the past ten minutes."

"Okay, fair enough," I yawn again. "But text me if anything comes up, okay?"

"I will. Promise."

I kiss him goodbye and head for the elevators. I'm heading towards the subway when I realize that I left my phone at the office. Probably in the bathroom. Probably because I almost fell asleep while peeing.

It doesn't take long for me to grab my phone once I get back in the building. Since it fell on the bathroom floor, I walk over to the kitchen to grab a disinfectant wipe so I can clean it off. But when I get there, I hear voices. I peek out into the other kitchen hallway—the one I didn't enter through—and notice a light on in Jessica's office. She usually doesn't stay this late the night before a show.

Maybe this has something to do with *Live From New York*'s future. It's probably not the most ethical thing in the world to eavesdrop on my boss, but this is too important. I have to see if I can find anything out, for the sake of my fellow writers. And myself.

"You know it's not show policy to comment on things like this," Jessica says. I'm hidden from view around a corner, but I can hear Jessica perfectly.

And then, the other person in her office speaks. "Our relationship isn't for public consumption."

It's Chris.

"*Live From New York* putting out a public statement denying any relationship is only going to add fuel to the fire, Chris. You've been in this business long enough to know that a denial only gets more tongues wagging. Besides, it wouldn't do anything. Everyone's already seen the pictures," Jessica points out.

"I don't care. I want a public statement denying our relationship."

I suck in a breath. Why wouldn't Chris talk to me about this before he asked Jessica?

"Right. And I'm assuming you want me to go ahead and do this without Emily ever finding out it was at your request." She pauses. "Just like I assume she doesn't know about our other deal?"

No. No. Chris would never go behind my back like this. There has to be some other explanation.

He sighs, and my stomach tightens. I know that sound. It's the one he makes when he's faced with a difficult decision. "Things got out of hand. I never meant for this to happen."

Jessica snorts indelicately. "All of that talk about integrity when you were both in my office, and yet you were the one who promised me that you would pretend to be attracted to her on the *Update* if it helped your chances of being chosen over her."

No. He wouldn't. But...after the *Update* on the second show bombed, we were desperate. Chris had agreed to work with me, but it still took time for us to trust each other. And yet every time we went on camera, it felt like there was something there. Some chemistry between us, a connection that spoke to how great we could be.

Was it all a lie? Him doing my makeup before the first show, comforting me, promising I wasn't alone. Tapping my knee with his before every show. That little ritual—was that all part of his plan?

Pretending. He was pretending. To convince Jessica why he was the right choice and to make people pay attention to the show. And it worked. On the audience, and on me.

I press a hand against my mouth, fighting my sob. Because Chris only looked at me like I was special to get people to pay attention to the *Weekend Update*. He did it to get Jessica to pick him.

Even when things changed about us, he didn't tell me the truth. He didn't admit that everything that made me fall in love with him was an act, part of his plan to get rid of me.

And then he tried to go behind my back and get Jessica to issue a statement denying our relationship. That would make it so easy. He could pretend we had to keep things under wraps because *Live From New York* wanted to, when really it was all him. He was pulling every string, manipulating me, making me fall in love without ever showing me who he truly was.

All I wanted was for him to show me all of himself. Now I know, and I feel like a fucking fool for ever believing in him. In us.

"I didn't mean to," Chris says, so quietly I can barely make it out. "I never meant to fall in love with her."

Of course. Of course. The universe truly has a sick, twisted sense of humor, to deliver me the words I want to hear from him now that I know we have no future.

"So, the pictures were an accident."

"Of course they were an accident," Chris snaps. "I would never manipulate Emily like that off-camera."

"You're such a fucking liar," I storm into Jessica's office, ready to make him pay.

"Emily," Chris breathes, jumping up. "Did you—"

"I heard everything." I'm practically shaking with rage.

"I never lied to you," he breathes. "I know I didn't tell you the whole truth, but—"

"Bullshit," I hiss. "You said you would never manipulate me off camera, but you just asked Jessica to lie for you and tell me it was her idea to issue a statement denying our relationship." I turn to Jessica. "But you can go ahead and do that, if you'd like. Because it's the fucking truth now."

"Emily," Chris looks chagrined. "Please."

"Please what?" I demand. "Do you know what your problem is?

You think you're such a good guy because you've spent most of your adult life watching out for Zoe. And that's great. But it doesn't make up for everything else you did. The only two people you have ever looked out for are her, and yourself. You let Alex run this show into the ground. You let him treat everyone like shit. You let me fuck you and fall in love with you." My voice catches, a sob tearing from my throat. "You're not a good guy. You're a passive coward."

Chris opens his mouth, but I cut him off. "Stop talking. I don't care what you have to say." I turn to Jessica. "Who would you have picked, if we hadn't told you we both wanted to stay?"

"Stop it. Emily, that doesn't matter," Chris protests. "None of that fucking matters. I didn't mean to hurt you."

"I wasn't talking to you," I retort.

"Emily, please don't throw this all away," he pleads. "I know I fucked up, but we have a future here."

"No," I say softly. "We don't have a future. Not as partners, or people in your twisted version of a relationship, or even as friends." I turn to face Chris, letting him see every bit of fury on my face. Every ounce of rage and hurt. Letting him finally face the fucking truth, the damage and pain that he's responsible for, even if he doesn't want to admit it. "I changed my mind. I'm not staying with him. It's him or me."

26

“You don't mean that," Chris says.

"Don't tell me what I mean," I seethe. "You did this. You ruined *everything*."

Everything we built is crumbling beneath us, and it's all his fault.

And whatever hatred I may have felt towards Chris when we first began pales in comparison to this: the red-hot slice of his betrayal, the emptiness left inside me after I had something perfect and lost it.

Jessica frowns at us. "This is becoming a bit messy for my taste."

"Maybe you should have thought of that before you encouraged Chris to seduce me for the purpose of good television," I snap.

"I think seduce is a bit of a strong word."

"Either way, it was wrong." I thrust my chin forward, waiting for the apology that I know will never come.

"I did what I had to do to save my show," Jessica replies evenly, not a hint of remorse in her expression. "And speaking of, I hope you can at least shove all of this down and put on a good performance on Saturday."

"Of course. It's my last shot to prove that I'm better than him," I reply, sticking my chin out defiantly.

"Don't do this, Emily," Jessica's expression softens, just a bit. "Don't walk away from the biggest opportunity of your career because someone hurt you."

"Then get rid of him." I jerk my head in Chris's general direction. He looks pained, and some savage part of me relishes that. It feels good, letting my words shoot to kill, hurting him because he hurt me.

"You're better together."

She's right.

It should be an easy choice. My pride, or my career? My heart, or my future as a writer?

The thought of just walking away from this show feels deeply wrong. But so does continuing to work with Chris, pretending everything is fine when it's not. It will never be fine. Even if we got through our final show tomorrow and I spent the summer away from him, it wouldn't be enough time. It doesn't matter if I had ten minutes or ten years. I will never be able to look at Chris Galloway without my heart breaking all over again.

"I've made my decision. And I won't change my mind," I tell Jessica. And then I turn on my heel and leave.

Chris doesn't follow me. At least, not right away. I've already reached the elevator by the time I hear the sound of him running after me.

I hit the down button. Maybe if I time this right, I can escape him.

"I told Jessica that I wouldn't stay without you," Chris says, coming to a stop several feet away from me. "No matter what. I meant what I said on New Year's Eve."

I laugh bitterly. "Fuck you, Chris. You didn't mean it. Not really. Or you would have told me that you played things up for the cameras."

"I knew you'd freak out," he says defensively. The elevator opens. I go to step on, but he rushes forward, blocking the entrance with his body. "I couldn't lose you. I *can't* lose you, Emily."

"Move, Chris," I try to sound angry, but it just comes out broken.

"No," he says, his jaw set, looking as stubborn as I've ever seen him. And I hate it, because I wanted that so badly. I wanted to be the thing, the person, that he fought for. But he didn't. Not until it was too late. "You said you heard everything," he pauses, as if waiting for me to say something. To acknowledge the words he said that could have changed everything, if only I had been the one he said them to. "I meant it."

"I'm sure you think you did," I reply, not meeting his gaze.

"I love you, Emily." He takes a small step forward, letting the elevator doors close behind him.

It was one thing hearing him tell Jessica that he loved me. Chris Galloway saying those words to my face—the ones I thought he might never be capable of saying—makes my knees weak. But I won't let it make *me* weak.

"No, you don't." I feel my eyes fill with tears. "If you loved me, you wouldn't be ashamed of me. You wouldn't have asked our boss to publicly deny our relationship."

"I didn't do that because I'm ashamed of you. I did it because I'm ashamed of myself." he shouts. "I wanted to tell you the truth about my deal with Jessica. But you're right. I was scared. I was terrified, because the majority of people that I've loved have walked away from me and I was fucking terrified that you would too."

"You don't think I was scared? Of course I was. Falling in love with you is the scariest thing that's ever happened to me." Tears slip down my cheeks, and I don't bother wiping them away. "That doesn't excuse what you did. You manipulated me. You admitted it yourself. You made me feel safe, and you pretended that it was because you cared about me, when it was all part of your plan to get rid of me." I scream, my voice shaking. "Was that why you did my makeup? Why you comforted me before our first show?"

"No. *No*," he breathes, his hands moving to grip the sides of my face. With heartbreaking gentleness, he brushes the tears from my face. "After we bombed the second show, I was desperate. That's when I went to Jessica."

"So, that was when it stopped being real."

"It was always real for me, Beckerman," Chris exhales sharply. "I wanted to comfort you, and flirt with you, and fight with you, against all of my better instincts. If it was part of my strategy to win that stupid fucking competition, I could justify it to myself. But I would have done it anyway, because you got under my skin. And I liked it," He leans forward, so our faces are only inches apart. I can see the truth of what he's saying written all over his face: in the paleness of his skin, the tears shining in his beautiful eyes, the desperate clench of his jaw and the breath catching in his throat.

It's the honesty I always wanted. But it's too late now. My heart is too broken beyond repair to appreciate it.

"How can you expect me to ever trust you again, after this?" I sniffle, hating how pathetic I sound.

"Would you have trusted me, if I told you earlier? Would you have forgiven me?"

"Of course I would have."

"Really?" He steps back, and even though I hate him now, I mourn the loss of his hands on my skin. "Or were you just waiting for me to fail? Waiting for me to fuck up and become human, instead of the perfect hero from one of your books, so that you could write me off without thinking twice?"

"If you'd bothered to read any of those books, you'd know that none of the people in them are perfect, or they'd be boring. I never asked for you to be perfect. I asked for you to be honest, and you couldn't even give me that, when I gave you everything."

"Fine, I fucked up. But don't pretend one thing I did would have changed things. It was a mistake, but if one lie was enough for you to consider everything ruined, maybe we never even had a future."

"At least I would have had a choice," I snap. "At least I would have known what kind of person I was falling in love with."

"And what kind of person is that?" he asks, his voice dangerously low.

"A liar."

Chris laughs bitterly. "If I'm a liar, then so are you."

"In what way?"

"You told me you wanted to be there for me, and now you're leaving."

"You were the one who wanted to hide our relationship. You were the one who walked away from me at Shabbat dinner when I asked you to stay. You've had one foot out the door since we started."

"You seemed fine with both of those things at the time."

"Because I was afraid of scaring you off," I exclaim. "Because even when you told me you were all in, something inside me knew it wasn't the truth."

"It was as much of myself as I could give," he replies furiously. "I fucking tried. Does that not count for anything?"

"Seriously, Chris? You told our boss that you loved me before you said it to my face. When were you planning on doing that, by the way? After you joined me in complaining that the show put out a statement denying our relationship?"

"I wanted to protect you," he says brokenly. "You looked so sad and scared after the news broke. After we heard all that stupid shit people were saying outside the building. I know you struggle with anxiety, and I just thought that this would keep you safe. Keep *us* safe."

"And I told you that I hate people trying to protect me just because I get anxious." I shake my head at him. "The way to protect me would have been to claim me, Chris. Not to push me away. If you wanted me to feel like you didn't care what anyone else said about us, you shouldn't have tried to hide me."

"You're right. I know that now." He looks stricken. "I fucked up. I shouldn't have gone behind your back. I should have asked what you wanted. But I can't change that now."

"No, you can't," I agree.

"All I can do is try to fix this. I *want* to fix this," he pleads, reaching for me.

"You can't. This was built on a lie."

"That's bullshit," he growls. "I told you I wasn't lying."

"We both know how good you are at lying to my face."

"Punish me all you want, Emily," he says, his strong jaw clenching. His eyes turn bright with unshed tears, and I have to fight every instinct in my body that's telling me to go to him. To comfort him, and tell him we can fix this. "I can take it. Hurt me as much as I hurt you."

"I don't want to hurt you anymore," I lie. "I just want you to leave me alone."

"You don't mean that." A single tear escapes, sliding down his cheek. "Please. Fuck, Emily. I don't know what to say. I don't know how to convince you that I can make you happy."

"There's nothing you can say to salvage this." Another lie.

"So you don't even want to give us a chance?" He asks, and I can see his heart breaking on his face. Some savage part of me is glad for it, glad to see that he's suffering as much as I am. Even if another, larger part hates causing him pain.

"There's nothing left worth saving," I repeat.

"Look, Emily, I can't guarantee you that we're going to have a happy ending if you stay. But I can guarantee you that we won't if you leave."

"Don't act like I'm just giving up for no reason after you betrayed me. You made me question everything you ever said to me, Chris!"

He surges forward, taking my hands in his, pressing them against his heart. "I know. And I hate that I hurt you, when you loved me in a way that I didn't think I would ever experience. I didn't believe in love because I didn't believe that I deserved it. Emily, you believed in me when I couldn't believe in myself. I'm asking you not to stop now."

"You said that you went to Jessica after our second show."

"I did." His brow crinkles in confusion at the sudden change in subject.

"And do you remember what happened, right after that show?"

He squeezes his eyes shut, as if bracing for a blow that he knows he cannot defend against. "I do."

"We promised to trust each other. And then you did the exact opposite."

His throat bobs. "I told you that night that *Live From New York* meant everything to me. I was wrong. This show means a lot, but it's not everything. You're everything. Zoe is everything. And I know that doesn't make sense, but what I'm trying to say is that you made me realize that I'm more than what happens inside these halls. You make me want to take risks. Not just in comedy. In life, Emily." Tears slip down his face. "I didn't tell you the other reason I left after Shabbat dinner."

"What was it?" I ask, even though it won't change anything.

"Because you told me you'd never brought anyone to meet your family before. I pushed you away then, but during dinner...I realized that I didn't want to be there as your coworker. I wanted to be there as your boyfriend. As the person who, maybe...maybe could be part of that family, one day."

He pauses, letting go of my hands. I stand, frozen, unable to form words. He's laid out his heart before me. All I have to do is take it.

But I can't. Because he's wrong. He wronged me.

He broke my heart. And no amount of pretty words will change that. He can't love me enough to undo the hurt he's caused, the lie he chose not to reveal.

"You had your chance to say all of this, and you waited until you needed to win me back."

"I know." He hangs his head. "I've done this all wrong. But you're the one who's throwing everything we have away like it meant nothing."

"It meant everything," I shout. "That's why I can't let you in again, Chris. Because it's too hard."

"It's worth it."

"You're not the one with the broken heart." My scream rips through my throat. "You have no idea how it feels, not to trust anything good you've ever said to me. To feel like I was so delusional and desperate to be loved that I couldn't see the truth."

"That's the thing. You saw the truth in me from the very start. And if you're desperate, then I'm desperate, too, because I would do anything to make you stay." Chris looks wild, almost unhinged. As if he can feel me slipping through his fingers and he refuses to let it happen. But is he only sure of his love for me now that he's losing me?

"Would you have told me you loved me, if I hadn't overheard it?"

The question catches him off guard. "I don't know."

"If you can't tell me you love me until you're about to lose me, then I can't be with you, Chris."

I wonder if it's as difficult for him to let me walk away as it is for me to leave. If every step breaks his heart the way that it's breaking mine. Pain builds upon pain as the distance between us grows larger and larger.

That distance will never be bridged again.

I arrive late the day of our last show, as late as I possibly could without being behind schedule.

Chris isn't there when I walk into our office, but I still feel his presence. I'll never not feel it here. The question is whether I can get past that enough to stay.

But that's not something I need to figure out tonight. Tonight, I'm only focused on survival. I'll get through this final episode. It'll be the performance of my life. I'll show my face at the afterparty and then go back home and let myself fall apart.

I don't see Chris at all as I head backstage, making sure everything is ready. Luckily, my friends are all busy enough that they don't notice. We exchange brief, celebratory backstage hugs with the promise of seeing each other at the afterparty. As hard as it is to hide how I'm feeling from them, seeing Faith, Mandy and Riley is a reminder of all that I'd lose if I leave the show behind.

In what feels like the blink of an eye, I'm done with hair and makeup. I'm in my costume, waiting to go on for the *Update*, when I feel Chris behind me.

"Hi," he says, a thousand meanings hidden within those two simple letters. His expression is carefully neutral, as if we didn't scream at each other just down the hall last night.

"Let's give them a good show," I reply. *Because it might just be our last.*

"Emily—" he starts.

"Five minutes," a production assistant interrupts.

"Thank you."

Chris gently grabs my elbow. "Are you going to be okay out there?"

"I'll be fine," I snap, wrenching it out of his grasp. "I know how to pretend, too."

His jaw tightens, but he stays silent as we reach our seats.

"We're on in five."

The noise of backstage fades, everything that isn't Chris blending into the background. *This could be my last Update.* The thought devastates me, and I take a deep, shaky breath, wondering how I'm going to get through this. Wondering how I can possibly tell these jokes we wrote together and smile at the man who broke my heart like it was nothing.

Beneath the desk, his knee taps mine. I grip the edge of the desk with white knuckles, closing my eyes for a moment. Our familiar gesture, designed to help the other person feel less alone.

Except it doesn't work anymore. I'm more alone than ever.

And then the red flashing light of the camera blinks to life, and I paste on a smile as if I'm not dying inside.

"Hi, I'm Chris Galloway."

"And I'm Emily Beckerman."

Our final *Update* goes off without a hitch. We do as Jessica asked. I wonder if it's killing him as much as it's killing me to fall back into our familiar banter, knowing that it doesn't fit anymore. Knowing that we're never going to do this again.

I try to enjoy it. Chris has taken so much from me. If this is the last time I'm here, I don't want to waste it hating him.

I've wasted too much time on him already.

But I can't appreciate the laughter. I don't feel that familiar rush of euphoria when a joke lands perfectly. I only feel empty, and alone, as we sit next to each other and deliver jokes together without even looking at each other.

Before I know it, it's over.

"This has been the *Weekend Update*," Chris's eyes land on me, and I can't help but meet them. There's regret simmering under the surface, hidden behind a congenial smile.

He'll miss it, too. If nothing else was real, this was. It was fucking perfect.

"I'm Emily Beckerman." I can only hope no one notices the sudden shininess in my eyes, the tears that I'm holding back by sheer force of will.

I thought I'd be relieved when our last *Update* together was over. When we were finally done with each other.

I'm not. I'm devastated.

"And I'm Chris Galloway."

"Thank you, and goodnight."

We smile and wave. Chris and Emily, one last time.

27

R iley, Faith, and Mandy corner me at the afterparty.

"Well?" Faith demands.

"Well, what?" I ask, taking a long sip of my whiskey. I've been fending off well-wishes all night from the kind of comedy legends I once would have killed to be in the same room as. I pictured tonight so many times. That moment when Chris and I reached the top of the hill, secure in our future together as head writers, *Update* anchors, and as two people in love.

Instead, we've been avoiding each other all night, careful to never cross paths. I stare at him when he isn't looking. I wonder if he does the same to me. It feels so wrong to accept praise I never could have earned without him. We did this together. We should be celebrating together, too.

Still, I'm not alone. I have my friends. That's something.

Except, they were Chris's friends first. Now that we're done, will they pick him over me? I don't exactly have a stellar track record of relationships on this show.

"Well, are we saved from cancellation?" Riley asks.

I take a gulp of my drink. Was that all they wanted from me?

Information? Has Chris already told them his version of events? Have they already decided it's the truth? "I don't know yet."

"No wonder you look like someone pissed in your drink," Mandy says. "How long is Braugher going to torture us?"

"Who knows." I can barely even think about *Live From New York*'s future. At this point, we've done everything we could. And as important as this show is to me, as much as it is a dream that belongs to me alone...my best season on it is inextricably tied up with a man I can't even look at. "Out of our hands now."

"Does Chris know anything?"

I laugh bitterly. "Probably. Even if he did, he wouldn't tell me."

Faith raises an eyebrow at me. "What the fuck does that mean?"

"I think I have an idea," Riley casts a meaningful glance across the room, to where Chris stands talking to a cluster of network executives. "The two of you are the most miserable pair in this room."

"We're not a pair anymore." The alcohol loosens my tongue. "Not in any sense of the word."

"Wait," Faith pauses, her eyebrows knitting together. "You mean...as head writers? And on the *Update*?"

"I guess," I shrug.

"Oh, no you don't." Faith grabs my hand. "You two, follow me," she instructs Mandy and Riley, pulling us along until we reach an empty hallway towards the back of the restaurant where tonight's afterparty is being hosted.

"Can we stop holding hands now?" I grumble.

"You are not quitting." Faith folds her arms over her chest. "And we're not leaving this hallway until you promise that." Riley and Mandy fall into step next to her, effectively blocking my exit.

"I don't want to quit. But I don't want to see *him* every day."

"What happened?" Mandy asks.

"Chris went to Jessica after the second show, and made a plan to flirt with me on camera to boost our ratings. It was all part of his strategy to get rid of me," I say glumly. "And then he went behind my back to try and get Jessica to release a statement denying we were dating after the pictures of us came out."

Faith whistles lowly.

"That is some shady shit," Mandy mutters. "Did he really think you wouldn't find out?"

"I don't know," I reply, hesitantly. They were Chris's friends first. I don't want to shit talk him in front of them. "But you don't have to choose between us, or anything."

They immediately burst into laughter.

"Oh, my god," Mandy wheezes. "We can love Chris and still think he acted like an idiot."

"This is classic Chris bullshit," Faith adds. "He thinks he has to fix everything by himself."

"We've been suggesting therapy for years," Mandy adds. "Maybe he'll finally listen."

"You mean...you still want to be my friends? All of you?" I ask, looking between them.

"Of course, dummy. One bad breakup doesn't change that," Riley smiles.

I immediately burst into tears.

"You're not getting rid of us," Mandy vows, as she, Riley and Faith envelop me in a group hug. "Even if this show gets canceled and I have to do something insane like move to L.A., you're stuck with me for life."

"You're the best," I sniffle.

"We know," Faith grins.

"I do have one question," Riley says. "Do you really think that Chris flirting with you on camera was an effective method of sabotage?"

"It doesn't matter if it was effective or not. He was trying to fuck with me." *But he said that he just wanted an excuse to do it.* His words in front of the elevator flood back to me, the desperation on his face as he begged me to give him another chance.

"Think about it. Playing up your chemistry for the *Update* only made viewers like you *both* more. He wasn't trying to get rid of you, Emily. He was trying to keep you."

"But he lied."

"He did. And you don't have to forgive him for it. But trust me when I say that the three of us saw the writing on the wall from day one."

I pause. "What do you mean?"

"Even when you two hated each other, there was something there," Mandy replies. "You were so busy hating each other that you couldn't see how much you had in common."

She's right. I thought the same thing once we started to become friends.

"I just don't know if I can do any of this without him," I admit.

"Of course you can!" Riley looks offended. "You work well together, but he doesn't make you. He compliments you. You're Emily fucking Beckerman."

"And I think you'll regret it for the rest of your life if you quit your dream job because of him," Faith adds.

"I don't want to leave," I admit. "But...every time I look at him, I want to fall apart. I don't know if I can handle it."

"You can," she insists. "It won't be easy. But what you feel for Chris—if you let it, it'll pass. What you feel for *Live From New York?* For comedy? For us? That shit is forever. That's love, too."

"You love me?"

They exchange glances. "We do."

"And you decided on it...as a unit?" I raise my eyebrows.

"Shut up," Mandy smirks. "We're trying to be nice. We love you, Emily. You're a pain in the ass, but you're our friend."

"And we all want you to stay," Faith adds.

"Three of us versus one of him," Riley nods. "The math checks out. You can't leave us. We'll never survive it."

"You survived a long time without me," I point out.

"Yeah, before we knew you." Faith rolls her eyes.

"It just feels like this show is so wrapped up in him,"

"Do me a favor. Close your eyes," Mandy instructs. I do, mainly because I have to pee and I know we're not leaving this corner until my friends are satisfied. "What's your favorite part of working on *Live From New York*?"

I pause, thinking about my answer.

I could say that it's writing with the three of them, and with Chris. The way we get goofy after a 5pm cup of coffee when we know we'll be working late. The rush of writing a sketch that kills at the table read. The gooey satisfaction when a host or musical guest that I love compliments my work, or defers to me as the expert. The post-table read meetings with Chris, Jessica, and a host when we put together a show, thinking about how everything fits together. The joy of seeing words I put on a page come to life.

Those are all things that I love, but they're not quite it.

I think of being backstage before the *Update*. I think of Chris's hand squeezing mine, and his reassuring presence. I think of the itchy suits that I thought would make me look like a middle school principal but somehow, behind that desk, transform me into the thing I always really wanted to be: a *Weekend Update* anchor.

I think of the joke swap, watching Chris read something audacious from the teleprompter and try to keep it together while we're on camera. I think of the characters we've created, the bits we've started, the way we've made the *Weekend Update* our own.

That first show, I was terrified. But there's one feeling that hasn't changed, even as I've grown more confident. Even as the man sitting beside me at the desk went from my enemy, to my ally, to my friend, and then the love of my life.

"The laughter after I tell a joke on the *Update*." One written by me, or one written by Chris, or one written by a combination of both of us. Sometimes even ones written with help from our friends. It doesn't matter who technically gets the credit. Once I tell it, the joke becomes mine. And there is no greater rush in the world than saying something deeply funny and deeply true, something that I believe in and that I know other people will enjoy, and then hearing the roar.

It's like nothing I ever experienced. And that feeling exists without Chris. It exists beyond him. It belongs only to me. It belongs to the little girl who dreamed of doing exactly what I'm doing. To the adult who gave up that dream because she thought it made her weak to wish for things that might never come true. To the woman who snuck a joke onto a teleprompter to humiliate an asshole, and then said "yes" to an idea that most people thought was crazy.

It belongs to Emily Beckerman, as a child, as an adult, as a staff writer and a head writer, behind the scenes and in front of the camera.

Those other things, they matter so much less—ratings and reactions, network notes and internet hot takes. I can't control how *Live From New York* is perceived. As head writer, I can only do my best to make it into something that I'm proud of. That matters to me. I love it. But it's not the best part.

For me, the best part is what I share with the audience when I say something, and they laugh. That moment when I'm behind the desk, alone, and yet somehow not. The lights are too bright to truly see them, but I can hear them laughing.

It's how I got into this in the first place. Because I love making people laugh. And when I open my eyes, my friends are nodding back at me. They get it, because they have that bug, too. We know that the best part is the laughter.

Because life is short, and sometimes painful. It can be full of assholes and heartbreak and hard things. But it's not *only* full of those things. And we can take those things, the frustrations and agonies of our lives, whether it's politics, family drama, loneliness, rejection, or any number of things that suck, and we can rewrite them. We can tell the truth of them in a different way, a way that acknowledges the pain but also acknowledges the humanity and the humor.

And once we laugh at something, it seems much less scary because of it.

"It's the best part," Faith says quietly, worshipfully. "The best part of any stage, any audience. And if you were capable of giving it up—if you really wanted to—you would have done it a long time ago. Because it's a hard road, to get to the place where you can enjoy the laughter. But I think…" she pauses, looking between the four of us, a smile stretching across her face. "I think it's worth it."

"Okay," I sigh. "You're right, all of you. It's worth it."

"So, you're not leaving?" Faith's hopeful expression kills me. A year ago, the three people in front of me were strangers. Now, they're some of my closest friends. And they've just saved me from potentially making a life-altering mistake.

"I owe you for helping me with this."

"Just keep looking out for us, head writer," Mandy winks.

"Fair enough."

"Should we get back to the afterparty? I need more sushi."

"I think that's an excellent idea." I loop my arm through Riley's. "And we haven't requested nearly enough songs yet,"

Mandy grins. "How much do you think we'll have to pay the DJ to play old Britney?"

"At least twenty bucks. Did you see her eyebrow ring? She's way too cool for that."

"Oh, yeah. Hot," Faith sighs dreamily. "Maybe I can win her over."

"If you do, those twenty dollars are yours," Riley declares.

Just before three, Jessica grabs the microphone. "I just want to thank everyone for their hard work next year. Enjoy summer hiatus," she pauses, just barely. "And I'll see you all in September."

My eyes find Chris's across the room. There's so much that I wish I could say. Instead, I just nod at him in acknowledgment of what we accomplished.

We saved this show. And even if he becomes a stranger to me, if we drift apart now that everything between us is over...at least we have that.

❧

The first few weeks of hiatus are agony. I try to distract myself, filling my days with the things that I love and never had time for during the *Live From New York* season. I go on long walks and catch up on podcasts. I do yoga, I meditate, I watch TV. I finally move into and decorate my condo, with the help of my mom and Rachel.

Every day, I wake up hoping that ache in my chest will grow smaller. Hating myself when it doesn't. Hating him, for being so wonderful and then so terrible.

I hate that I can't forget him. I hate that I fall asleep every night and feel the ghost of his body against my skin, as real as the last night we spent together. I hate that he's ruined my favorite stories, that I can't read even a page of a book without remembering how close I got to my own happy ending. Remembering that brief, perfect period where I thought that I had found the love I'd always dreamed about.

I hate how much of my brain space is devoted to thinking of him. I don't want to be consumed. I don't want to be that person who lets heartbreak define her. But the hurting has overtaken me entirely, and I don't know how to make it stop.

"You're looking at sadness as a sign of failure. You can't fault yourself for feeling emotions, especially when you consider the intensity of the positive experience," my therapist says when I bring it up to her.

"But what if this feeling never goes away?"

"It may never go away."

"That doesn't help me!"

She gives me a familiar let-me-finish look. "Think about other times that you have felt similar emotions."

I do. I remember the trauma of weighing myself every morning in high school, of crying when the numbers weren't what I wanted them to be and vowing to be better. I think about the pit inside of me that would never be filled by a flat stomach or wearing a smaller size, the anguish of wondering whether I would feel that emptiness forever. I remember gaining weight as I got older, the torture of doing everything "right" and still seeing my body change, feeling that control over how I looked slip away from me. I remember going shopping and not fitting into anything at my old favorite stores. I remember my zayde dying, watching my bubbe and my mother sob at his funeral, and feeling both my own grief and theirs, witnessing the two strongest women I had ever known fall apart. I remember those early months of college when I was so homesick that I cried every day, terrified of adulthood and missing my family, unsure if I'd ever be happy again.

"Thinking about the things in our lives that have been unbearably painful or difficult might always carry an echo of that sadness. But there is a difference between the grief that smothers you and the grief that you make peace with. Romantic heartbreak is devastating. To have that happiness and then to lose it, to see someone that you love hurt you—even if they didn't mean to—it is excruciating."

"I just wish I knew how long it would last."

"Well, if you keep fighting it, that will only prolong your grief. Feel your fucking feelings. You are strong enough to sit with the pain. I promise. And you don't have to do it alone."

And so, I do. Bit by bit, I sink into the well of despair inside of me. I face it head-on. It fucking sucks, and yet, it's also a relief. A relief from the exhaustion of fighting my pain. I let it wash over me. I sink beneath the waves. I let myself drown.

Day by day, it gets easier. The sadness lingers underneath the surface, but it no longer consumes me. When the ache recedes, it makes room for other things. I drink cheap wine on outdoor patios in the middle of the weekday with Faith, Mandy, and Riley, reminiscing about the season. Even when I'm not telling a joke for an audience, the laughter makes the pain easier to deal with.

It gets easier. But it never goes away.

28

"You're quiet today," my mother remarks offhandedly. "You've been quiet all summer. I thought I'd be hearing about that big raise by now."

I wince. If there's one person I can never hide what I'm feeling from, it's my mother. I've been avoiding her all summer for that exact reason, and because I know she'll ask me about Chris.

"Just focusing," I say evasively, focusing all my attention on the challah dough in front of me. I'm no baker, and my challah braiding skills are passable at best. But I've been doing it all of my life, so pretending that it requires every ounce of my concentration isn't fooling anyone.

"Have you decided what to do about next season yet?"

"No," I admit, biting the inside of my cheek. "My agents are still negotiating on salary, so I've been putting off my decision."

"Ah, yes. Procrastination always solves everything," she says sarcastically, tucking the last strand of her challah into its braid and turning to face me.

"It's complicated," I finish braiding my challah and brush egg wash over it. I open the oven, setting both our challahs inside to finish rising.

"Love always is."

"Who said anything about love?"

"Please, Emily." She rolls her eyes. "I saw those pictures. It was love."

"Key word: was."

"You broke up."

"We did."

"And that's why you haven't made a decision about next season yet."

"No." She raises an eyebrow at me. "Well, yes. Maybe. Kind of," I sigh. "I don't want it to. But the thought of seeing him every day, working with him like that again...I don't know if I can do it. I don't want to go back. But I also don't want to *not* go back."

"I can see why that would make things difficult."

"Is it embarrassing that I'm scared to see him?"

"Not at all." She reaches over to grasp my hand. "It's scary to face people who have hurt us. But you can do it."

"I can?"

"You can," Mom says, squeezing tightly. "I know I've treated you delicately because of your past struggles. But you're strong, Emily. You can do hard things. You've done hard things. And I knew the moment I saw you on the *Weekend Update* this fall that you were where you were meant to be."

"Then why didn't you tell me?" My voice wobbles. "I thought you didn't support me. I thought...I thought you wanted me to give up."

"Oh, Emily. I *never* wanted you to give up. I was only trying to make sure that you didn't sacrifice your happiness and mental health while you worked so hard to make your dreams come true." She hugs me tightly. My tears turn into sobs as I lay my head on her shoulder and let the emotions that have been weighing me down make their way out now that I'm safe in her arms. "I hate seeing you sad. That's my right as a mother, but I never want you to stop fighting for what you believe in."

"I'm going to go back next season." I lift my head so that I can meet her eyes. "But I have to talk to him first," I add, gratefully taking the tissue she offers me when we pull apart. I don't know how she somehow always has tissues on her—it's one of those magical mom powers that I've never been able to crack.

"And what are you going to say?"

"I don't know." I frown, and her arm tightens around me, her hand rubbing soothing circles against my shoulder. "We have to decide who will take the head writer job, and the *Update* desk." The thought of doing either without him makes me sick to my stomach, but I don't have a choice.

"I wouldn't worry too much," she advises. "It'll all work out."

"At least now I can find a nice Jewish boy."

"I'm sure when you get back together, Chris will convert," she replies, as if it's simply a matter of fact.

"If he does convert to Judaism, it's not gonna be on my behalf."

"We'll see," she shrugs. "I have faith."

"You met him twice."

"And that was all it took for me to see that he loves my only child the way she deserves to be loved."

"He was pretending, Mom. He flirted with me on the *Update* for show, not because he meant it."

"Well, god forbid someone ever flirts without intending to propose marriage." She rolls her eyes.

"He played me. He was doing it to try and make himself the only *Update* anchor next season."

"I seem to recall you trying to do the same thing."

"It's different."

She makes a disbelieving noise in her throat. "Do you remember your father's friend Larry?"

"Larry with the mustache?"

"No, Larry who plays racquetball," she clarifies. "Before your father and I became official, as your generation likes to refer to it, I asked Larry out. While I was still dating your father."

"Well, if you weren't exclusive, you didn't really do anything wrong,"

Tracey smiles. "That's true. But I did it because I knew it would hurt your father's feelings. I wanted to push him into being serious with me, so I did something underhanded. And now we've been married for twenty-five years."

"I assume there's some lesson in this for me to figure out?" I say dryly.

"Don't sass me." She swats me with a dish towel. "But yes, there is. The lesson is that we all do foolish things when we're first falling in love. It's scary, and people make mistakes. But those mistakes don't make a relationship. It's not about what you do wrong. It's about what you both do right."

I pause, rocking back on my heels as I take in her words.

All this time, I thought learning about Chris's initial deception meant that the foundation of our relationship was a lie, in a way that we could never overcome. I thought it meant I couldn't trust my instincts, because everything between us had felt so right.

It doesn't fix all of our problems. I still don't know if he would have told me about his initial lie, or that he loved me, if I hadn't overheard him saying it to Jessica. He still tried to go behind my back and convince our boss to deny our relationship.

"I don't know if I can trust him." My throat bobs with emotion. "I only found out the truth by accident. He should have been honest with me."

"He should have been," she agrees. "But you can be intimidating. You inherited that from me."

"That and the flat feet," I mutter.

"You should be grateful that you're not still in the shtetl that gave you those flat feet," she replies indignantly.

"Oh, my god," I groan. "Is this conversation over yet?"

"Not quite." She smirks at me. "See, I've known you your whole life, and we still have our disagreements. No relationship is perfect. That doesn't mean it's broken, or not worth saving."

"That's different. I can't get rid of you. You're my mother."

"Fair enough. But can you really look me in the eyes and tell me that you want to be rid of him? That you'd rather have your pride and have him be out of your life then try to fix things?"

"I don't know." We both know I'm lying. I'd rather have Chris. "He didn't trust me."

"Really, Emily, you've known each other for a few months. You expect that kind of trust to just fall into your lap? These things take time."

"I don't know if I have that kind of time."

"Please. You're young." She waves a hand dismissively. "You have time for second chances. Especially when it's love. Just like I predicted."

My eyes nearly bug out of my head. "Like you *predicted*?"

"I told you at the beginning of the year that I'd be sending you your husband."

"And you think that's Chris."

"It could be. He came to Shabbat dinner, Emily."

"Maybe he just wanted to get a free meal out of you."

"Maybe he just wanted to get you out of your underwear."

"Mom!"

"Don't be a prude. Not after you insisted I read that Tessa Bailey novel."

"Fair enough." Once again I'm reminded that it's hard to avoid talking about sex with your mother when you regularly swap romance novel recommendations.

"All I'm asking is for you to try, darling. If you try and he isn't able to give you what you need, then you move on. And you'll be fine. I've never worried about you finding love. I only fear that you might have found it already and lost it because you're afraid to fight."

Almost an exact echo of Chris's words to me the night before our last show. I've always been a fighter, so why couldn't I this time?

I accused him of being a coward, but I've been acting like one, too. The depth of my feelings for him terrifies me. After spending so long dreaming of finding what we have together, it still felt safer to push him away than to risk getting hurt again. If he could hurt me this deeply after only a few months together, what could he do to me if we stayed together for years?

He could break me.

Or he could make me happy, if I let him.

The Monday after my weekend with my parents, I call Chris and ask him if we can talk. He answers on the first ring and promises to meet me somewhere by my place in half an hour.

Even though I spend the walk over mentally preparing myself, the sight of Chris standing casually and holding our coffees makes my chest ache. Several angry New Yorkers bump into me when I stop walking right in the middle of the sidewalk, stunned into immobility by my first glimpse of him. He's wearing a faded Celtics T-shirt and a Harvard hat. He smiles as he sees me, and I feel like crying.

I drink him in for as long as I can without it being obvious. Three seconds is all I need. I haven't forgotten so much as a freckle on his face.

"Hey." I stop in front of him, both of us just reveling in the mutual awkwardness of the situation.

"This is for you." He holds one of the coffees out to me robotically.

"Thank you," I reply with equal lifelessness. I sip it, because I need something to do with my body aside from ogle at him and think about how much I want to be in his arms. I nearly spit it out. It's way too sweet and definitely contains real milk.

"This is yours," I offer it back to him. "I don't have an STI, don't worry."

"Probably a little late if you did," We swap coffees, and I nearly drop mine at the words. The casual reference to our intimacy as if it's already in the past. As if he's already moved on.

But then I notice his hand shaking slightly as he lifts his drink, and the pit in my stomach recedes. Maybe if I were a better person, I wouldn't feel knee-wobbling relief to know that he's as affected by me as I am by him. It's a small comfort, but a comfort nonetheless, to know that even if I have been suffering, I wasn't the only one.

Chris and I find an empty table in the shade and sit. We're quiet for a few minutes before I realize that I should probably be the one to start this conversation, since I asked him to meet. I should have practiced how I wanted this to go. But even imagining being face-to-face with him again was too painful.

"So, how are you?" I ask when the silence grows truly unbearable.

"Great." His easy grin doesn't reach his eyes. "I've just been enjoying my time off."

I swallow the lump in my throat, and refuse to let myself dwell on those words. It's too late for them to make any difference, and pretending otherwise will only hurt us both more. "Is this the part where you ask me why I invited you to get coffee?"

"I was wondering. The last time we talked, I got the impression that you never wanted to see me again."

"I should apologize."

"We both hurt each other," he says gently. "We hurt each other for a long time, professionally and personally."

"We did," I agree, taking a sip of coffee. It tastes bitter on my tongue, and not just because it's unsweetened. I hate that he's basically a stranger to me now. "I'm coming back next year."

"Good. *Live From New York* needs you," Chris pauses, his eyes glazing over with something like longing. "It wouldn't be the same without you."

"It won't be the same."

"You're right," Chris inhales, and my eyes track the way the breath travels in his throat. "I told Jessica to give you the head writer job. And the *Update*."

"What?" I nearly spit out my sip of coffee. "You're not serious."

"I am."

"You can't do that!"

"Why not?" He smiles sadly. "You deserve it."

"But you shouldn't be the one who decides."

"No," he agrees. "I probably shouldn't. But I spoke to Jessica, and she refused to choose, so I had to take matters into my own hands."

"But…what about you?"

Chris's eyes widen. "Are you really worried about me?"

"And Zoe," I say quickly. "What if she wants to go to law school? What if you need money?"

"Don't worry. I'm not getting a pay cut," he chuckles softly. "After we fought at Shabbat dinner, Zoe and I talked. I realized—because she told me, and I finally listened—that I've been pushing her to follow in my footsteps because I wanted to protect her," he pauses. "I've fucked up a lot of things out of a misguided desire to protect the people I love."

My eyes burn with unshed tears. I open my mouth, but I can't find words to say.

"She was right. If she needs to take out student loans, it's not the end of the world. I want her life to be easy, but it should still be hers."

"You've done a lot of soul searching," I say thickly.

"Therapy." Chris smiles, that dimple on the left side of his mouth popping into view. God, I missed it. "It's worth the hype."

"It really is," I pause. "You're really giving up the *Update*, and head writer? For me?"

"You deserve it."

"So do you."

"That might be true. But I spent a lot of time watching other people lose out on things that they had earned when I was Alex's writing partner. You were right, Emily. I protected myself. I don't want to be that person anymore."

"I still love you," I blurt, the words just falling out of my mouth. *Fuck*. Why does he have to be so goddamn wonderful?

"Emily," he breathes.

"You were right, too. You told me I was running away, and I was. Because I was terrified that you had the power to hurt me so badly."

A muscle in his jaw feathers. "I hate that I hurt you. Every time I picture your face that night—" He chokes up, emotion overcoming him, and my gut twists.

"We both hurt each other. But that was the past," I say. "I forgive you, Chris. On one condition."

He pauses, remembering when he said those same words to me. "What is it?"

"Be my partner again. On the *Update*, and as head writer," I pause, working up the courage to finish my thought. "And...in life. If you want that."

"Emily," he inhales sharply. "You couldn't have said this two months ago?"

"I needed time, to figure out what I wanted. If you still want me."

"I do," he groans. "But it's not that simple."

"Can't it be?" I plead.

"I'll do the *Update* and head writer jobs with you. But that's it," he says firmly. "I love you, Emily. But things got so messy between us. If we're going to be partners again, I can't risk things going badly again."

"But what if they don't?"

"You didn't fight for me before." His chest heaves slightly, his throat bobbing with emotion. "I said everything I needed to say, and it wasn't enough for you. *I* wasn't enough for you."

"That's not true," I reply, stricken. "You are exactly enough, Chris."

"I begged you." His voice is quiet, distant. It feels like I've already lost him, and I hate that. "I put everything on the line for us."

"You did. And I should have listened. I should have trusted you.

But I'm trusting you now," I plead. "You told me on New Year's that you wanted to believe things wouldn't end badly."

"And look where that got me." He laughs bitterly, the sound sending ice skittering through my veins. It's so cold, so unlike the man I've come to love. "Fuck, Emily," He drags a hand down his face. "You don't know what you're asking of me."

"I do," I insist. "Because it's the same thing I'm asking of myself. You broke my heart, Chris."

"You broke mine too," he whispers. "When you walked away from me."

"I want to make it right. I want to put us back together. I think about you all the time. I thought it would get easier, but it didn't. And I don't want it to. I don't want to keep missing you."

"So, we'll move on."

"I can't."

"You will." He gives me a sad smile.

"So, what? I just have to watch you move on?" My heart twists. "Watch you fall in love with someone else someday?"

"No." He shakes his head. "Because I'm never doing any of this again. Not with anyone."

"You're wrong," I pause, the wheels in my mind turning. "You're wrong about love, and you're wrong about us. And I'm going to prove it to you."

"How, exactly, are you going to do that? What makes you so sure that it's all going to be okay? We wrecked each other, Beckerman."

"We did," I nod.

"And yet you still think there's something left to fight for between us? A future?" The words have an edge of anger to them, but I see something different flickering behind his green eyes. Hope. Just a hint, but it's enough. I want to sink to my knees with relief that he's not lost to me forever.

"I do, Chris. Because I love you. And if someone as extraordinary as you could love me too, then I think I have no choice but to be worthy of that love. That means fighting for you."

"So, what exactly do you expect me to do? Wait around for you to do some miraculous thing that will win me over and fix everything between us?"

"It's called a grand gesture."

"What, like telling me you love me on the Jumbotron at a Red Sox game?"

An infuriating grin is my only response. "If that's what you want."

He sighs. "I want you to be okay with my decision."

"I will never be okay with you choosing unhappiness. If you don't want me, then fine."

"I want you too much," he confesses, his voice full of raw emotion.

"You want me exactly the right amount," I reply fiercely. "I can't guarantee you that we're never going to hurt each other again. But I can promise that I'm not giving you up without a fight. Our love is worth trying to save. You're worth fighting for. Just let me try."

"You are so goddamned stubborn," he mutters, although his hint of a smile reveals that he might not be as annoyed as he's trying to sound.

"I know," I grin, holding on desperately to that hint of a smile. "But that's why this isn't over yet."

Rosh Hashanah falls at the end of August, exactly a month before our first episode of *Live From New York*.

It's not the kind of holiday people usually associate with romantic gestures. But I wanted to do something unique, and meaningful.

I wanted Chris to know that I love him, and want him to be a part of my life. And Judaism is part of my life.

So, I sent him a ticket to the late morning Rosh Hashanah service at my synagogue.

I spend the walk to the synagogue from Rachel's apartment full of nervous energy. She and my mom squeeze my hands for support before they walk inside.

I wait on the front steps, knowing how difficult it will be for Chris to find us once we're inside. I'm wearing a simple purple slip skirt with a fabric motorcycle jacket and my favorite black booties. I even put on makeup and ran some curl cream through my waves to make them look manageable.

Right before services are scheduled to start, Rachel comes outside.

"No sign of him?"

"No," I shake my head, anxiety bubbling up in my gut. I really thought this would do it. "Maybe this was stupid."

"No, it wasn't. It was brave." Rachel pulls me in for a quick hug. "If he doesn't show up today, it's his loss."

I nod glumly.

"Do you want to stay outside, or come in?" she asks, the gentleness of her voice making me want to crumple into a ball and cry.

"I'll come in." Rosh Hashanah is the Jewish new year. That was what made me think of it in relation to Chris. I thought it would be a sweet allusion to our relationship beginning on the non-Jewish new year. But it wasn't enough. At least now I have two hours of services to reflect on that, and think about new beginnings.

We head inside, my mom's face falling when she sees that Chris isn't with us. "I'm sorry, my love," She hugs me tightly. "You did everything you could."

"I know," I whisper against her hair, fighting the urge to cry. Music starts to play, an indication that the services will begin shortly, and I spot the rabbi approaching the pulpit.

"Excuse me," the older woman next to us says loudly. "Are you using that seat? Because the congregation policy is that we're not supposed to save them."

It's true, although no one listens to it.

"No. We don't need it," I say quietly.

"WAIT!" someone shouts loudly from the synagogue entrance. Chris comes sprinting down the main aisle, every eye on him.

"Chris?" I stand on my chair.

"Emily," he cries. The room is enormous, and he's on the opposite end of it from us.

"Don't take that seat," I snap as my neighbor reaches for it. "It's for him."

"He's late," she grumbles.

"He's *here*. And he's the love of my life," I declare, feeling the truth of those words in my very bones.

"Fine, fine. No need to make such a fuss," she says, backing off.

"Am I too late?" Chris shouts as he runs down the aisle, one hand holding onto his *kippah* so it doesn't fly off of his head as he runs towards our seats.

"We can wait," the rabbi says into the pulpit's microphone, her voice full of amusement.

"You're here," I breathe, jumping down from the chair just as he reaches our row.

"I'm here." His face is flushed, and he's breathing heavily, but his navy suit looks perfect. "I'm sorry. The subway was delayed. I should have taken a cab. I should have left earlier. I should—"

"It doesn't matter. You're here."

"I am. Because you were right, Beckerman. I know that this is a risk. But it's one worth taking. Before I met you, I was so afraid of getting hurt. But you taught me that the best things in life are when I do exactly that. From being vulnerable, and trying new things, and pushing myself. As a writer, and a comedian, but also as a man."

"I'm sorry, too," I say, my voice full of emotion. "I shouldn't have pushed you away at the first sign of trouble. I should have trusted you and kept my own promises."

"I should have told you the truth from the beginning," he says, his eyes shining with emotion. "I want to be the kind of man you deserve."

"I'm the one who doesn't deserve you," I say thickly. "I didn't trust you. I put my pride before our relationship, and thought one mistake would define our story. But it doesn't. We're going to make more. We're going to fuck up—"

"Language," my mother reminds me.

"Mess up," I amend. "And I'm glad for it, because that's how we're going to learn, and grow, and get better at this. You make me want to be better, too. You make me laugh. You help me trust myself, and trust others. You've shown me again and again the kind of person that you are, Chris Galloway. And once I knew you, there was nothing in the world that could stop me from loving you." I bite my lip nervously. "I should never have walked away from you."

"I should have been honest."

"Yes," I agree. "But I ran the second I started to doubt. I let one moment erase everything we'd built, because I loved you enough that I knew you could break my heart. And that scared me, more than anything."

His eyes glisten with unshed tears. "I hate that I ever gave you reason not to trust me with it. I promise, it will never happen again. I was afraid, too."

"Afraid of me?"

"Afraid of what you mean to me." He takes a step closer, although it's still not nearly close enough. "I've never felt this way before about anyone. Em, you make me so happy. There's no one else's opinion that I value more. When I'm with you, I feel safe. I don't feel alone."

"You have never let me feel alone," I say fiercely, staring up at him. "And neither of us are ever going to be alone again."

"I want to be with you, Emily," Chris says, pulling me into his arms. "I want to write with you, and fight with you, and make up. I want you by my side. On the show, in my life, at Am Shalom." He gestures to the synagogue we're inside of.

"There's a waitlist," someone shouts.

"Oh, let him cut! They're in love," someone else interjects from the crowd.

He smiles softly, and my heart feels full enough to burst. "I'm just a boy, standing in front of a girl, asking her to take an extremely Catholic male shiksa with her to five hours of Rosh Hashanah services."

"We're reform, so it's only two," the rabbi clarifies into the microphone.

"So, what do you say, Beckerman?" He traces the pad of his thumb down my palm, and I'm overcome by a strong temptation to ditch services and drag him back to Josh and Rachel's apartment so we can take full advantage of its emptiness. "This is our happy ending, if you want it to be."

"I don't," his face falls until I continue, "I won't accept an ending with you, Chris. This is our happy beginning."

"You had me worried there," he murmurs.

"I'm sorry," I tease. "I just love messing with you. I love *you*, Chris Galloway. So much."

"Oh, honey, kiss him," my mother exclaims.

"Yes, kiss him, please, so we can start on time," the Rabbi deadpans.

There's a giddiness inside me that I've never felt before, the kind of effervescent joy that comes from knowing that the person you want to be with wants to be with you, too. He's here, standing in front of me, just as willing as I am to admit mistakes and find a way forward.

I wrap my arms around his neck. "I can't believe this is real."

"At the risk of sounding like a cheesy, lovesick idiot, this is the realest thing I've ever felt."

"I love cheesy, lovesick idiots. Especially the one I'm about to kiss."

Our lips meet, and the world falls away. Or it would, if not for the loud whoops and cheers of excitement from the synagoguegoers assembled around us.

"Oh, goodness." My mom sniffles loudly, my dad handing her a tissue.

"The early morning service is going to be so mad they missed this," Rachel says with a laugh.

"Alright, if the grand romantic reconciliation is finished, can we get on with services?" the rabbi asks.

"We're good," I call. I turn to whisper to Chris, "Should we just get out of here? The apartment is empty…"

"As tempting as that offer is, I think we should stay. After all, this is important to you. And I want to learn about Judaism before I convert one day."

"You're so sure we're going to get that far?"

"I am." He reaches for my hand as we sit down. "Besides, I look hot in a *kippah*."

And he really, really does.

Unfortunately, any ideas that I have about ripping Chris's clothes off and showing him exactly how much I've missed him over these past few months are quickly checked by the reality of a relatively un-sexy holiday. Rosh Hashanah isn't as bad as Yom Kippur, but it's definitely not the sexiest Jewish holiday. That's Purim, hands down.

What I get, instead, is what comes after. After the declaration of love, the chase through the airport, the snow, or the streets of New York City. It's Zoe, who justifiably showed up for the meal and not for the services because, as she put it—in front of my entire family— "I don't need to go the extra mile to get into Emily's pants."

"Are you kidding me, Josh?" Rachel stares daggers at her husband. "Four aces? You're sleeping on the couch tonight."

"If you stayed angry at me every time I beat you at Rummy 500, we wouldn't have any children," Josh replies.

"Have you made a deal with some sort of Rummy 500 devil? Did you sell your soul?" Zoe demands. "I have to know. You can't just be *that* good."

"We've attempted to learn his secrets for the past twelve years," I inform her. "But you're welcome to try."

"I see. By any means necessary?"

"Nothing illegal," I say quickly.

"I am *deeply* offended!" Zoe places a hand on her chest. "I was simply going to offer my services as a babysitter."

"I'll think about it. Now, who's in for another game?" Josh asks, and we all eagerly agree.

From the kitchen, I hear the loud peals of my mother's laughter, joined by Chris's. From the hallway, I hear Alex and Amy's squeals as my dad chases them around. My insides are light and fizzy with a happiness that seems too wonderful for this world, as if my very being has been filled with champagne. "I knew this would happen," Rachel says.

"Because I told you I was buying the ticket."

"Okay, but I still *knew*," Rachel defends herself as her husband sighs, before leaning forward to kiss the top of her head.

"You two are adorable," Zoe grins. "I love it."

I have to tear my gaze away from the radiant expression on her face, the pure joy she feels. Seeing my family through Zoe's eyes gives me a newfound appreciation for them. We're a wild bunch, but we're accepting of each other, and ourselves.

"Not as adorable as Chris and Emily," Rachel waggles her eyebrows at me. "I've never made out with someone in front of a synagogue before Rosh Hashanah services."

"We did not *make out*," I protest. "It was a peck."

Josh snorts. "I think it had a bit too much tongue to be classified as a peck."

"Can we please stop talking about my brother's love life? No offense, Emily, but I don't want details." She shudders.

"None taken. I don't want to give them!" I direct that comment at my cousin, who only sticks her tongue out at me in response.

As if on cue, Chris emerges from the kitchen, still wearing my mother's apron. I find it unspeakably adorable. It just makes my heart swell with emotion to see him fitting right in with the Beckerman clan. There's a common expression among Jews that when you marry someone, you marry their family. And I'm not trying to put the cart before the horse, but being here with Chris…I love that it's not just him and me in a bubble. That he's part of my world, and I'm part of his.

"We were just talking about you," Rachel grins. "So, Chris, are you ready to tell me everything there is to know about you?"

"That should probably wait until dinner when the whole family's there, so you only have to do it once," I reply. "And I'm sorry in advance."

"I don't even know what I'm going to say."

"They'll ask the questions, you just have to answer them." Josh gives Chris a sympathetic pat on the back. "It's like a job interview without any legal protections or boundaries."

"Remember the first time I brought you to a Rosh Hashanah dinner?" Rachel asks Josh, laughing, as they begin to reminisce.

"You can still escape if you want to," I whisper in Chris's ear.

"No chance. You're stuck with us forever," he says, gesturing to Zoe.

"Yeah, even if you two break up, I'm keeping the Beckermans," she declares.

"We're keeping you, too."

"And we're never breaking up," Chris interjects.

"Dinner's ready," my mother shouts from the kitchen. "Mark, can you get the good wine, please? We're celebrating! *Bubbe* says Chris is the best sous chef she's ever had."

"That is high praise indeed." Chris stands, extending a hand to me. "Well, Emily, are you ready?"

"To try the chicken noodle soup that you helped make? Absolutely." I place my hand in his as I stand up and we walk toward the dining room.

"And for everything else after."

"Yeah? Do you know exactly what happens after tonight?" I raise an eyebrow at him.

"I have no idea. All that I need to know is we'll face it together."

ACKNOWLEDGMENTS

Thank you so much to my incredible cover designer Ashley, for bringing Chris and Emily to life. Thank you to my wonderful proofreader and formatter, Kristen, for not only correcting my nonsensical typos but also helping me navigate the sometimes scary world of self-promotion. Thank you to Gabby Ginsburg for taking my beautiful author photos and to Emily Joachim for making my amazing website.

Thank you so much to Gabi Conti, for your kind and thoughtful notes on an earlier draft of this story. Thank you to Lauren Hochhauser. And endless thank-yous to Emma Noyes for all of your self-publishing wisdom, writing wisdom, and general wisdom about every aspect of being an author.

Sydney, Cammie, and Ellie, thank you for being my friends even when I was an annoying teenager and staying my friend now that I am a slightly less annoying adult. I am so lucky to have friends that feel like family, and even when I'm not in Chicago, I hope you remember that the Wolfberg door is always open to you (literally). Thank you to all of my Tulane friends for making a magical time in a magical city that much more wonderful. Emily Silverman, thank you for letting me use your name for my main character and sharing my enthusiasm for John Mulaney, history, and Taylor Swift. And endless thank yous to Raimy, Laura, Bekah, Yael, and Francesca, the best Pham a girl could ask for. Thank you to Hannah Moses, Marissa Levey, and Steph Hausman for your years of friendship, and thank you to BBYO for bringing us together.

Thank you to Zoe Brown. I never imagined when I met you in the summer of 2019 that we would still be friends nearly five years later, but it also shouldn't have surprised me because you are the kind of person that lasts a lifetime. Thank you for helping me make LA my home and your endless support. Thank you to Marnie, Mel, and Loie, my Chicago Baddies. Thank you to Nathan Glovinsky for believing in my writing and only making fun of me a little bit for my email typos. Thank you to Simon for making me laugh. Thank you to Maddie Powell for your expert design skills, and being an incredible friend. To Jamie Kerner, I'm so glad you're my neighbor and my friend. To Hannah Petosa, I'm grateful that we share a brain and I can't wait to have my name next to yours on a script one day. And to Dani, the final California Cowgirl, your friendship has been such a gift.

To the rest of my LA friends, there are too many of you to name, and for that I am so grateful. Your support means the world to me and I am so, so grateful to have you beside me in this chapter of my life. Pun intended.

Thank you to Jewish Bookstagram. I found this community after the most traumatic moment in Jewish history since the Shoah, at a time when I felt terrified and alone. I am so grateful to you all for your activism, support, and bravery in the face of indifference and antisemitism.

Thank you to Grandpa Joe, Grandmom Gerri, and Grandmom Sue for your endless love and support. And to Grandpa Earl, I love and miss you. Thank you for giving me my love for stories, and my appreciation for bad jokes. Thank you to Aunt Linette, Uncle Dan, Uncle Scott, and my cousins Amber, Sammi, and Chase. And thank you to the Ettelsons and Coans. I am so grateful to have such an incredible family.

Thank you to my siblings. David, I'm so grateful for your love, support, and kindness. Eli, thank you for making me laugh. And Zoe, my sister and best friend, I am so lucky to have you in my life. Thank you for reading this and giving me helpful notes about how to be less "cringe", and sharing my love for Taylor Swift, New Girl, and Brooklyn 99.

To my parents, you are the reason I was able to write this book. I wouldn't be who I am today without you, and I am so proud and lucky to be your daughter. Your support means everything to me. Thank you for encouraging me to dream big and never give up. I love you both so much.

ABOUT THE AUTHOR

Chayla Wolfberg (pronounced like Kay-luh) is a writer originally from Chicago, but now living in LA. By day, she works as an assistant in the entertainment industry. By night, she fights crime. Just kidding—she watches TV, reads romance novels, and tries to find the perfect chocolate chip cookie recipe.

instagram.com/chaylawolfbergwrites
tiktok.com/@chaylawolfbergwrites